THE
PERFECT
GUEST

BOOKS BY CASEY KELLEHER

THE
PERFECT
GUEST

CASEY KELLEHER

bookouture

Published by Bookouture in 2025

An imprint of Storyfire Ltd.
Carmelite House
50 Victoria Embankment
London EC4Y 0DZ

www.bookouture.com

The authorised representative in the EEA is Hachette Ireland
8 Castlecourt Centre
Dublin 15 D15 XTP3
Ireland
(email: info@hbgi.ie)

ISBN: 978-1-83618-918-3
eBook ISBN: 978-1-83618-917-6

For Kay Bull
The doggies at Healing Paws Animal Rescue in Greece send big slobbery kisses!

I hope you love Kay Wyldes as much as I do!
X

PROLOGUE

She's gone.

Her eyes, once a striking, vibrant blue stare vacantly ahead. They're pale and watery now that there is no longer anyone shining out from behind them. Drained of blood, her once blush-pink lips are tinged grey. Her skin ashen and waxy.

She looks like a broken doll.

As if she's been stripped of all colour and soul.

'Can you hear me?' Panic rises inside me as I stare down at the lifeless body, only to be met with a deathly silence.

Of course she can't hear me. I have killed her.

'Get up! Come on. Get up!' I grab at one of her arms and vigorously shake it in a desperate, pathetic attempt to will her back to life.

Only it's no use.

Of course it's no bloody use!

I can't shake someone back to life. What's done is done.

Murderer.

My hands tremble as the word forms inside my head. The realisation hitting me like a thunderbolt.

I *am* a murderer.

Shock gives way to blind terror as adrenaline courses through me. My whole body vibrating now, as if a swarm of bees are buzzing aggressively around inside me, trying to protect their nest.

I can't stay here. In this house. With her like this.

I should call the police, only my fingers are rigid and numb like the rest of me. Because the police will not help me. They won't believe that it was an accident.

I move towards the door, but my legs, already weak and jittery, give way beneath me and I drop to the floor. A strained, muted screech leaves my mouth.

This isn't real. This can't *be real.*

No matter how many times I repeat this mantra she'll never hear it.

She's never coming back.

1

KAY

I push open the front door, the dim hallway light spilling out as I turn to look at Stephanie. In this half-light, my granddaughter seems even more broken and fragile. Her lank blonde hair covers most of her face, but I can just about see her eyes, sunken and hollow.

She hesitates in the doorway, clutching her rucksack to her chest as if it's a shield. Wavering at the threshold of my house, as if crossing it might be the point of no return.

I see it, the wave of apprehension that washes over her and I understand how overwhelming this must all feel. But I want her to know that she has me now. I'm here. I'll take care of her no matter what.

'Come on in!' I smile warmly and wrap my arms around her shoulders as I guide her inside. 'Make yourself at home, love.'

Stephanie's eyes widen as she scans the room, taking in the endless piles of bags and boxes stacked up along the walls. I flush in embarrassment, it's been so long since I saw my home through a stranger's eyes, I'd forgotten what a shock it can be. I see her nose wrinkle in distaste. My chest tightens. Perhaps if

I'd have known tonight would unfold like this, I might have tidied up a bit. But really – where would I have put everything?

'Oh this! This is all just organised chaos! Don't mind any of it.' I babble, as Stephanie tries to hide the judgement in her eyes.

I don't understand. Surely my warm, comfortable home is better than where I just picked her up from? The awful things I saw in that house... what's a little mess by comparison?

She'll adjust, I tell myself. If the clutter doesn't bother me, it needn't bother Stephanie either.

As though he senses the tension, my beloved dog Max bounds towards us, tail wagging excitedly.

'Aww, here he is! My main man!' I beam, as he turns his adorable chocolate eyes to my guest.

'Max, this is Stephanie. She's going to be staying with us for a while.'

Max circles Stephanie's legs before jumping up at her as if citing his approval and my heart swells with affection for him.

Stephanie however, clearly doesn't feel the same, looking at my sweet little Yorkshire Terrier like he's a rabid animal.

'No! Get down, Max.' She waves him away with the back of her hand as if swatting away an annoying wasp. 'Go on, down!'

'He's only saying hello!' I say, my voice a little too tight.

'Sorry... I'm allergic,' Stephanie mumbles, but as she glances away, a part of me knows she's lying. Her mother would have the same look on her face when she fibbed.

'Well, Max is a hypoallergenic breed,' I inform her. 'And he only means well, he can probably sense that you're... a little out of sorts, with everything that's happened.'

She nods vaguely, her eyes moving around the room, not meeting mine.

It's just growing pains, I tell myself. I shouldn't be too hard on her. We're basically strangers after all. Yet we are both painfully aware of how tonight has changed everything. Everything.

Here we are, both dancing around each other, playing the roles that are expected of us. Grandmother and Granddaughter. I should know her allergies, her hopes and fears. I should know the name of her best friend and how she likes her tea. But instead I hardly recognise the sixteen-year-old girl in front of me. We have ten years to catch up on, and I can't let us blow this chance.

'How about I make us both a nice hot drink and then perhaps we can talk?' I suggest, only Stephanie purses her mouth and the expression on her face tells me that talking is the last thing she wants to do.

'Come on, lovely. You're shaking. A bit of sugar will do you some good!'

Reluctantly she nods, more out of politeness than anything else and I retreat into the kitchen.

I busy myself preparing the cups as the kettle boils and listen as the girl moves around my lounge in my absence. Snooping through my things as she tries to suss me out.

I imagine Stephanie peering into boxes and bags, trying to make sense of my clutter. The stacks of books that tower in large piles, old landline telephones with their tangled mass of wires. Chipped photo frames. I imagine her sizing me up, wondering what sort of woman can live in such mess.

'Here we go! Have you ever tried Ovaltine before? Because I swear by it...' I say, coming back into the room with the tray in my hand. Just in time to catch Stephanie shove something into her pocket. 'Everything all right?'

'I was just admiring all the little china dogs you've got. Cute!' Stephanie quips, the picture of innocence.

I stare at the shelf and do a quick inventory, realising quickly that none of them are missing, but unable to forget what I saw.

It's been a long night though. Perhaps I imagined it?

'Actually, Kay, I'm really tired. If you don't mind, I might give the drink a miss...'

'Are you sure? It's not even eight?' I say, unable to hide my disappointment. Stephanie hasn't even taken her coat off and already she wants to shut herself away from me.

'I'm shattered. I just want to sleep.'

Sleep? As if there would be any sleep for either of us tonight? After what we just witnessed?

Before I can breathe a word, Stephanie grabs her things and disappears into the dark stairwell. Sighing, I go to follow her, ready to show her her new room.

It's only then as I glance at the shelf once more, that I realise what's missing. The little pot of pills hidden carefully behind the King Charles Spaniel. The space sits empty now. My medication is gone.

2

KAY

Rap-tap-tap. Rap-tap-tap.

Homing in on the faint tapping sound from inside the coffin, I immediately dismiss the sound as nonsense. I am hearing things. The enormous stress of the last few days is finally catching up with me. Or perhaps it is wishful thinking.

My gaze fixes on the extortionately overpriced oak coffin, as it is lowered slowly down into the cold, damp earth.

Rap-tap-tap. Rap-tap-tap.

I hear it again. Louder now. Clearer.

But that's impossible, isn't it? That can't be real.

Of course it's not real! I tell myself sternly, sifting through the only few rational explanations I can think of.

My imagination is simply playing tricks on me.

Grief has finally sent me mad.

RAP-TAP-TAP. RAP-TAP-TAP.

This time when I hear it, I purposely block it out. Only it just gets louder.

Amanda is dead. Dead, I tell myself.

I've seen her with my own two eyes, cocooned inside that coffin, wearing the dark violet fitted dress that I picked out for her especially. Her long fiery red hair cascading down over her thin, bony shoulders. Her frail, waif-like hands clasped together neatly on her lap. As if she was merely just resting.

A modern-day Sleeping Beauty.

In a dress that I never thought would see the light of day.

A dress that had spent so many years neatly wrapped in tissue paper at the bottom of Amanda's childhood wardrobe, because Amanda had never returned any of my calls or agreed to let me see her in order to gift it to her.

Shocked at the frightful state of Amanda's own clothes, when I'd gone to pick out something suitable for her to wear for her funeral, how the threadbare rags, full of cigarette burns, holes and stains that my daughter was used to bore no comparison to the beautiful dress that I had bought for her. It had felt like fate.

My God, how Amanda would have hated it if she had still been here to see it. Because I bought the dress for her. I had chosen it. She'd hate it just to spite me, like she bloody hates me too. And who could blame her?

Dead to me! I wince at the last words I had ever spoken aloud to my daughter. Words I had screamed into her face.

DEAD TO ME.

And now she really is. My daughter's lifeless corpse laid out inside that coffin, about to be buried beneath a mountain of soil.

Rap-tap-tap. Rap-tap-tap.

The noise keeps coming. Louder. Harder. Faster. So severe that I am almost certain that I can't be the only one to hear it.

Allowing my gaze to sweep the rest of the congregation, I take in the sea of shocked, horrified faces. Their frantic gasps and hurried whispers fill my ears like waves slowly rolling before they crash against the shore, as if trying to wake me up. Make me take notice. I am not alone or going mad in fact.

They can all hear it too.

The dull thuds, delivered with force now as if a pair of

clenched fists are frantically smacking against the inside the coffin in desperation to be heard. To be saved. TO GET OUT.

A muffled voice.

'Help me, Mum! Get me out!'

'Amanda?' The words leave my mouth in a strange, twisted high-pitch screech as I stare down to where the mound of soil is already being poured down on top of the grave. Trapping her inside for all of eternity. It's too late.

'Earth to earth, ashes to ashes.' The priest's mournful voice carries in the bitterly cold wind, across the congregation.

Doesn't he hear her too?

'She's not dead,' I mumble, trying to make some sense out of the madness. 'SHE'S NOT DEAD. SHE'S NOT DEAD.' The words burst from my mouth and without thinking I am sinking down to the wet ground. Swinging my legs over the side of the graveside, and scrambling down into the deep, vast hole. Landing with a thump, I am on my knees, frantically clawing back huge handfuls of dirt from where it's settled on the lid of the coffin before I throw it back up to the grass verge above me.

'Don't just stand there, help me get her out,' I scream at the horrified faces that all stare down at me.

A chorus of panic and shrieks echoing out above me, confirming what I know now to be true.

My daughter is not dead. She's being buried alive.

'I'm here, Amanda, I'm coming. Hold on.' I am shouting now. Blind panic flooding out from every part of my body as I scrape and claw at the soil.

'She's not dead. Amanda is not dead.'

It's my own screams that wake me.

Disorientated, I fling myself forward, only to find myself alone in the dark. My skin is hot and prickled with a thin film of sweat and my nightdress is soaked through. I frantically stare around the room, the thin slither of light creeps in from the gap beneath the bedroom door lighting the way as I gather my bearings.

I am in my bed, I realise as I grip the wall with one hand in a bid to steady myself as the room begins to sway. Gulping down huge greedy lungsful of air as panic floods my veins, I remind myself to focus. I need to pull myself back from yet another awful nightmare.

I am wide awake now. It wasn't real. Amanda is dead. Gone. Her funeral had only been yesterday. This information does nothing to comfort me, if anything it makes me feel worse. Because my waking reality is more agonising than my very worst nightmares. There was no relief in saying my goodbyes yesterday. No closure like they'd all said there would be. If anything I feel even more despondent now, my chest tight, my heart plagued with grief. Riddled with it, in fact.

'You're dead to me. DEAD.' I flinch at the memory of those final angry words. That *had* happened. I *had* said that.

I'd only ever said them out loud that once. But that once had been enough it seemed, for God to pay attention and grant me my one, sullen wish. It didn't matter that Amanda had said it back, or that Amanda had said worse. A lot worse in fact. Always telling me that she hated me, despised my very being. Blaming me for ruining her life. It was yet another of our charged and complex fights, full of bitter names and nasty words. How was I to know it would be our last? How was I to know I could never take my angry words back?

Breathe! I instruct myself.

In through my nose and out through my mouth, inhaling as I do the familiar remnant of the lavender air freshener that lingers in the air around me, but it's overpowering now, so sweet and cloying that I fight the urge to be sick.

I need to get up. I need to get out of this room.

My eyes go to the red glow of my alarm clock that sits on the bedside cabinet beside me. Two a.m. Is that it? Is that all that I had slept for? One whole hour? If it wasn't so tragic I would laugh at the fact that, even now, Amanda is still tormenting me. Haunting me. Tears threaten, and I shut my eyes to keep them from pouring out, because this is all part of my punishment, isn't it?

This is what I am owed.

BAD MOTHER.

I focus on the sound of rain outside, the heavy droplets splattering loudly with force against the windowpane. The weather forecast has predicted a storm brewing over London in the next few days. Storm Kathleen is set to batter the city, with its gale force winds and heavy downpours of torrential rain. Is it here already? Judging by how the wind has picked up, sending gusts whirling down the open fireplace opposite my bed, a cold chill blasting out around the room, I think it must be. Though I like the feel of the cool air on my skin and the way that it pulls me back, away from all the insular thoughts that swim inside my mind.

As I look down at my hands and note how they are trembling, I accept that I am done with sleep for tonight. I can't relax, let alone switch off, so I decide to get up. Swinging my legs over the side of the bed, I reach for my dressing gown. I tuck the edges of my duvet neatly down into the groove between the mattress and the metal bed frame as if making my bed means I won't be tempted to sleep in it later. I think about making some nice Ovaltine and finishing my knitting, before crossing the room and yanking up the bedroom blinds for good measure. Only outside, there's no daylight just yet, it's much too early for that.

But it's out there. The 'nothingness' as I often aptly refer to the view from my window at this time of the morning. The vastness of Highgate Woods that spills out for miles behind my home. A blanket of green by day, sitting boldly against London's grey-blue skies, hidden underneath the blanket of complete darkness now. The woodlands are one of the things that I have grown to love the most about living in this house. My view from up here, on a clear sunny day, allows me to pretend that I live somewhere far away from the real chaos and noise of this busy residential London street. Somewhere rural and idyllic.

Only tonight, the nothingness is broken by the flash of something glowing white and unfamiliar. A light of some sort, flickering in the distance. And movement. Grabbing my glasses from the bedside table, I position my face nearer to the window, straining to see out past the driving rain streaking its way down the glass. My eyes adjust to the darkness. A faint glow of yellow blinks on the horizon. Like that from a lamp or torch that has been muted slightly. As if something or someone is stopping the illumination from radiating out too brightly. It's coming from inside a tent. A tent that appears to be pitched up on the wood-lands' edge, purposely set among the tress in a bid to stay hidden. Only it's not hidden now. It's literally glowing in the dark. Who in their right mind would choose to sleep out there tonight in this weather?

Focus.

My attention is back on the tent now, held by an emerging figure. A young woman, I guess, going by the slight of her frame and glimpse of long hair peeking out from the large, hooded coat wrapped tightly around her. What is she doing out there? Why would she leave the sacred shelter of her tent, right now, just as the rain drives down harder?

It's only when the girl attempts to hide herself further, squatting down in the overgrowth that I realise to my utter horror that the woman is emptying her bowels. And I, like some perverted weirdo, am stood at the window blatantly spying on her.

Mind your business, Kay. Don't interfere. Concentrate on your own mess of a life.

Another image of Amanda fills my head.

My daughter stood on the front doorstep; her hair stuck limply to her face with the pouring rain. Amanda is screaming at me, telling me that I am a Bad Mother. That I don't deserve her as a daughter. That I don't deserve Stephanie as a granddaughter.

DEAD TO ME.

My words. Right before I slammed the front door in her face.

3

ROSIE

I tug at the zip, making sure that the tent is closed behind me, before glancing over to where Ash lies, huddled inside his sleeping bag, snoring soundly.

So much for him protecting me. Protecting us. He doesn't even know I've been out, let alone come back. Angry now, I crouch down and crawl across the damp, cold ground sheet towards my own bed. Anyone could be in here with us right now and Ash would be none the wiser. He's completely out of it. His chiselled, handsome features relaxed now that he is deep in sleep. His sharp jawline softened. He looks calm in sleep. Angelic almost. As if he doesn't have a care in the world.

There's irony in that, because he is the very reason we are here, pitched up in this shoddy old tent on the edge of the woods in the first place. He'd convinced me that we'd be safer here, that if we set up after dark and stayed hidden among the trees and bushes that lined the woodlands' edge, there would be less chance of anyone bothering us.

Only Ash is wrong about that.

Here, unlike the dimly lit shop doorways we'd taken refuge in at Highgate Wood High Street, we actually stand out more. If anything, we've made ourselves more vulnerable if anyone does spot us. It's only a matter of time until we attract trouble, or unwanted attention from the police.

I wipe my dirt-stained hands on my jogging bottoms, before peeling the wet layers of clothing away from my skin thanks to the downpour I just endured while relieving myself outside. Another degrading part of living out here on the streets is the basic hygiene, or lack of. I stink.

Pulling on one of Ash's huge, oversized jumpers I let out an involuntary groan as I realise that it's as damp and smelly as the one I've just taken off. Though his jumper is slightly thicker, so it will do for now. Irritated, I slip silently back inside my makeshift bed. Ash, of course, continues to sleep through all of this while I lay alone again in the darkness.

The silence is deafening. I've heard that expression before, but I never fully appreciated its real meaning until now. The blue tarpaulin walls are closing in on me, crushing me. Forcing me to go inside myself and face my deepest, most terrifying thoughts. I try to shake the image of Ash's face as he had stared down at the body at his feet. How his expressions had flashed so quickly from rage, to guilt, then to something else? Gripped with fear or panic? I'm not sure which, all I remember is how he begged me, pleaded with me.

'Please, Rosie. Don't phone the police. Please don't call them.'

And foolishly, like always, I had listened to him.

'We need to go.'

Stupid, stupid girl. I silently berate myself, because I know now that we should never have run. We should have stayed and faced the consequences of our actions. We should have done the right thing.

Head floppy, body lifeless. Dead.

I tightly squeeze my eyes shut, trying my hardest to block that last harrowing image of her out of my head. Because I can't do this, I can't think about her right now. Just the thought of what we did makes me feel physically sick.

I try to think about something else. Anything else. Concentrating on the relentless storm outside. Grateful for the distraction of sporadic rain droplets bouncing loudly against the taut material of the tent's roof. Then seconds later an almighty loud crack of thunder whips at the skies directly above me, making me physically jump with fright.

Still Ash sleeps.

Shivering violently from the cold and utter exhaustion, I sink down further inside the old musty sleeping bag, following Ash's lead in the hope that I too will give in to sleep soon. The thin, frayed material does little to keep the icy cold chill from my skin, and I can't help but think about the old man that Ash stole it from. How he'd be freezing right now without it. I force down the heavy flurry of guilt that rises up from the pit of my stomach, because I can't deal with the guilt of that too. Ash's actions, not mine. *He'll be fine*, I tell myself. Especially if the weather is all the old man has to contend with. He would have found some kind of shelter. The streets are different for men. Safer, without the added fear of being tormented or hurt as they slept.

Deep down I know that isn't strictly true. Anyone sleeping rough on London's bitterly cold streets sets themselves up to be an unwilling target. That's just the way it is out here. I'd witnessed that cruelty with my very own eyes these past few days, yet I still can't seem to get my head around it. How the homeless, already so down on their luck are seen by some as fair game. Singled out and set upon by drunken mobs purely for their own entertainment. Kicked awake, spat on, laughed at. Pissed on too.

It feels worse for me. The streets are a far more dangerous place for a young woman at night. There is no denying that. I've barely slept at all since we've been out here, gripped with paranoia at every sound or sudden movement, as I've huddled in dark crevices of shop doorways and alleyways in a bid to stay small and invisible. I've had to stay on my guard and be cautious, though trouble seems to constantly have a way of seeking me out.

'*What's a pretty young girl like you doing out here all by herself?*'

Chancers mainly. Opportunists. Lone men crawling out from the darkness in their droves. Believing that I could be theirs for the taking.

Stupid, stupid girl.

'I'm not out here on my own.' My well-rehearsed response always the same as I waited for Ash to return with food, or blankets or some money he'd begged from strangers further down the street. I'd done my best to do as Ash told me. Holding their eye contact and standing tall as I spoke. Making it look as though I could handle myself, that I wasn't a stranger to these streets or the kind of predators that roamed them, preying on young women like me.

'My boyfriend will be back any second.'

That's what usually did it. The mention of a boyfriend. That alone irritated me. How the word 'No' from a woman was never enough, how I needed to give them a valid reason to go with it.

The rain begins to slow, and the night becomes quiet again. Too quiet. I am suddenly engulfed with an unsettling feeling of being isolated. It's a good thing I suppose. The awful weather means that people are avoiding coming out in it. Tonight, there's a good chance of me actually getting some sleep finally. God, I need it. I close my eyes to stop tears from pouring out. Feeling sorry for myself now, I suppress the sob that I can feel threatening in the back of my throat, managing to hold it in.

Ash lied to me. This isn't going to be all right, is it? Not if we keep doing things his way.

I concentrate on the soft, hypnotic sound of the wind outside, whipping through the trees, I know that even the rhythmic and soothing lull of what sounds like white noise will not be enough for me to give in to my exhaustion.

There'll be no sleep for me tonight.

I need to think of a new plan. I can't depend on Ash to get us out of this mess. I know he wants to, but I'm not sure he's capable. Silently, I tug my sleeping bag back down over my legs and get up. Bracing myself to face the treacherous elements once more, I keep my head low, crouching quietly until I'm back outside the tent.

I need to find a way out of this nightmare. And I need to do it myself.

4

STEPHANIE

The sound of something smashing startles me wide awake. Disorientated, I sit up in my bed and take a moment or two to realise where I am.

Not in my bed.

The sickly, chemical smelling plug-in air freshener that Kay insists on planting in every room of her house is so overwhelming and pungent that I fight the urge not to be sick. But the smell propels with me with full force back into my newfound reality. Waking up in Kay Wyldes' spare room. My mother's old room, in fact. I flick the bedroom lamp on and prop myself up onto one arm, straining to listen so I can work out what it is that has woken me.

Only I am met with silence.

Shivering, I stare around the dimly lit bedroom, my eyes following the light as it casts its long, foreboding shadows into every darkened corner. I thought it was sweet at first. When Kay had proudly showed me this room for the very first time. How she'd kept my mum's childhood bedroom just as she'd left it.

In all these years Kay hadn't moved a single thing. It's immaculate. Sacred. One of the only rooms in Kay's entire house that she hasn't filled to the brim with mess and boxes and clutter. Which I suspect is the real reason for Kay's obsession with pungent air fresheners all over her house. It's her poor attempt to mask the musty, sour smell of all her things everywhere. The endless clutter that takes up so much space, it squeezes out all of the air from the rest of the house.

Now, at this early hour, in this light, Kay's showroom looks more like a creepy shrine. My mother's old things, stuck here on display, lost in time. In limbo. The tatty stuffed toys of her childhood placed in a neat careful row at the end of the bed. An old dressing table still set up in the corner, with brightly coloured hair scrunchies discarded messily among the pots of lotions and tubes of make-up that are strewn about, some of the lids remain off.

That's odd isn't it? Leaving a room so staged for all these years, in the hope that one day my mother might finally come back here. How Kay's homage to her estranged daughter has now become a creepy memorial for the dead. A place for my mother's ghost to visit. The last time she would have been here, in this room, would have been when she was the same age that I am now. Sweet Sixteen.

I've avoided it until now. Looking at her things, studying all her stuff. But I'm feeling a little braver this morning, stronger somehow since the funeral yesterday and I feel the pull of it all. As I wonder what she would have looked like back then. As a young girl, before she had me. I'm curious about how she would have dressed, what kind of books she would have read.

Getting out of bed, I walk over to the dresser and pick up one of my mother's lipsticks, gliding the dark, frosted purply brown smudge of colour in a neat line across the pale skin of the back of my hand. 'Heather Shimmer.' Hmm, not keen, I purse my lips as I replace the lid and set it back down on the dressing table. It would have probably suited my mother's colouring much better than mine. Her complexion had been darker, her lips full and pink. While I am pale and sickly looking. My lips a thin, straight line.

Picking up the black and white Exclamation shaped perfume bottle, I spray it sparingly into the air around me, coughing and spluttering as the sickly potent combination of peaches and vanilla catch in the back of my throat. Worse than the air freshener.

It makes me think about a time my mum took me shopping when I was ten. How she'd distracted the lady behind the counter in the department store, asking for something high up on a shelf, before quickly emptying the entire basket of perfume testers into her handbag then grabbing my hand and running from the shop. We'd smelled heavenly for months after that. I smile but am quickly overcome by sadness, and the sudden pang of grief that catches me is all encompassing, all consuming.

God, how I miss her.

I miss her. I miss her. I miss her.

There are so many emotions that come with that thought that I can barely think straight to differentiate between them. I am sorry, and sad, and terrified all at once. But more than anything I feel the overwhelming feeling of guilt.

She's dead because of me.

Now, I'm here seeking solace with the one woman that my mother had spent a lifetime warning me against.

They are complete opposites of one another.

Kay, surrounding herself with all these things, while my mother had always chosen to surround herself with people. Always the wrong kind, granted. An endless stream of visitors. Untrustworthy people, users mainly, most of whom I had always hated. All those incoherent drunken conversations and drug-fuelled arguments I'd been forced to endure from such a young age. I'd grown up on that, hadn't I? The constant noise and chaos of our flat. All of that crying.

My mother's tears mainly, after one of her so-called friends had disappeared along with the last twenty-pound note that she had managed to squirrel away in the back of her purse. Or another time, when the sparse contents of our fridge had gone missing. One of my mother's so-called friends thanking her for her hospitality by taking the last of our food with him when he left. Food that was supposed to see us through until my mother's next Universal Credit payment was due.

I shouldn't miss my old life. But I do, I realise as a deranged screech escapes from my mouth. Because my old life came with my mother. To be without it, means being without her and I'm not sure I can do it. I am yearning for it. The familiarity of the one shambolic life I'd ever known. I think of the silences then too, how I didn't miss those. My mother enthralled in another one of her 'episodes.' Bed-bound for days on end. Unable to function or cope.

Then that very last time I'd seen her. She'd been completely silent then too. Not breathing. Dead.

I take a moment, allowing my new reality to sink in. The realisation that she's never coming back. Not for all this crap that Kay has laid out on display and not for me. For now, this is my new life and I need to accept that. Living here with my estranged grandmother Kay. Allowing her to help me.

SMASH!

The earlier sound that woke me comes again, reminding me that something had pulled me from my sleep. I hadn't imagined it. It's louder this time, more defined. The sound of glass smashing and instantly I am worried about Kay.

Plagued with insomnia, Kay has a habit of bustling around downstairs in the early hours of the morning. Making herself endless cups of that gross smelling malt drink that she is addicted to, before spending a few hours getting stuck into whatever her current knitting project is, while the rest of the world sleeps. Another shapeless boxy looking jumper no doubt or a pair of hideous stripy socks that she'll insist on gifting me, that we both know I'll never wear.

Either that or I'm woken by the loud slam of the backdoor, as Kay goes off out on one of her ridiculously early morning walks with her dog, Max. As if pounding the pavement outside will somehow bring the woman some much-needed solace or release from the grief she is feeling. It won't. I know that first-hand, but I also know that there is no point telling Kay that, because people deal with grief in different ways and how Kay deals with hers is none of my business. But I should go and check on her and make sure she's okay. Dog walking, drink making and knitting were Kay's usual tricks. Glass breaking, however, wasn't the norm around here and I'm worried that Kay may have fallen and hurt herself.

Deciding to investigate, I pull a jumper over my pyjamas, and I am about to leave the room when the noise comes again, stopping me in my tracks. It's not coming from inside the house at all. It's coming from directly outside my bedroom window. Pulling back the curtain to get a better look, I stare out into the street, right on cue as the streetlights flicker off, making way for the sun now slowly rising in the sky.

The noise comes again.

Glass shattering accompanied this time by a woman's voice. High-pitched and defensive as if she is arguing with someone. Alert now, I search the street, and it takes me a few seconds before I see them. The couple stood next to a parked car, a few doors down. They are arguing. The man leaning in, towering menacingly over the woman, jabbing his finger towards the passenger side window, and the shattered spider web crack that is splayed across the remainder of the glass. There's a huge chunk of it missing. That's what must have woken me. They've broken into the car.

My first instinct is to go out there and investigate, but I know from experience not to get involved in other people's business. I'd witnessed enough of my mother's over the years and it never fared well. Instead, quietly, carefully, I slide the window upwards before grabbing my iPhone and leaning out. I start recording instead.

'Stephanie?'

'Shit.'

The unexpected sound of Kay's voice behind me makes me jump. A pain exploding inside my head as my forehead connects with the sharp edge of the sash window. I step backward into the room, cradling my head in my hands, just as Kay turns the bedroom light on and the bright sudden glare of the main light almost blinds me. I flinch.

'God, Kay. You scared the bloody life out of me.'

I see the flicker of hurt flash across Kay's face at my insistence on calling her by her first name instead of 'nan', as she insists.

'I heard a noise up here and thought maybe you couldn't sleep either. Thought you might like a nice hot drink.' Kay places the steaming hot mug down on the dresser and goes back to standing in the doorway. Awkward now and fidgety, like an intruder in her own home, her arms hang loosely down at her sides as if she doesn't know what to do with them. It's only in this sharp, unflattering light that I notice the heavy lines imprinted across the older woman's face, how they seem so much deeper and defined than they appeared yesterday.

Kay looks as if she's aged an eternity overnight.

I soften slightly because I can see that she is in pain too. It's not just me that's hurting.

'I'm sorry. I didn't mean to worry you. I heard a noise outside,' I explain, nodding towards the open window, my phone still recording, only when I look outside, the street is empty now. The two figures I'd seen just minutes earlier, are long gone.

'Someone broke into one of the neighbours' cars. They smashed one of the windows.'

'Oh dear.' Kay makes her way over to where I am standing so that she can take a better look. 'Maybe we should call the police?'

She stops, quickly changing her mind. 'Though, aren't they always saying on the news how the police are already stretched for their resources? Besides, the car looks ancient, it doesn't even have an alarm,' Kay says knowingly, as she too peers out of the window as if for confirmation that this is in fact true. 'It's probably just kids having some harmless fun. Nothing sinister.'

I nod my head. Aware of how reasonable and rational Kay is trying to sound. Only the slight shake of the older woman's voice gives her away. She doesn't fool me in the slightest. We both know this is exactly the sort of thing that Kay would be hyperventilating about usually. Some snippet of gossip or drama to fixate on. Anything to add some excitement to the quiet, unremarkable little life inside these four cluttered walls. Normally, Kay would be one of the first people to call something like this in, I bet.

'We shouldn't waste their time, not when they have real crimes to solve.'

Real crimes.

The words hang in the air between us and I'm almost certain that I can hear it. A flicker of a warning to Kay's tone. Telling me that we cannot get the police involved. We don't need any more police round here.

'Yeah, you're probably right. It's probably just kids. Nicking loose change and a few spare cigarettes is hardly the crime of the century, is it? Whoever broke in is probably long gone by now anyway. They'd never catch them.'

Kay nods her head, happy we are both in agreement before

she finally leaves the room. The relief evident in the woman's body as she hurries to get back to her tepid cup of Ovaltine and her knitting project and her beloved dog.

I'm not stupid though. I know the real reason Kay doesn't want to call the police. She doesn't want them here, snooping around and asking any more questions. Because more questions only mean more lies.

5

KAY

It's still out here. The blue tent that had magically appeared out of nowhere in the early hours of this morning. I'd started to think that perhaps I'd imagined it. Not noticing it initially, as me and Max had done our usual lap of the park.

Highgate Woods' park is my favourite walk, especially at this early hour. Dawn. That perfect half-light of the early morning when the streetlamps have flickered off, the sun isn't fully up and most of the world is tucked up in their beds still fast asleep. The park is void of its usual influx of dog walkers I normally politely say hello to, there's no one here riding their bikes or young mothers with their children in pushchairs. For now, there is no one else around to interrupt the peacefulness I crave as I grip Max's lead tightly, allowing him to lead me in a dazed stupor around the field, as he wags his tail excitedly. Only, today it isn't just me and Max. There is a filthy blue tent to contend with. An ugly blip on the horizon that the trees and bushes it stands among do nothing to conceal. It bothers me, how now I've spotted it, it stands out like a sore thumb. Ruining the tranquil illusion of my little piece of oasis among the chaotic concrete jungle that is the rest of London.

Teenagers.

That had been my first thought, when I'd set eyes on the monstrosity from my bedroom window. Kids inside, playing camp. Teenagers who had probably told their parents they were sleeping at each other's houses, when really, they are rebelling. Braving the elements to set about having some form of adventure. They'd be gone soon.

Only they haven't gone and now in the cold harsh light of day it doesn't look like the kind of place for fun or adventure. I listen out, noting how there's no sound of any laughter or chatter. There's no sign of life at all inside. Though there had been signs, I think of the girl I'd seen late last night. Leaving the tent before squatting down in the bushes. What if she's out here all on her own? I should go and check on her, shouldn't I? See if she's still inside and if she's okay, because she might be genuinely homeless and has nowhere else to go. She might need some real help.

Thoughts of Amanda burst into my mind. Had she ever had to sleep rough out in the cold like this? What would I want someone to do if they'd have found her?

Help her.

Pulling Max's lead in tightly, I gather up all my courage to go to do exactly that.

'Hello?' I call out loudly, my tone laced with a bravado I don't really feel as I reach the front of the tent. My confidence disintegrating now as I see the zip is pulled down tightly. I am suddenly aware of my blatant intrusion.

'Hello?' I wait patiently for an answer. When I don't receive one, I wonder if whoever might be inside is still fast asleep. Perhaps that's why they haven't heard me? Though the sheet of flimsy material between me and them does little to convince me of that.

'I'm sorry to bother you. I just wanted to check and see if

you're okay?' I call out again, only still there is no reply and there doesn't seem to be any signs of movement inside either.

It might be empty, I think, wondering if whoever has been camping out here last night has already cut their losses and moved on. And who could blame them? Very few people would be able to withstand the freezing cold temperatures and heavy downpour of the past few days. They may have upped and left, leaving their filthy looking tent behind them. Littering, I tut loudly to myself.

The tent would sit here for days, if not weeks if that was the case. Other homeless people might take up residence in it. Or children might discover it. They might climb inside, and God knows what's been left behind in there for them to find if they do. I should look, I think as I turn and scan the rest of the park, checking that the coast is clear. That no one else is approaching or watching me. That I'm safe to look, before I bend down at the door and tug at the zip.

'Hello, is anyone in here?' I sink down to my knees straight into the puddle of slushy mud outside the tent's door and silently curse to myself as it smears up my leggings. I'll have to shove all my clothes in the washing machine when I get home. Now isn't the time to be worrying about a bit of mud.

'I just wanted to check and see if you're okay...' I call out again, this time more assertively as I pull at the zip. I'm relieved when I push the tarpaulin doors open to see that the tent is empty inside. There's no one here. Though the putrid, acrid stench that spills out causes me to physically recoil and I clamp my hand over my mouth in a bid to retain the pool of watery bile that's instantly formed, as I try my hardest not to gag. I inspect the tent, because the smell is so potent, so vile that I half expect to have stumbled upon a dead body. Max must smell it too, because he begins barking excitedly, scurrying his way past me to get inside.

'No, Max. Out,' I command, tugging his lead to forbid him from scampering into the small, cramped living quarters. Placing Max's lead down on the floor, I hold out my palm instructing Max not to follow me inside before I turn, crouching, still not sure what I have happened upon as I eye the heap of blankets in the far corner.

Concealing something. Or someone.

I cautiously step forward, acutely aware of how I shouldn't be here. Snooping through this person's things. Invading their privacy like this. How I should mind my own business, but my curiosity has got the better of me and I can't go back now, not now that I have come this far. I need to look, need to take this chance while I can. Only I am scared. Scared to take another step but I know that I must because that God-awful smell is coming from somewhere. Stepping over a carrier bag, its contents strewn across the tarpaulin floor, I eye the supermarket value brand biscuit wrapper and empty cans of baked beans on the floor. There doesn't seem to be any sign of cooking appliances in here, so I assume that whoever has eaten them, has eaten them cold straight from the tin.

They are not pungent enough to create this smell. Something black is sticking out from beneath what looks like the sleeve of a wet jumper. Kicking out with my shoe, I see that it's a torch. Most likely the same light I'd seen shining brightly across the park from my bedroom window. I keep moving, the smell so much worse the longer I am in here. Even with my fingers locked firmly over my mouth. I step towards the pile of damp and dirty blankets that are heaped into a corner.

My heart pounds inside my chest and I am full of trepidation as I lift the thin sleeping bag that has been placed on top of the pile. A knot of fear tightly twisting inside my stomach as I force myself to look at what might be beneath. *Who* might be beneath it. I flick up the first few layers and narrow my eyes. To my utter relief what I see is not that of a body, or a person. I am staring down at a long, tatty cardboard box.

Then I see it, where the smell is coming from. The soiled, grimy looking nappy that has been left on top of the colourful knitted blankets the cot's lined with inside. I realise to my horror that this is what the box is being used as. It's a makeshift cot. The girl I saw last night isn't alone.

6

ROSIE

I place the syringe full of liquid paracetamol to my son's mouth, though of course George refuses it. Crying hysterically now because of the pain and discomfort he is in, he squirms defiantly in my arms as if in a bid to get away from me, as he wails loudly in pure disgust that I would even dare place anything other than his bottle of milk to his lips. Well, I can be just as stubborn and obstinate, and I'm not prepared to give in either. I tilt his head back, expertly, and part his pursed, angry lips with the teat of his bottle, waiting patiently for him to give into the temptation of suckling, before I quickly replace the teat with the plastic syringe.

'There you go. Good boy,' I whisper, administering the liquid before George even has time to register that I have just tricked him in to swallowing his medicine down. Then quickly, I place his bottle of milk to his mouth, just in time to catch the defiant scream that I know is coming.

And I do catch it.

His loud screech is quickly replaced by the greedy sucking sound as George latches on to his bottle, and despite my angst I smile down at my boy who is distracted now by the comfort of his milk. I feel his tiny, rigid body finally soften and sink into mine and it's only then that I allow myself to relax too. Exhausted from the past few days, I slump back against the makeshift bed of blankets and sleeping bags that are screwed up into a messy heap behind me and close my eyes. Not for long, I promise myself, just a few minutes so that I can rest for a while. Relish the warmth of George's body against mine. Absorb the blissful silence that has descended inside the tent now that his frenzied cries have finally stopped. Praying silently to myself that it will stay like this now. That the medicine will work its magic and make my son better. It has to.

'Someone's been here.'

My eyes flicker open at Ash's sudden accusation, thinking that I must have misheard him. The angry look on his face tells me I haven't.

'They've been through our stuff,' he adds then with a certainty.

'How do you know?' Unable to keep the scepticism from my tone, I follow Ash's steely gaze as it darts around the small space and he scans the contents of the tiny tent.

We don't have much stuff to go through and even if someone did come in here, there is nothing of any value worth taking. A pile of blankets, our tatty, stolen sleeping bags and our damp, dirty clothing. The cardboard box Ash swiped from behind a supermarket, that we've been using as a makeshift crib for George is shoved in the corner, taking up most of the room in here. We don't have anything else.

'Nothing's missing, is it?' I ask, but even as I say this I am second guessing myself. Ash is shrewd and nothing ever gets past him. He doesn't miss a trick. Whereas, according to him, half the time, I'm 'away with the fairies.' Barely registering what's going on around me. What am I not seeing now?

'George's shitty nappy and that bag of rubbish are gone.'

'Okay...?' A small smile teeters on the edge of my lips at

Ash's attempt at a stupid joke, only the thunderous look that flashes across his face stops me dead in my tracks. This isn't his attempt at being humorous. He isn't messing around. He means it. He really believes that someone has been in our tent. That they've taken our rubbish and George's soiled nappy.

'But why would someone come in here and steal a baby's dirty nappy?'

'I have no idea.' He shrugs. 'But it's gone. Look.'

Ash points to the space on the floor where the carrier bag, full of old baked bean cans and biscuit wrappers, had been dumped last night. It's not there now.

Clambering to my knees, I peer inside the cardboard cot and note how the nappy that I'd left there last night at George's feet has in fact gone. It had been there, I know this for a fact, because I'd remembered after I'd left the tent that I had meant to take it with me and throw it in one of the bins that sits on the park's perimeter, only I'd been in such a hurry to leave, so worried about George that I'd forgotten. The tent had stunk. A rancid reminder of George's upset tummy lingering in the air.

It isn't as pungent in here now and I hadn't noticed, probably because I'm so used to the acrid stench of baby shit from the past few days, almost as if it has seeped into the pores of my skin, engraining itself into my clothes and my hair.

'But why?' I shake my head as if I'm missing something. 'I don't understand. Why would anyone take a dirty nappy and a bag full of rubbish? It doesn't make any sense. They're hardly highly theft-able items, are they?'

'DNA? Maybe it's the police poking about, looking for evidence of who's been staying here. Maybe they're on to us, Rosie. Maybe they know we're here and they're going to come back? Or maybe they think we've left for good?'

'The police?' My voice quivers as I subconsciously tighten my grip around George as he continues to finish his bottle. Ash warned me what would happen if the police found us, why we can't ever go back. They'll say we're bad parents, that we put George in danger. Exposed him to the elements, that we made him sick. They'll take him away from us.

Looking down at him now as his fat little cheeks glow a deep red, the sound of phlegm rattling at each rise and fall of George's chest as he fights to draw breath through his snot-encrusted nostrils, as he gulps at his milk I can't help but wonder if perhaps they might be right about that. We are bad parents, aren't we? We did this to him. It is madness. Camping out here in the woodlands on the edge of the park with our newborn baby. Hiding the tent among the trees and bushes. What had we been thinking?

'You really think they've found us?'

'Found us?' Ash laughs but the sound is stilted and the half smile he offers looks more of an angry grimace. 'Are you for real? No one has just randomly *found* us, Rosie. They've been led straight to us, by you.' Ash shakes his head in dismay, a look of frustration spreading across his face that somehow, I can't see it without him having to spell it out for me.

'Me? How is this my fault?' I shoot back, defensive now. Unsure how Ash is managing to turn this all back on me.

'I told you not to do anything that would draw any attention to us. But once again you didn't listen. That's the problem, Rosie, you never listen. I told you we need to lay low, didn't I?'

'And I am laying low...' I hold my hands up and indicate the crappy, basic living quarters that I've had to endure for the past few days. 'It doesn't get much lower than this.'

'Oh, come on, Rosie. Smashing car windows with rocks and stealing people's money isn't laying low. Someone must have seen you. They've seen the tent. It doesn't take a genius to put the two things together.' Ash's voice is taut with anger, and he doesn't bother waiting for a reply.

He doesn't need or want one. He is already busy gathering up our things and shoving them into carrier bags. My heart sinks, because I know what's coming. We're going to have to move on again. Pack up everything in this tent and find somewhere else to pitch up before whoever it was that was snooping around in here comes back. Only I don't think I have the energy to move anywhere. Because where would we go, really? Another shop doorway or park? God, I wish I'd never agreed to any of this.

Ash's bright idea of running away doesn't seem so bright any more. He'd been the one to persuade me to do this. He has a way about him like that. Knowing all the right things to say to me at just the right time. How on earth had he managed to persuade me that sleeping on London's bitterly cold streets, then moving here, to this pokey little tent in the park were our only choices?

We're trapped out here. I'm trapped. The tarpaulin walls of this flimsy tent feel as if they are closing in around me. I just want my old life back. Before any of this happened, only I know I can't have it.

I could be at home now in the warm, slobbing out on the sofa in a pair of my comfy pyjamas with George lying next to me, while I binge an entire new series on Netflix. Something dark and crimey, while I absently scroll on my phone. Mum would come home from work and moan at me for getting nothing done. She'd call me lazy and I'd tell her that looking after George had left me exhausted, and she'd do her usual, huffing and puffing to herself, just loud enough for me to hear, as if to make a point. But in her element really, as she'd fuss over what to make us both for dinner.

I'd taken my old life for granted and that life has gone for good now. I can't have it back. It's impossible. Hadn't Ash drummed that into me from the minute we'd both gone off grid? Warning me that I needed to do what he told me. That any fuck-ups could cost us everything. Had I cost us everything? Were the police going to come back and take George?

It's all my fault. Oh God! It's all my fault.

'I'm sorry, Ash. I didn't purposely try and draw any attention to us. George is sick. He needed his medicine. What was I supposed to do?'

Still Ash doesn't reply. He's angry with me and I get it.

I never had any intention of breaking into someone's car and stealing the money. I'd been hoping to find someone to beg for some loose change. Only the roads had been quieter than I'd anticipated at five this morning and then I saw the loose change on the front seat. Gleaming up at me. The opportunity had kind of presented itself to me via a shiny glow from the nearby street-lamp, illuminating something sparkly on the front passenger seat as I'd peered through the car window as I'd passed it.

More than enough to buy George the medicine that I knew he needed. I'd convinced myself that it would only take a minute, and no one would really miss it. Not if they were just leaving coins lying about. No real harm would be done. That was the truth. In that moment, all rational, reasonable thinking seemingly evaporated from inside my head and all I wanted was to get George better again.

At whatever cost.

I remember picking up the huge chunk of stone that had crumbled from a nearby resident's wall, but after that, my memory is vague. It all happened so fast, as if I was outside of my body. I don't even know how many slams it had taken before the explosion of shattered glass had landed at my feet. I'd leant in through the broken, fragmented window carefully, so that I wouldn't cut myself. Greedily scooping up the pile of money, before loading it into my pockets.

'Rosie. What the fuck are you doing?'

I'd almost jumped out of my own skin at the sound of Ash's voice creeping up behind me, catching me red-handed. Staring to where our son was nestled in Ash's arms, George had still been crying, I'd never felt so much shame at what I'd become.

'What are you doing, Rosie? I woke up and you were nowhere to be seen.' Ash had glowered at me.

'I was getting money for George. He needs food and medicine.'

We'd argued then. Again. But that's nothing new, because all we seem to do lately is argue. Though this particular argument had been short lived. Interrupted by a nearby neighbouring light flickering on. A beam of bright yellow light pouring out onto the street. Illuminating us both as well as the newly smashed car window.

'Move!' Ash had commanded, taking control of the situation once again as he'd grabbed at my arm and told me to run. We hadn't stopped until we reached the all-night chemist back at Highgate Wood High Street. Both of us panting and spluttering from lack of breath, our lungs burning. I'd spent all of the money on a bottle of paracetamol and a small tub of formula milk. I stalled the pharmacist with questions about the ingredients and enquiring how long the paracetamol would start to take effect, as Ash shoved a pack of nappies up inside his coat.

'You stole this tent, Ash. You stole these sleeping bags. You stole George's nappies. How is it okay for you to steal and lie and not me?' I say, wondering how Ash can't seem to see the double standards here. We are both doing what we can to survive.

Whatever it takes.

I want to tell him that he is a hypocrite and this is all his fault. Us being here in the first place. That his stupid, bloody brainwave of stealing some unsuspecting person's tent, of camping here on the secluded borders of the freezing cold park on the edge of the woodlands was the worst idea he'd ever had. I don't want to antagonise him any more than I have already, so instead I try to reason with him. Make him see that this isn't my fault, that his plan to stay out here was never going to work.

'We're sleeping rough in a park with a tiny baby, Ash. The

tent you stole is bright bloody blue. No matter how hard you try and hide it among the bushes and trees, it stands out like a beacon. Anyone can see us out here. Anyone could have reported us. I think—'

'That's just the problem though, Rosie. You don't think, do you? It seems to be a habit of yours...' He interrupts me and I close my eyes, just wanting to sleep.

Wanting to shut all my problems out for a little while and pretend that we are not really here, living this waking nightmare. I feel the numb, aching hollowness of my empty stomach as it rumbles noisily. I can't remember the last time I ate. It's all I can do not to cry, because I don't even have the energy to deal with yet another argument right now. I'm beyond exhausted. I can't cope with another thing, not one more word.

When I open my eyes again, I stare down at George. Still now, limp in my arms now that his bottle is empty. His little mouth hanging open and there's a tiny drop of milk perfectly balanced on the corner of his lips. His face bursts into a huge smile, which I know is wind, but even so, my heart melts at the sight of it. He looks content, angelic almost, and I will myself to believe that he is dreaming of something nice.

A noise drags my attention away from him and I listen to the crunch of twigs and leaves just outside the tent. I am about to warn Ash, but he hears it too. He moves towards the tent door, a forefinger pressed firmly against his lips as he silently commands me not to make a sound. Someone is moving around out there. Quietly. We both see it, the shadowy figure lurking on the other side of the tent. Not the police or a social worker like Ash had said, because they wouldn't skulk about out there, not wanting to be seen. Would they?

Ash must be thinking the same thing as me, because quickly, silently he removes the tent pole from the centre of the tent, leaving the roof's material to sag down in the middle just above our heads, before gripping the pole tightly in his fist,

ready to use it if he has to. And the look on his face says that he
might have to. Fear floods through me at the thought of that. Of
whoever is out there, forcing their way in here and taking my
child from me. A stranger ripping George from my arms.
Because I won't just give him up.

'Hello?' The voice that calls out is female and I catch Ash's
eye in the hope that he'll know what to do, only he just shakes
his head. Telling me that under no circumstances am I to reply.

We wait then in silence, physically holding our breath, too
scared to make a sound. I pull the woollen blanket tightly up
around George, to keep him warm. To keep him safe. I'm
grateful that he is sleeping now. That he isn't aware of what is
going on.

'Hello? I know you're in there.' The woman's voice calls out
again.

Her voice sounds gentle, kind. She doesn't sound authoritative, and she hasn't given out any official titles or form of ID.
Though that doesn't mean it isn't the police or someone from
social services. I had seen that tactic on the streets too. The
undercover officers had pretended to be concerned about us,
when really all they'd wanted was to is move us on. Stop the
busy London streets looking so untidy for all the tourists and
shoppers that flocked to the capital.

Clearing up the riffraff, that's what Ash had said. That the
police didn't really want to help any of them. They couldn't be
trusted.

'I don't mean to pry, but I live just over there, on the edge of
the park, and well, I saw you out of my window...'

Ash glares at me as if his warning had come true.

Smashing windows, breaking into cars, stealing money. This
woman had seen us from her bedroom window. Had she seen
me breaking into the car too? Someone had switched a light on
and peered out at us. Maybe she's already called the police and

is keeping us here, cornered inside this tent like caged animals, awaiting our fate.

'I just wanted to see if you were okay.'

'I don't believe her,' Ash whispers, but there is an uncertain edge to his voice and I see him waver. 'What do you think?'

I shrug, because if I'm honest I'm not sure what to think. What to believe. Who to trust. Ash might be wrong. This might not be the police. Maybe this woman is genuinely checking that we are okay. There is only one way we were going to find out for sure.

'Answer her,' I whisper, clutching George closer to me now, only as I do so, I must somehow dislodge a large, painful burst of wind because instantly his eyes flicker open and he begins to wail loudly.

'For fucksake!' Ash shuts his eyes despairingly, both of us knowing that George has just given us away. We can't pretend that no one is in here. The woman isn't going to get bored and walk away.

'I can hear you. Is everything okay?' the woman exclaims, and I see the raw panicked expression creep its way up Ash's face as the tent's zip is yanked up. The doors part open, and instinctively I push myself backward, away from the doorway. Away from Ash, who is still holding the metal tent pole just above his head.

The haunting flashback from just a few days ago fills my mind. The lifeless body at my feet. All of that blood. The way Ash had screamed at me to move. Roughly grabbing at my arm, commanding me to run. Bile threatens at the back of my throat as I fight to shake away that awful image from my head. It's happening again, I think as I stare at the manic grimace that spreads across Ash's face as he readies himself to protect us.

Because he promised that he would.

No matter what.

Even if that means bringing the bar down with force, on this woman's head if she dares to come in here.

7

STEPHANIE

'Are you sure you won't come with me, Stephanie? Some fresh air might do you the world of good. You've been cooped up in here for days. It's not healthy.' I hear the desperation in Kay's voice, the way she's still trying so hard to persuade me to spend some 'good quality time' with her. Only right now, I don't even want to spend quality time with myself. I'm exhausted and my head is a mess.

'If you don't mind, Kay, I think I'll just stay here for a bit. My head is banging.' It's not a complete lie.

Kay spent ages earlier, trying to entice me into having a cookery lesson with her. When I'd said no, she'd insisted on talking me through the entire process regardless of whether I was interested or not, as she'd set about making a big, fresh pot of her 'speciality' leek and potato soup and some homemade soda bread.

'Suit yourself.' There's a tightness to her words now, a hardness there. Immediately defensive at yet another of my rejections. I do feel bad about that, but I don't have the energy to do anything other than lie around the house and mope.

Even so, I wait until I hear the click of the front door shutting behind Kay, before I go to the window and peer out from behind her yellow-tinged net curtains to make sure that she's really gone.

Watching as Kay bounds down the front path, with her little dog Max in tow. On their way to the park for their second walk of the day. Only this time Kay is equipped with provisions. Her 'good deed for the day', she'd gleefully announced before she'd left, as she'd yanked a heavy looking rucksack onto her shoulders. Full of all the food she'd just spent ages making for some random homeless person in the park. Good old Saint Kay, I think bitterly, wondering if this too is all part of the woman's act.

Because she must be acting.

My mother had spent a lifetime warning me about what a hard, mean and bitter woman Kay was. Always telling me how controlling she'd been. How she hadn't allowed my mother out of her sight as a child, not even for a second. And as my mum had grown older, how she'd become jealous of her friendships, ruining them for her. Kay had even sabotaged my mother's first love, forbidding my mum from seeing her boyfriend. Which had been the catalyst in the end, that had driven my mother to leave home at sixteen.

Only so far, this isn't the Kay I've seen. This woman is the complete opposite of everything I've ever been told and I'm not sure what to believe. Has Kay changed? Has a lifetime on her own made her change her ways for the better? Was she ever that person to begin with? I ponder this as I hover, peering out as Kay and Max both reach the gate, watching as Kay bends down to pat Max affectionately on his head before commanding him to sit as she holds out a treat. Spoilt little Max clearly has other plans. Jumping wildly with excitement in a bid to reach the dog biscuit, he claws his two muddy paws up her leggings. She simply laughs before giving Max the treat anyway and I scoff loudly, mildly irritated at how Kay has rewarded her bratty little dog's bad behaviour. I wait, watching as they set off again, matching each other's pace as they stroll out the gate and down the road. Then they are gone.

It's endearing, I suppose. How besotted the two are with each other. Or at least, it would be to anyone else, other than me, watching. But for some reason, Kay's obvious affection towards her little canine companion only seems to creep beneath my skin and annoy the hell out of me and I'm not quite sure why.

Jealousy perhaps?

Maybe.

Growing up, I'd never really experienced the unconditional love that a pet could bring me. Ha! I'd never really known the unconditional love and joy a human could bring me either. My mother had always meant well, but my childhood had never been easy and I think perhaps a small part of me feels as if I've somehow missed out. Is that it?

No. No. It isn't that.

This isn't about the dog, because if I'm being honest, unlike the rest of the world, I don't really like dogs. They smell and always seem to leave a trail of mess and destruction in their wake. Leaving tufts of moulting hair, or chewed-up, manky, drooled-on toys. I only have to cast a vague eye around Kay's house to see proof of that. The dirt and mess and fur sprinkled over everything. No. Max is annoying but this isn't about him. It's Kay that bothers me. Kay and her obvious, unwavering love that she constantly showers the mangey creature with. The woman treats that animal more like her own child than a pet. Better than her own child in fact, going by my mother's experience.

I'd never really had that either.

My mother had tried her best, but her own half-arsed way just wasn't good enough. If anything it had been me, from a very young age, that had been forced to be the caregiver out of the two of us. I'd always subconsciously watched out for my mother. Rolling her onto her side in the middle of the night, after she'd blacked out. So that she didn't throw up in her sleep and choke on her own vomit. I was the one who was left petrified that she wasn't coming home, all the times she'd gone off on one of her drunken benders and didn't come back for days.

I had to endure the endless stream of strangers she brought into our home. Often before she passed out and left me in their care. Odd, weird, vile people who had no real interest in her or me. They just needed somewhere to stay for a while. Which always ended in trouble. I'd seen physical altercations between people with my mother. Shouting about stupid things like money or alcohol or something as mundane and pathetic as who was going to have the last cigarette. It was repeated behaviour. The only life I'd ever known, but still I knew that it wasn't normal. I knew that we weren't normal. Making those same mistakes and bad decisions day after day.

The worst though, had been all the times I had been forced to live through the deafening silences that descended on the house like a black fog, when my mother suffered one of her 'episodes'. Gone in spirit and only seemingly there in body, somehow lost somewhere inside her own head, she'd lay in bed in a drug induced haze, completely unresponsive for days at a time, staring blankly back at me as if I wasn't even there. That had scared me the most because they always led to one thing.

The two of us being sent away again.

My mother, whisked away in an ambulance to some mental health facility, while I was dumped in yet another foster home, full of unfamiliar faces.

How long this time? I'd ask whichever social worker had been assigned to drive me each time.

Just until your mother is better, came the same, vague noncommittal answer. Spoken with just enough conviction to silence my questions further.

Only experience taught me that they were wrong about that. My mother would never get better, not really. She'd just become better at hiding it. A master at concealing her illness in the end, fooling everyone in authority into believing that she'd managed to somehow extinguish the demons crawling around inside her head. She'd found a way to silence their voices. And being cured meant that she was allowed home again. She was allowed to have me back home again too. Until the next time, of course. And there was always a next time. When all those dark nasty thoughts that squirmed and wriggled around inside her mind like infectious maggots reared their ugly heads again.

That was our life, our pattern. Dancing to the same tune over and over again. Only, it's over now. She's gone. I still can't get my head around it. That this isn't some awful dream I've yet to wake up from. She's really never coming back. Grief hits me once again and I try to shake the feeling off. Refusing to let it in.

I need to get my head straight.

I remind myself that I'm alone now in Kay's house. The house that my mother had always said would one day be ours. How Kay would leave it to her, in her Will, when she passed.

'We'll paint that whole bloody place a bright, hot pink. Every single room. My mother hates pink.'

I smile sadly at the memory of my mother. How outspoken she had been. How oblivious she had been too, of course, that she would be leaving this world first.

There would be no dream home for us now, I think as I stare at the bland colour pallet of creams and beiges that Kay has used for her walls throughout, though most of the décor is concealed by the amount of bags and boxes that Kay has stacked up against the walls. There's so much stuff. What does she keep in all these boxes? It's the perfect opportunity for me to take a proper look around and find out. To really try to get a feel for who Kay Wyldes really is.

I don't have long.

Despite having no idea where to begin, I decide to start making my way through the mammoth task of searching through the endless piles of junk and books and clutter that Kay hoards in each room. My gaze sweeps the sparse display of cards scattered along Kay's windowsill, each of them displaying religious images of holy crosses, or beautiful white doves and pretty bouquets of flowers. This will do, I think, this is a good enough place to start as any. I take my time, thumbing my way through each one reading the messages full of heartfelt sympathy and condolences. Trying to get a sense of this woman who keeps insisting that I call her nan.

We're so sorry for your loss. Sending you all our love at this sad time. Thinking of you.

A dog walker. A neighbour. The funeral director. Acquaintances really, none of them real friends. Still, it stings that the few cards here are addressed only to Kay. That even her dog, Max, gets the odd mention here and there. Yet my name is nowhere to be seen.

How is that fair?

I am a daughter who tragically lost her mother. I am the one who has suffered the most. I'm the one who found her in that awful state. OD'ing on the bathroom floor. I'm the one who tried to help her, tried to save her. And failed. Where are my cards full of love and condolence? It's as if I don't even exist, though I guess that up until ten days ago, in Kay's world, I didn't. Not really.

The one and only fleeting memory I really have of seeing Kay before now, had been when me and my mum were both stood out on Kay's doorstep, trying to shelter ourselves from the pouring rain. Kay had refused to let us in. I'd been too little to know what was going on back then. Too young to understand the angry words that were being flung about just above my head, but I knew the sentiment behind them as my mother and grandmother had become louder and angrier, exchanging obscenities, until Kay had enough and slammed the door in our faces.

I've never forgotten the hurt look on my mother's face.

Who does that? she'd muttered. *Who slams the door on their own daughter and young grandchild? The nasty old witch.*

My mother had barely mentioned Kay after that, apart from the occasional time she'd allowed her anger to boil over and get the better of her, and Kay's name had seeped out from my mother's lips like a toxic, venomous poison she could no longer contain.

Which looking back, was irony in itself, I think now. How hard my mother had tried not to subconsciously express any of the resentment and bitterness that festered inside her. Not to focus on the negatives in case it made her sick. Only by holding it all in, it had consumed her in the end anyway.

I'd hated Kay for that.

For ruining my mother's life.

For ruining both our lives.

Only it was the methadone that had destroyed my mother in the end.

And me.

The one person who was supposed to help her but didn't. The one person who, in my panic, had made everything so much worse. Seeing how my mother had been struggling, how hard she'd fought to get clean from not only heroin over the years, but methadone too. And it was me who had helped pour it down her throat.

I stare at the sparse line of Kay's cards.

A woman without a heart. That is how my mother had once

described Kay. Only, going by the fact that Kay had been sent cards at all, meant that she must be liked. Especially someone like Kay who claims to live like she is a recluse. Maybe Kay does have a heart after all, albeit a religiously guarded one.

Just like her and this house. I stare around at the piles of mess and chaos that Kay hoards. She's put walls up. I think. Huge, bulky, thickly built walls of 'stuff' that she amasses. Stacked up high all around her. To keep herself safe inside perhaps. Or to keep people out? Only she'd let me in, hadn't she? That must count for something. Telling me that this could finally be our chance to get to know one another properly. To form a proper bond. We're family after all. Blood.

Pulling open one of the lounge dresser's drawers, I rummage around inside. Sifting through the mounds of paperwork. Bills mainly, and messily scrawled reminders. Unsure exactly what it is that I am looking for. Get bread. Pay electricity bill. Max vet appointment 2 p.m. None of this stuff reveals anything about who Kay is as a person. None of it tells me anything at all.

It's the same in the kitchen, I discover, as I root through every drawer and cupboard. Disappointed at finding nothing. How can someone have so much stuff, yet none of it says anything at all about them?

Maybe I'll have more luck in her bedroom, I think, as I finally take the stairs, aware that time is running out and it won't be long until Kay is back. The last thing I want is for her to come back and catch me red-handed, going through all of her things. Kay's bedroom is even worse, and all the enthusiasm I felt earlier at discovering her secrets disappears as I step inside the cluttered room and eye the dusty stacked up boxes that line the edge of her room. Lids open, allowing the mountains of books and shoes and clothes to spill out. It would take me ages to make my way through all of this. I turn, about to leave the room only as I do, I almost walk into the tall, dark, frail figure that's snuck up directly behind me.

I scream.

My shock's short lived as I let out a small smile, feeling stupid, as I realise that it's not a real person standing there at all. It's the dress that Kay wore for my mother's funeral, hanging on her wardrobe door. I know this because I'd spent enough time studying it. Studying her. Taking in every word, every mannerism throughout my mother's eulogy, both intrigued and suspicious in equal measure, as I'd tried to work out if the woman's grief had been real.

Because it had looked real. The pain from her sudden loss etched across Kay's face for all to see as she'd sobbed loudly. Uncontrollably distraught as my mother's coffin had been slowly lowered down into the ground. Her tears had been real, she hadn't been pretending.

The funeral had been hard on us both. The ceremony itself had been such a small, intimate affair. Strictly close family, which was funny because none of us were close. Kay and I, still practically strangers, and other than a couple of Kay's long-distance cousins that I've never seen or met before, there wasn't anyone else.

It was as tragic as her death, how my mother's final farewell had been such a morbid, pitiful goodbye. Celebrated by just a small handful of people, it hadn't reflected her vibrant, chaotic life at all. Where were all those waifs and strays my mother had collected along her way, generously labelling them as friends, when she'd needed them? None of them had been there for her in the end. I was glad when it was over. Glad when I could stop exchanging fake pleasantries and the general awkwardness and I could skulk off to the silence of Kay's spare room.

My mother's old bedroom.

Where I'd lain in my mother's old bed analysing how Kay had come and helped me when I needed her the most.

'You need to come. I think she's dead.'

That's how I had broken the awful news to Kay. That's how she learned about the death of her daughter. Me, frantic on the phone in my trance-like daze. The shock of finding my mother like that had stopped me from thinking properly. Stopped me from recalling anything much about that harrowing night at all. It's all slowly coming back to me now, as I dissect every moment, every word, every possible outcome. Wishing desperately that I'd done things differently.

Give her due, Kay had arrived in minutes, taking control of the situation and keeping me calm. She hadn't even blamed me.

'It's not your fault, Stephanie.' Her words spin inside my head. 'Your mother didn't want to be helped, you know that. She was stubborn. It was always her way or nothing. It wasn't your fault. It wasn't anyone's fault.'

Only it was and I wonder now that the shock had started to wear off and our bleak reality was setting in, if Kay blames me now too. For not being capable of saving my mother. For making it all so much worse and fucking everything up.

No mother should ever have to bury her child.

Her words, later at the wake, were laced with so much sadness. But I'd heard bitterness in them too. I couldn't blame her for that. She was only human after all. Yet still she let me stay. She still hadn't told a single soul my secret.

And here I am skulking around her house, searching for dirt on her. Acting mean and untrusting and suspicious when all Kay had shown me in the past ten days was kindness and love.

Good, kind, Kay.

A changed woman, which wouldn't be impossible. Not after all these years alone without her family. She wanted to make amends. Make things right. Spend quality time finally getting to know each other, yet I was doing everything in my power to fend her advances off.

God. What had I been thinking?

What was I doing? Silly, silly, girl.

I step quietly out of Kay's bedroom and close the door behind me.

If the woman is an actor or a fraud, I would know it. I'd seen enough of that type in my lifetime. Kay was good and kind and caring and somehow, somewhere along the line, I think my mother must have had her all wrong.

8

KAY

I shouldn't have come here.

Those are the first thoughts that enter my head, as I squat down in the tent, poking my head inside only to see someone purposely blocking the doorway, to stop me from crawling any further inside.

'I'm not here to cause trouble,' I say, sensing the immediate danger as I spread my palms wide above my head like a shield, staring up at the figure that looms over me.

A man.

I hadn't been expecting that. To find a man in here. I'd only expected to see the girl and the baby. I'd assumed that they were out here alone. But he is here too and his stance is hostile. Poised and twisted, as the metal tent pole hovers just above his head and he readies himself to use it.

On me, I realise with horror. For my sudden uninvited intrusion. He is going to cave my skull in.

'I came by earlier, except there was no one here,' I explain quickly, instantly regretting my decision to impose as I show him that I'm not armed with anything. That I have come here empty handed.

Only I'm not empty handed. Forgetting all about the bag that I am holding, until I lift my arms to show him as much, the rucksack that is hooked around my wrist is too heavy. The weight of it pulling my arms back down, I extend the bag out towards the man as a peace offering, so that he'll believe me when I say that I mean him no harm. That there is no threat here.

'I brought you some things,' I say. 'It's just a couple of spare blankets I had in the airing cupboard and I made you some hot soup. Leek and potato, it's my favourite. I baked some soda bread too. Fresh out of the oven, it's probably still warm.' I am rambling now, desperately mumbling my words. Aware that the pole is still high in the air above the man's head and that time is running out for me.

'It's not much...' I say, not adding that I hadn't expected to see him here. How I'd thought it was just the young woman and a baby. 'I just thought that maybe you were hungry. And well, it's comfort food. And you both look as though you could do with some comfort. I just wanted to help.' I stare over to where the carrier bag full of empty cans of cold baked beans had been earlier, that I'd taken. The stinky nappy too. Only by doing so I realise that I have just unwittingly told the man that I have already been in here. Snooping around inside their tent.

'I got rid of your rubbish for you. There was an awful smell in here... I wasn't snooping, honest.'

Though I am not being honest, of course I snooped. Isn't that the reason I'm back here, after all? Because I'd seen the scruffy looking cardboard box, lined with a dirty folded blanket and realised there was a tiny baby out here. I'm concerned for the child's welfare. For the mother's too. Though I'd barely taken my eyes off the man for fear of getting hurt. For a few minutes, I'd forgotten all about the girl and the baby.

'You have a baby here, don't you?'

And it's these words that finally do it. Igniting the man's

growing fear that I am here because I have other motives. His knuckles flash a bright white as he grips the bar tighter.

'Our business is none of yours.'

Sensing his fury, I close my eyes, flinching as I wait for the blow.

'Ash, NO.'

Finally, I allow myself to drag my gaze away from 'Ash'. I stare over to where the woman is cowering in the corner. I take her in properly, realising that she is younger than I had expected. Her youthful appearance makes me think that she can't be much older than Stephanie. Sixteen at the most. Her blonde hair is matted and dirty and her clothes look filthy too, but it's the girl's vivid green eyes that I am drawn to. The way she's staring back at me, her gaze ablaze with something that looks like fear as she huddles in the corner of the tent like a scared animal, protectively clutching her tiny baby in her arms.

She's scared of me, I realise. These people are scared of me.

'I'm not here to cause you any harm.' I try again.

'Put the bar down, Ash.' The girl's eyes glare past me, her words an order not a request and to my surprise, Ash drops the bar. It lands loudly with a clang on the ground behind him. The sudden jolt of noise startling the baby awake. Then the crying starts.

'For Christ's sake!' the young woman mutters angrily, clutching the infant tightly in a bid to soothe his hysterical cries.

Too tightly, I think as I see how the infant squirms despite his mother's protective hold. His face puce, as if all the air is being squeezed out from him by the young woman's bony fingers. The young woman loosens her grip as if she realises it too.

'Is he okay?' I ask, homing in on the child, I guess by the blue blanket wrapped around him and the little red embroidered car sewn onto the hat he is wearing that the child is a boy. Though he is much younger than I had anticipated. Not much more than a newborn, a week or so old at least. Far too young to be subjected to sleeping outside in a tent in these bitterly cold temperatures.

'He's fine. He's just tired,' the young woman answers tightly, though she doesn't look me in the eye when she speaks, and we both know why.

She can't.

Because if she does, I'll see the lie that resides there. Only I see and hear it regardless. How this baby is far from okay. He looks sickly pale and scrawny, his face encrusted with dry snot and even from this distance, the other side of the tent, with my heart thudding so loudly that the blood rushes noisily inside my ears, I can hear how wheezy the child's breathing is.

'There are charities out there, people who can help you...'

'We're fine. We don't need anyone's charity.' Her eyes flash a warning as they fix on mine. Seeing my concern, she glances nervously over in Ash's direction. For my benefit this time. She's warning me that Ash is volatile. That I'm not safe yet.

'I'm sorry. I shouldn't have come,' I start, knowing that I've outstayed an already unwanted welcome. 'I just wanted to check you were okay, and to bring you a few things. I don't want to cause any trouble. I'll go.'

The statement leaves my mouth as if it's a question, as if I am waiting for these people to grant me permission.

Am I?

I wait, hoping that they both see me how the rest of the world sees me when they look at me. Like I'm nothing more than a sad, lonely, old lady. A busybody at worst. Poking my nose in matters that don't really concern me because I have nothing better to do with my time.

'Who else knows we're here?' Ash's voice pulls me back to the present, his tone as cold as his expression. But the threat that flashes in his eyes tells me everything I need to know. Despite the bag of food and blankets I've just handed to them, he still thinks that I'm capable of making trouble for them. For him. He doesn't trust that I haven't already. That I'm not acting as a decoy, to keep them here while waiting for the cavalry to arrive.

'No one knows you're here. At least, not through me. I haven't told anyone...'

There's no one to tell.

That is what I'm about to say, because for much of my life that's been the painful reality for me. I have no one to share anything with. No one to confide in. Only I stop myself, my words sticking in the back of my throat, as I realise how vulnerable that truth will leave me. If I admit that no one knows I'm here, there'll be no one out there looking if anything happens to me. Besides, that's not strictly true any more, is it? Someone would be missing me now, wouldn't they?

Stephanie.

'My granddaughter, Stephanie. She's at home, waiting for me. She's back at the house. Just over there...' I point across the park to the very last house on the row that lines the front of the parkland, closest to the main gate.

'That's how I knew you were here, you see. I saw you from my bedroom window. Last night. I saw the light shining from the torch.'

I see the look that the woman shoots Ash, only I can't quite interpret what is being said in the unspoken conversation they are having now.

'I told her I wouldn't be long. She'll be up there, watching, waiting for me,' I say boldly, pointing up to the loft room window before giving a half wave as if I can see Stephanie from all the way here. Up there, watching me. That wasn't strictly a lie though either. Stephanie does know I'm here. She knows I'm visiting the homeless girl I spotted here in the park. Though the chances of her being up there now, in my bedroom staring out at me, were slim to zero. It was more likely that Stephanie had skulked back off to bed, to mope about there all day. The girl was in turmoil, too consumed by her grief, to take much notice of what I'm up to, but these people didn't need to know that.

Outside the tent, an impatient Max tugs at his lead and begins to whine loudly so I take this as my cue to go.

'Well, I guess I'll leave you both to it. I won't disturb you again,' I say cautiously, though when neither of the couple answer, I take my opportunity to leave.

Backing out of the tent slowly, all the while, my eyes are fixed on the couple. Half expecting to be stopped in my tracks by Ash, leaping forward to stop me from getting out. Though neither of them moves so much as an inch and I am relieved when I am finally, safely back outside and I hear the sound of the zip being yanked back down behind me.

Shutting me out.

Good. I move fast, clutching Max's lead tightly to me as I traipse my way back across the waterlogged park, towards my house.

The sound of the crying baby carries on the wind around me, along with the mother's gentle attempts at comforting the child. Only nothing is working. The baby's cries don't stop.

9

KAY

The storm that has been brewing for the past few days is finally here, descending directly over the house, the air charged with the same heavy intense energy that matches my mood. Which is perhaps why I am still unable to sleep. I'm beyond tired now. I have laid here in my bed for what feels like hours, listening as the thick walls of this old house tremble against the blustering strength of the howling winds that somehow manage to seep their way inside. Huge gusts of air screaming down the chimney like a wild banshee, before sweeping around my bedroom. The chilling sound mimicking that of a crying woman sets Max immediately on edge as he growls.

'There there, Max. It's only a bit of wind. It's not going to hurt you.'

I give him a gentle pat of reassurance that I wish I felt myself, before pulling my duvet tightly up around me, in a bid to keep the cold out, just as an almighty clap of thunder crashes violently down from above me.

Max howls loudly, and I physically leap from my bed.

Wide awake now, I pace the room, knowing only too well that the intense electric charge of the storm is only part of the reason I haven't slept tonight. I can't stop thinking about *them*. That young mother and her boyfriend, and that poor tiny baby. Sleeping rough out there, in this. With only that grubby, makeshift tent as protection from the lashing rain and ferocious wind.

I should leave it well alone, leave them well alone, I think, as I anxiously tear at the jagged edges of my cuticles with my teeth. Willing myself to do exactly that. To not lift the blinds and look out of the window. The storm sounds bad enough from in here, I can't even begin to imagine how it must sound out there, in the very thick of it. How cold and wet and fed up they all must be. The baby had looked so sickly earlier. He'll be even worse come the morning, after enduring a night like this. I bite down on my lip, aware now that my efforts weren't enough. That one measly flask of hot soup and an extra blanket, my so-called good deed for the day, wasn't nearly enough.

You stupid old cow. What had you been thinking?

As if a mug of vegetable soup and a couple of slices of bread would make any real difference to their lives. That it would be of help in any real way. No wonder they had seemed unimpressed at my intrusion. I'd seen the squalor and poverty that they were living in, how little they had between them. How desperate they were, and I'd simply walked away when I should have called someone for help.

I had offered to put them in touch with a charity, with people who could organise refuge for them in a local hostel or a B&B only they'd refused. I could still do that, I think, glancing over to my mobile phone that sits on my bedside cabinet. I can still call someone for help, but I know deep down that they wouldn't want that.

Who else knows we're here? Ash had asked, his question loaded and his tone full of anger as he'd glared right through me.

And I got it. How vulnerable I'd made them feel by just turning up there like that. I could have been anybody standing there. That's what they'd both been thinking. I hadn't imagined it, had I? The fear in their eyes at my sudden presence. That they didn't want to be found. I'd done what I'm so good at, turning my back on them and pretending that they weren't my problem.

I'd spent the rest of the afternoon trying to push all thoughts of them to the back of my mind. Stephanie was still refusing to spend any time with me, refusing my suggestion of a movie marathon, or Netflix binge as the kids call them these days, so I had kept myself busy trawling through the entire contents of the local charity shop. A much-needed distraction from all the noise in my head. I'd ended up buying up half the shop and by the time I'd got it all home and added it all to my ever-growing pile of things, I felt even worse. Flooded with a self-loathing and emptiness that I can't seem to fill.

More stuff. More things.

More books that I hadn't yet read and probably never will. More magazines that look almost new that will no doubt stay that way. A purple scarf that might come in handy when I'm out on one of my walks with Max. Though even that had looked familiar, and I'm almost certain that I've already got something similar stuffed inside one of my boxes.

By the time I'd finally got into my pyjamas tonight and lay down in bed, I'd known instantly that I wouldn't sleep a wink. Unable to shake the feeling of trepidation growing inside me even before the storm had arrived, I had lain in the darkness berating myself for not doing more. For not offering to help. For walking away. They'd be freezing out there now, wouldn't they? The baby might catch his death.

Catch his death.

The words snag inside my head.

Catch his death.

Just like Amanda. Only it had been death that had captured Amanda in the end. I'd always known it was coming. The phone call that I'd spent the last sixteen years equally expecting and dreading.

You need to come. I think she's dead.

Stephanie's voice on the end of my phone. The first and only time she's ever called me. I hadn't recognised the number that flashed up on my screen and I almost dropped the phone when the voice at the end had told me that she was my grand-daughter. Instantly, I'd felt so full of hope that Stephanie was finally reaching out to me. I'd wondered if she'd decided to do that all by herself, if perhaps she'd gone against her mother's wishes now that she had turned sixteen. Or perhaps Amanda had finally had a change of heart? Maybe she no longer wanted to cut me off and keep my beautiful grandchild from me?

Better late than never, I had so foolishly thought. Sat there in my flannelled pyjamas, doing yet another tedious jigsaw puzzle to stave off the boredom of another lonely Saturday night with only Max for company.

You need to come. I think she's dead.

I must have gone silent, unsure if I'd heard her right, because Stephanie had been forced to repeat herself, and I can't remember what I had said in reply, but I know that I'd somehow managed to stay cool and calm and in control. That I'd stifled the immense feeling of relief I'd felt at learning that Amanda might be dead. There was no real shock, no surprise, no grief. Amanda would have finally found some kind of peace, if it was true. The kind of peace in death that she was never able to obtain in life.

'Kay? Please. I need your help.'

I shouldn't have gone. I shouldn't have told Stephanie I would help her. I close my eyes at the memory, shutting them out. No. I can't think of this now. I can't think of her now. My Amanda.

It's too painful.

I need to stay in the moment I decide as my mind goes back

to them. Ash, and the young woman with the baby. They are not my problem, I know that. Whatever reason they have to be out there, it's down to their own doing. We all have choices and being out there in a tent is theirs.

Besides, I can't possibly make any difference, can I? But even as I think this, I know that I can. I could make a huge difference if I really wanted to. Of course, I bloody could. But I can't just invite them into my home, can I? These perfect strangers? Ash is dangerous, unhinged. I had witnessed that first-hand. How reactive he is, how he'd happily use violence against me if he had to. He is the type of person that I should keep away from my home, from my granddaughter, at all costs. Yet I was happy to leave him out there with that young girl and her baby, wasn't I? Even after I'd seen the fear in her eyes.

I'd assumed it was at my presence, but I've been thinking about that look she shot me all evening. How her eyes had flashed me a warning, that if I didn't leave, Ash might actually hurt me. If he was capable of doing that, were the girl and her baby at risk from him too?

Damn it.

Reluctantly, I do the one thing I promised myself I wouldn't do, and I tug at the blinds. Squinting out into the sea of black nothingness that expands out, way beyond my window, as I wait for my eyes to adjust so that I can see past the heavy downpour, I focus on a spot over by the far trees where I know the tent sits.

A warm glow of amber from the streetlamp lights up the nearby bushes and branches as they sway wildly in the wind. Only I can't see the tent now. It's gone? I scan the length of the woodland convinced that my eyesight is playing tricks on me but there's no sign of them. Has this dreadful storm finally brought them to their senses? Have they packed their things and gone back home?

I hope so.

I should feel relieved that they have moved on, that they are no longer my problem. Only I'm surprised to feel the tiniest flicker of disappointment too. That I hadn't acted sooner. That I hadn't done as much as I could have. Should have. I can go back to bed now. I can sleep. Get my head down for a few hours before the morning without fretting about how they're doing.

And just as I am about to, another roar of thunder explodes overhead, sending a jagged fork of lightning down, cracking open the darkened skies above me. A bright, brilliant flash of light illuminating the entire park. I see them then. They are not gone. The force of the wind has moved the tent about twenty feet to the left and I watch in pure fascination at the two figures that appear to be dancing wildly in quick circles around the perimeter of the tent. What's left of it, I realise, as another huge gust of wind takes hold, picks up the tent's slack material, before flapping it wildly around in the air. The torch sending a strobed attempt of an SOS through the treacherous, endless rain as the two figures fight desperately, to hold the tent down in place.

I'm too far away to say for certain, but I can't see the baby and I hope that despite the way the tent is flapping wildly in the wind, he is safely tucked away in his cot inside, shielded from the elements, protected from the relentless downpour. I watch as the couple finally manage to pin the tent down, frantically hammering the pegs securely back into the ground, before they clamber inside once more. Seconds later the tent is plunged into darkness and I can't see anything now but black. Which means neither can they.

They'll be completely soaked through, as would most of their belongings that are now strewn all around the tent. They would have wanted to check on the baby. Their torch battery must have run out.

A feeling of unsettlement descends upon me and I can only imagine the despair and helplessness they both must be feeling right now. Sitting out there in the darkness, exposed to all the elements. All their things soaked. Would the baby be wet through too? I think about him lying in his little makeshift cardboard box for a cot. His babygrow soiled and dirty.

Shit.

Shit. Shit. Shit.

What sort of a person just stands back and watches while a couple and a baby suffer?

You, Kay, YOU. You bury your head in the sand like you always do. Pretending that it's not your problem. Nothing's your problem, is it? That's why you live like this, alone, like a recluse.

Well not tonight, not any more.

'Come on, Max boy. Walkies,' I say as I quickly make my way down the stairs. Tugging my raincoat over my nightclothes and shoving my bare feet into my wellington boots, I attach Max's lead to his collar. I grab the keys from the hallway dresser and I open the front door. The wind so strong now that it blows the rain sideways, into my doorway, all over me. I pull my hood up in preparation because I can't just stand back and do nothing.

I'd done that before and look where that had got me.

10

STEPHANIE

'Does anyone actually ever sleep in this bloody house?' Muttering, I drag the pillow over my head and hug it tightly over my ears in a futile attempt to block the sound of Kay bustling noisily around the kitchen again at ridiculous-o-clock in the morning.

Ignore her, I think as I silently will myself to drift back to sleep.

It's no good, I'm wide awake now. Exasperated, I roll onto my back and stare up at the ceiling, homing in on the sound of Kay's voice as it floats up from the kitchen below. Kay has a habit of mumbling loudly to herself when she thinks no one is listening, and I wonder if she's doing that now. Or if perhaps it's Max that she's talking so animatedly to this morning, as she clangs cups together noisily with no care or thought that I might still be sleeping.

Fat chance of that.

I sigh bitterly, unable to remember the last time that I'd slept so deeply. Last night had been the first time in a long time that I'd had no bad dreams.

No dreams at all in fact.

I wonder if the sleeping pills I'd taken had been the main reason for that. The events of the last few weeks had taken their toll on me, so much so that my recent burnout was inevitable really.

I'm lost without my mother.

It all feels too much. Her death, the funeral, moving in here, to this strange house, with this even stranger woman and all of her odd ways. There's only so much one person can cope with and I'm at breaking point. Trying my hardest to hold it all together. I'd spent hours last night tossing and turning, tormented by the dark thoughts in my head, convinced I'd never be able to drift off. Convinced I'd never be able to sleep ever again. I wondered if Kay feels that way too. If what happened to my mother is eating her up inside as well? Though, unlike me, Kay is fighting it. Getting up and carrying on, regardless. Keeping herself busy, doing all her mundane daily tasks at the crack of dawn, rather than choosing the warmth and comfort of her duvet. Not wanting to sit with her grief, instead she chooses to pretend that everything is normal. Whereas I can barely function. I'm a mess. I only leave this bedroom for food or to use the toilet, but other than the funeral, I haven't left this house. I barely even talk to Kay.

I can't.

I couldn't save her daughter. It was all my fault, despite Kay constantly telling me otherwise. Which only makes me feel worse. At least if there was blame or anger or disappointment from Kay, I'd have something to defend myself against. Something to fight back with. But with Kay, there is only love.

I listen to the sound of running water in the kitchen, the click of the kettle. A metal teaspoon repeatedly tapping against a porcelain cup. Normal noises, in a normal house, though being here in Kay's home feels anything but normal to me. It's alien in comparison to my upbringing. Nothing like the house that I'd grown up in and being here only seems to magnify the differences in our two worlds, which doesn't sit easy with me.

In my mother's home, I was surrounded by so many people. So-called 'friends' that were always passing through. I'd grown used to that, the chaos and madness of sharing our house and my mother with random strangers.

Kay's house and life were chaotic in different ways. Instead of choosing people to stave off her loneliness, she fills hers with things. Surrounding herself with books and ornaments and clothes and pointless gadgets. Which is why she has so much stuff cluttering up her home. Chintzy animal figurines that Kay has collected over the years seem to adorn every inch of exposed surface of her house. Books piled high on the shelves, and over-flowing into great big, towering stacks on the floor. Pot plants. So many bloody plants that the place looks a bit like a jungle. Though to give Kay her due, none of the plants show any signs of wilting or dying like they would have if I was left in charge of their wellbeing. Each and every one of her beloved plants bloom vibrant and green. A sign they were very much loved and cared for despite the chaos.

Organised chaos.

That's how Kay had described her home, when she'd mistakenly taken my long silence at the sight of all her worldly possessions cluttering up her house for something like awe when I'd first arrived here. What was the saying about one man's rubbish being another man's treasure? Kay's treasures were nothing more than junk from what I'd seen so far. Bits of old tat that simply took up space, while gathering dust, but it's how she survives I realise. Having all these things everywhere gives her purpose. They are part of her identity.

Kay's laughter grows louder. A real, throaty belly laugh that makes me wonder what Max has done to create such a reaction, only as I strain to listen, it's another voice that I hear, drifting up through the floorboards. Another voice. Not Kay's this time.

A man's voice.

There is someone else here at the house. I glance at the clock and see that it's barely even six. A visitor? At this early hour of the morning?

On edge now, the same familiar feeling ripples inside me, reminding me of when I used to wake to strange noises back at home. In fear of who else was in the house with me. That fear is irrational here at Kay's, I know that. A trauma response, no doubt, from having so many strange men in the house from such a young age.

Wide awake now, I throw on some clothes, deciding to investigate. Ignoring the growls of hunger that rumble inside my stomach as I follow the smell of hot, buttered toast and fresh coffee towards the kitchen, I focus only on the voices.

'George doesn't need to go to the hospital, he just needs some rest. He'll be fine.'

I don't recognise the male voice. Nor do I know anyone by the name of George, but as I reach the kitchen doorway, and hear the small, strained cry of what sounds like an injured kitten, I home in on Kay's voice again.

Cooing.

'Ahh poor little George.'

She sees me then, stopping mid-sentence before beaming with pride as she announces my presence.

'Ahh here she is. This is Stephanie, my granddaughter. Stephanie this is Rosie and Ash.' Kay introduces the couple as if saying their names might help to explain who these people actually are. It doesn't, and I feel as if I'm missing something, as Kay stares back at me with arched brows and an expectant look on her face.

'Hi...' I nod in polite acknowledgement at the two strangers, wishing I didn't sound so self-conscious and that I could place these people, as they smile back at me knowingly. As if they already know who I am.

The couple are young. If I were to hazard a guess, I'd say that girl is about my age, sixteen. Seventeen at the most. The man, though, with his stubbly chin and deep-set eyes, looks a few years older. Nineteen or twenty perhaps. They both look as if they haven't slept for days and are carrying the weight of the world on their shoulders. Their clothes are crumpled and stained, and their skin looks dirty. As if they're both in need of a good wash. And it's only then, as I crinkle my nose, that I am aware suddenly of the smell that lingers in the room. A sour, pungent smell of something putrid that even the smell of hot toast and strong coffee can't mask.

I don't know these people, I am certain of that. If I did know them, if they were of any relevance, surely they would have been at my mother's funeral. So, they can't be family or close friends of Kay's. No, that seems unlikely, especially seeing how young they both are and the fact that they look as if they are homeless.

Homeless. Oh God.

'They're from the tent,' Kay says, as if she's just read my mind. Plonking a plate of toast down between them both on the kitchen table.

'From the tent?' I repeat, and I hear the slight nervousness in my laugh that slips out with my words. 'Sorry... I thought you said that these are the people from the tent. In the park?' I continue, once I have managed to compose myself. Still half-convinced that I must have heard Kay wrong.

Because that would be madness, wouldn't it? That these people are the homeless people from the park, that Kay had taken food to the day before. The same people she'd been spying on from her bedroom window. That they are sat here now, at Kay's kitchen table, greedily gulping down huge mouthfuls of toast and marmalade as if they are worried that someone will steal it out from under them.

Only I see it then. How I haven't misheard at all.

'That's what I said,' Kay exclaims matter-of-factly. 'Seventy mile an hour winds last night, the weather man predicted. Only I suspect they hit near on eighty. Did you hear it? Awful storm it was. The wind almost took the tent away with it. It was like a mini tornado and these poor things were drenched right through. I couldn't just leave them out there, could I?'

Kay says this as if it's the most perfectly normal scenario in the world to wake up to. And maybe it is. Maybe Kay isn't so different from my mother at all. Maybe Kay doesn't just surround herself with things, maybe she surrounds herself with people too. Hadn't she invited me into her home? Weren't we also strangers?

My mother and Kay had fallen out. They'd cut each other off. But now, my mother's death means that this is our chance to finally get to know one another. Isn't that how Kay had worded it when she'd offered to let me stay here? Insisted that I stay here.

Your mother's death shouldn't be in vain. Some good can come from this. We can salvage something from this mess. You and me. If you want to?

I did want to, didn't I? Only it's hard to try and force a bond that just isn't there. Hard to fake a connection.

'You could have actually.' That's what I really want to say. 'You could have left them out there. Because they are not our business. They've got nothing to do with us.'

I snap back into reality as Kay drones on, oblivious to my reaction, the woman is already off on a tangent and isn't listening now.

'And as for this little one, well, he couldn't stay out there in that cold. Listen to his chest. Poor mite. I still think that he needs a doctor,' Kay says, nodding down towards the little bundle nestled in the crook of the young woman's arms.

Not a kitten, I realise as I see the tiny face almost completely covered with a blanket. The only part of him exposed are his eyes and his nose as he sleeps. It's a baby. Sleeping soundly, though his chest sounds loud as it bubbles with a thick congested mucus every time he takes a breath, so loud that I can hear it even from where I'm stood, still lingering in the kitchen doorway.

'No. We don't need a doctor. Honestly, I don't want to cause any fuss,' Rosie says tightly. 'He'll be fine. He's just got a bit of a cold and he needs some rest. He'll be fine after he's had a nice hot bath and a feed. Especially now that I can warm his milk up. He'll sleep then, he'll be better after that. Thanks to you, Kay.'

I hear the defensive edge to Rosie's tone and guess that she is riddled with guilt for allowing her child to get so bad. For making him sleep out there in the freezing cold, in a tent. No wonder! What sort of people would do that to a child? To a baby?

'Yeah, he doesn't need a doctor.' Ash speaks now. Though unlike Rosie, he has more conviction in his voice when he talks. His decision final. There will be no negotiations.

'A good sleep? You really think that a good sleep is all he...' I start, wondering how these people can be so oblivious to how sick the child sounds. Only Ash shuts me down.

'I said he's fine. Thank you, Kay, for taking us in and letting us stay here for a couple of days.'

He puts all his emphasis on the word 'Kay', as if reminding me that it's her decision to make and not mine, as he holds my gaze for just a few seconds longer than feels comfortable, as if challenging me to say more.

'Oh, don't be so silly. Anyone else would have done the same.' Kay preens, flicking her hand as if batting the compliment away, before busying herself gathering cups from the table.

She's secretly lapping up the praise, I think, though I catch her sing-song tone as she desperately tries to defuse the growing tension in the room.

'You said that they can stay for a few days?' I ask through gritted teeth, as I follow Kay over to the sink. My voice low, so that the couple at the kitchen table don't overhear me. 'Are you sure about this, Kay? Inviting complete strangers into your home?'

'It's just for a night or two. Yes. And they're not strangers now. That's Rosie and Ash, and baby George. They're practically kids, Stephanie, your age. What harm will it do?' Kay says vaguely, concentrating on tipping the contents of the cups down the drain before she re-boils the kettle ready to make a fresh round of tea. 'I've got some diced lamb in the fridge. There's way too much for just me and you, so maybe I can do us all a nice stew and dumplings for dinner later. What do you think?' she adds, as if she hadn't really thought further ahead than the initial invitation to this couple into her home and now she is trying to work out the logistics of it all.

That's Kay all over. Wanting to keep busy. Cooking, cleaning, walking Max. Anyone would think that nothing of any significance had happened in the past couple of weeks. But Kay isn't fooling me. Anything to keep her mind off her grief about my mum. While all I want to do is fester. To be alone with my grief. To revel in it. I certainly don't want two strangers in the house as spectators to it.

'A night or two?'

Not one night. Two. Maybe more than that? Kay is being too vague and I know from bitter experience that this is how it starts. I'd seen it time and time again with my mother's friends. How one or two nights often ended up being months on end. How if you give people so much as an inch, they'd often overstay their welcome like the self-serving parasites that they were and take a mile.

'I just don't think you've thought this through...' I start, trying to reason with Kay, to make her see that these people are life's takers. That they're willing to take advantage of Kay's generosity.

'Look, I know it's not ideal, but that little baby is poorly and they've got nowhere else to go. I couldn't just leave them out there. And Ash...'

It's Kay's turn to speak quietly now, her voice turning to barely a whisper.

'I think Rosie is scared of him. I thought maybe it would be safety in numbers and all that,' Kay reasons. 'I think that's why they're out there. In that tent. The girl doesn't want to be, only she's not the one in charge. If I can get the girl alone and speak with her, I can find out for sure...'

'Kay, you don't need to do this. There are organisations out there for that, charities. People who are specially trained to help them.'

'They don't want me to call anyone. They insisted. Were adamant in fact. They don't want the fuss.'

'Yet here you are fussing anyway,' I mutter, as Kay starts adding teabags and sugar to the mugs.

'It's just a few nights,' Kay says a little firmer now, as she pours out the boiling water. An edge to her voice that is telling me to stand down.

'Okay. Okay.'

This is Kay's house. Kay's choice. I have no right to tell her what to do here. Kay smiles then and nods.

'And look, I know it's not ideal but, there's three of them. Would you mind if I give them your bedroom? It's only for a few nights, and the sofa isn't that bad. Or I could give them my room? Maybe that would be better? I'm up half the night anyway...'

Kay starts backtracking. As if she's read the look of obvious discomfort that is written all over my face at the thought of these two strangers and their baby taking over my bedroom. Taking over the house.

'No. No. It's fine.' I reluctantly agree, unhappy about the arrangement, only I'm not heartless enough to let the older woman sleep on the sofa in her own home. Especially not after Kay being so good to me. Besides, it's only a couple of nights. I'm sure that I can manage that.

'Oh good. Well, there you go, Stephanie, looks like we've both done our good deeds for the day, huh.' Kay smiles at me warmly, before picking up the cups of hot tea and carrying them back over to the table.

I stand with my back against the sink, hugging my own hot drink tightly in my hands, as I observe the scene unfolding before me. Kay serving her constant cups of hot, sugary tea. She's practically drip-fed me with the stuff since I arrived here, because Kay is from a generation of women that believes there's nothing a nice cup of tea can't fix.

Only she's mistaken if she thinks it will fix me.

Kay is right about Rosie. The girl seems anxious, and I catch the way she shoots Ash a nervous look every time she speaks, as if she's checking for his approval. Ash's gaze is steely, boring into hers as if commanding her with his eyes not to disclose too much.

I take a sip of my tea, unable to shake the bad feeling that swirls in the pit of my stomach. The sooner these people are gone from here, the better. They say no good deed goes unpunished. Or something like that, and I have an awful feeling that this one good deed could end up costing Kay much more than the woman bargained for.

11

KAY

The rich smell of the meaty lamb stew fills the kitchen making me feel suddenly nostalgic. I stare over towards the kitchen table, and I am instantly transported back in time.

I see the image of my beloved six-year-old Amanda sitting there and I feel a tug of thick emotion expand inside my chest. The pull of something fierce in my heart at the memory of my daughter's dainty sparrow-like legs, swinging impatiently beneath the chair, as she waits for me to join her, so that she can talk incessantly about anything and everything she did at school that day.

I smile sadly to myself. Recalling fondly how as a young child, once Amanda started talking she couldn't seem to stop. My God, how I wish I had soaked that all up. Hung on my child's every word, her every story. I remember all of it though. The tales of her little school friends and all their petty dramas. Which books the teacher read to her that had quickly become her favourites. How much effort and love had gone into all those bold, beautiful paintings that she'd insisted on me displaying proudly on the fridge.

Simpler times. No. I correct myself. The happiest of times.

I'd taken it all for granted. Naively believing that it would be like that between us forever. That we'd still have time.

I think of her now. Inside that coffin. Ashes to ashes. Dust to dust.

Biting my lip, I fight back the tears that threaten as I recall the dramatic, profound shift in Amanda just a few short years later, when she'd become a teenager.

'I'm not eating that. Eating dead animals is cruel. I'm a vegetarian.'

Amanda's words the very last time that I had batch cooked an enormous pot of lamb stew like this. Amanda's favourite. Or so I had thought until she'd stubbornly refused to eat so much as a single bite. Stirring the bowl of thick, rich gravy while lifting out each huge, tender piece of lamb with a look of disgust on her face. Picking only at whatever vegetables I'd served with it, nibbling at the thickly cut wedges of buttered bread.

That had just been the start. She'd battled so wilfully against me over just about everything after that. Arguing with me about what clothes she did or did not want to wear. How much make-up was acceptable. What time she should be allowed out until.

Preoccupied with what I'd assumed had been the angst of teenage hormones, her mood swings were erratic and her energy levels low. I'd guessed that she'd become consumed with other things preoccupying her teenage mind. Like the pressure of her imminent exams. Dramas with her friendship groups. The trials and tribulations of navigating her way through puberty.

Boys had been the reality though. Just one boy in fact. The wrong kind. The kind that took up all of her time and her attention. The kind that distracted her from her studies, from her home life. From me. I'd soon put a stop to that though and when I look back, it's that which had been my downfall. Meddling in Amanda's relationship when her boyfriend had come to the house. I'd told him to go away, that Amanda didn't want to see or speak to him again. That she'd moved on and met somebody else.

Everything had fallen apart after that.

Overnight, Amanda's animated chatter simply disappeared. Replaced with irritated shrugs and grunts of annoyance at even my presence. At the mere audacity of my existence. She'd accused me of interfering in her life and if I dared to even ask about her day, she'd claim that I was interrogating her. Dinnertime became a mundane chore to the girl, as Amanda shovelled her food down, clock-watching the entire time. As if she had somewhere better to be than here with me, when in reality all she had wanted to do was skulk back off to the solace of her bedroom.

The teenage years had been the worst and I had foolishly believed back then, that in time, if I waited patiently, things would change back. Because your children always come back to you again, eventually. Isn't that what the 'so-called' experts in all the magazines say? All those smug parents that have already been dragged through the process, and have lived to tell the tale, now that they'd been spat out again on the other side.

No one warns you how painful the lead up before that is though, do they? About the constant daily rejection you endure while you help navigate your child's transition between childhood and adulthood. While you patiently wait for them to find their own way in the world.

No one warns you about how they stop sharing all those little stories and anecdotes about their day, until eventually they stop confiding in you completely. How they start disclosing their secrets to others instead. Growing up, that's what they call it. But really it's growing up, and away and apart, then one day they leave you completely.

That's the truth.

And my God, it had hurt like hell. Even now all these years later, the emotional aftertaste sticks to my tongue like bitter, soured lemons. I can still recall that same crushing sensation in my chest as I'd naively, painstakingly waited for the day that Amanda would return to me.

Only she never came back.

The distance between us as adults drove a bigger, and vaster wedge. I had pushed my daughter too hard, apparently. Put too much pressure on her to spend time with me. Become too demanding. Too overbearing. Too needy. Too clingy.

The list of Amanda's contempt for me had been relentless. Accusing me of following her when she was out with her friends so that I could keep tabs on her, of spying on her and barely giving her any space to breathe. Of being jealous of her making relationships outside of me.

The more intensely I had clung to Amanda, the more determined she'd been to pull away.

Amanda had punished me for simply loving her. I feel a lump form in my throat, tears pooling in my eyes. No, I think as I quickly wipe them away, I need to stop this. Stop tormenting myself by going over it again and again, and again. I blink and the vision of my perfect six-year-old Amanda disappears. Evaporating into nothingness before my very eyes once more. The kitchen is empty again and I am back in the room.

Turning my attention back to the bubbling stew, I give the sauce a stir to stop it sticking to the edges of the pan. Comfort food, I resolve as I set about dishing up huge bowls of boiling hot stew. Everyone here could do with this.

These days I am all about comfort. If there is one thing that my daughter's recent, tragic death has taught me, it's that life is too short and haven't I already wasted far too much of mine feeling exactly the opposite of that. Uncomfortable. Unable to find my place in the world, unable to find my people. Alone. Though I'm not alone any more.

'Dinner is ready.' I smile, enjoying the rare sound of the

footsteps and chair legs padding and scraping across the kitchen floor as they are pulled out from around the table.

Glimmers.

That's what my counsellor once told me to look out for. Those tiny micro-moments of joy, that's what I needed to hold on to. Not all those negative thoughts that fill my head, telling me that I'm not good enough. That I'll never be good enough, because if I focus on them, they'll consume me completely and I'll be lost again in my bad thoughts forever.

Trapped there.

This is a glimmer I decide, setting the food down on the table before placing a huge plated pile of buttered bread, in the centre. Here, tonight, sat at my kitchen table, enjoying my dinner surrounded by these people. People who actually want to be here. People who need me.

'I hope you're hungry?' I ask as Stephanie sits down last, reluctant to join us all at the table. Still not happy about me letting Rosie, Ash and the baby stay.

'Yeah, and it smells lovely,' she says, only the smile that she fixes to her face doesn't reach her eyes.

Another glimmer.

She is making an effort for me. Going through the motions of being polite because I asked her to.

'Good? It smells A-mazing.' Rosie beams good-naturedly as she tucks into the food despite the steam pouring from her fork.

Ash sits opposite us, holding baby George tightly in his arms as if he's afraid to let the child out of his sight for so much as a second.

'How's he doing? He looks a little more settled now you've all had a bit of rest.' Noting how after a day of resting in the warmth here, George seems a little calmer now.

'I think he's a little bit better now that he's had a sleep—' Rosie starts, only to be interrupted by Ash, who purposely talks over her.

'He's still not great though. Still full of cold. He's got a bit of a temperature too. He won't be put down.'

'Why don't you let me hold him for a little while, so you can eat?' I hold out my hands, only Ash shakes his head, refusing my offer of help.

I lower my arms awkwardly, wondering if despite me letting this family into my home, of doing whatever I can to help them, Ash still doesn't trust me.

'He's a right old Daddy's boy, isn't he, Rosie? Won't go to anyone without getting himself worked up again,' Ash says, seeing the look that flashes across my face, before glancing over at Rosie as if willing her to back him up.

Which of course, Rosie does.

'Yeah, he is being super clingy at the moment. Won't go to anyone but us.'

'That's okay. I only wanted to help, but I understand,' I say, shrugging off the feeling of being rejected once more. I am just being silly. Ridiculous in fact. This is not personal. I know that really. Babies can be vulnerable like that. I remember it only too well, how they only want the familiarity and comfort of their parents when they are sick. No one else will do.

'Well, a couple of nights and he should be right as rain,' Stephanie states. 'Where are you going after here?'

'Stephanie.' I let out a tight chuckle, hoping to take the edge off her blunt questioning tone. 'They've only just got themselves settled in. You make it sound as if you're in a hurry to get rid of them already...'

Stephanie shrugs, not denying my insinuation, and I shift awkwardly in my chair.

'Well, it's a fair question, isn't it? You said they could stay for a couple of nights. I'm just wondering where they're planning on going after here. I mean, you both can't have that many options if you've been sleeping in a tent in the park. And you can't just send them back out there again to that, Kay. So where are you going?'

'Stephanie!' I raise my voice, my words harder now as I flash the girl a warning. It is not Stephanie's place to interrogate these people. This is my house and my decision to let them stay here.

'Don't worry.' Ash grins at me, while batting the back of his hand in Stephanie's direction, as if fending off an unwelcome pest.

'We've got a friend we can stay with.' Ash holds eye contact with Stephanie while he speaks. Only breaking it to glance over at Rosie, so that she will once again nod in all the right places and back him up.

'Oh really? How come you didn't stay with them in the first place, then?' Stephanie continues, determined to poke at the couple.

'They've been away on holiday. Didn't leave a spare key...'

Ash talks fast, clearly rattled, he manages to keep his expression neutral, but I see it. The protruding vein throbbing at his temple, the small, tight smile that is fixed to his face, more of a grimace. The gesture full of insincerity just like the man wearing it. He is visibly riled at the way Stephanie has just put him on the spot. That she is so intent on calling him out. That she can sniff his lies from a mile away. Though he won't give her the satisfaction of knowing that.

I make a mental note at how Ash is so good at that.

Acting.

I should know, I do it often enough myself. Pushing my real feelings and emotions down for fear of them pouring out of me. Because that would make me seem weak and I am anything but weak. The solitary, tough life I've been forced to lead has hardened me.

'Yeah, they'll be back soon. And we'll be going there for a bit. So, that will be nice...' Rosie chips in and Stephanie turns her attention to her.

'Where did they go?'

'Spain.'

'Portugal.'

Contradicting each other in unison, Rosie quickly corrects herself.

'Spain. That's it. Sorry, I always get the two mixed up.' She diverts her gaze from mine and looks down at the table, and I appreciate that. How the girl is unable to look me in the eye when she lies.

It means that she has some level of integrity. That she doesn't take me for the old fool that Ash seemingly does. It's something I suppose, as I take a mouthful of the food, and chew on it slowly. Digesting it along with the fact that Stephanie is right, when these people have to leave here in a few days' time, they'll have nowhere else to go. They'll both be back to square one again.

I'm their only option and Stephanie is worried that I'll end up stuck with them. That *we'll* end up stuck with them.

'Don't you have family that might be missing you? Missing George? Can't you just go home?' Stephanie continues brazenly. Knowing full well how uncomfortable she is making Ash as she continues to prod at him.

'We're not all as lucky as you. Having family to *rely* on,' Ash bites back and there's an unmistakable sharp, spiteful edge to the words *rely on* which instantly triggers Stephanie, just as Ash had probably hoped.

'Rely? You don't know anything about me or my life. So please don't assume. I don't *rely* on Kay. I don't rely on anyone.' She glances at me then and pauses. As if trying to get her words in the right order, as she recites the story that we both agreed on.

'I've been staying here for a few months, because things were difficult at home. My mum was having some problems and I thought it was best to give her some space.'

Stephanie glances at me and it's my turn to look down at the table.

'I found her dead one night when I went to visit her and I knew that I could never go back there again after that. Kay said I could stay. I'm not relying on her.'

'Oh, I'm sure that's not the way Ash means it, Stephanie.' I raise a hand as if to insist on a mutual truce as I see Stephanie's emotions start to get the better of her.

Her cheeks burning bright red, angry tears glistening in her eyes.

'Then how does he mean it? Because he sounds defensive to me,' Stephanie repeats, shaking her head. 'And all I'm doing is asking questions. I'm allowed to do that, aren't I? One of us should be,' Stephanie says stubbornly. A parting shot before she takes the hint and drops the subject, concentrating on her food once more.

Only Ash, spotting a chink in Stephanie's reinforced armour, can't let it go.

'Yet here you are taking handouts just like the rest of us. Living off Kay's generous nature. At least we are only willing to do that for a couple of days.'

'Fuck you.' Stephanie slams her cutlery down hard against her bowl sending hot, thick gravy splashing out across the table. 'I'm nothing like you. My mother died. I had no other option.'

'I'm so sorry,' Rosie says, the tremor of emotion in her words showing that she is being genuine.

Only Stephanie clearly doesn't care for either of these people's sympathy, and glares back at her.

'Why are you sorry? You didn't kill my mother, did you?'

'What?' Rosie stammers, visibly taken aback at the curtness of Stephanie's response. 'No. I just meant that I'm sorry for your loss. For your mother, that must be awful. To have found her like that. To have seen her…' Rosie is crying now, her hands visibly shaking as she speaks.

I watch as she sets them down on the table and Ash places his palm over hers. A kind, small gesture I think at first, only I see how firm he is. How he's pushing her hands flat to stop the shaking. He's not offering her compassion or support, he just doesn't want us to see.

'Christ. What is wrong with you?' Ash raises his voice, visibly defensive at Stephanie's unprovoked attack on Rosie when the girl was only being kind. 'She's sorry for your loss. She's being nice. Maybe you should try that sometime...'

'Don't, Ash. Please, just leave it, yeah?' Rosie pulls her hand out from under his in a bid to silence him, offering Stephanie an excuse as she does. 'She's grieving her mum.'

'Grief doesn't give you the excuse to turn into a bitch.'

'Do you know what, I can't do this. Sorry, Kay, but I'm not hungry. I'm going to my...' Stephanie stands up, stopping still suddenly, her words filtering off mid-sentence and I realise she is about to say, 'my bedroom', only it isn't her room any more.

It's Ash and Rosie's bedroom for now.

'Stephanie, please...' I hold out my hand, feeling guilty. Aware that Stephanie, like me, suffered a terrible loss and that she needs her space except now she has nowhere to go and grieve privately.

'I'll be in the lounge.' Dismissing my hand, Stephanie scrapes her chair out from behind her defiantly.

I follow her gaze, as she looks over at Ash, physically smarting at the smug expression on the young man's face. A look that says he has won. He'd poked at her and got the reaction he was looking for.

Stephanie storms from the room, slamming the kitchen door loudly behind her, which of course sets baby George off crying again loudly. The lovely intimate dinner that I hoped to give everyone, bowls of comfort food, ruined now.

'I'm sorry...' I begin, watching as the two young parents fuss around their baby, trying to calm and console him once more.

'She's having a really difficult time right now. Her mother's death really hit her hard.'

'Don't be sorry. We understand. That must be awful for her. For you both,' Rosie says.

I nod my head unable to say the words that stick in the back of my throat.

More than you can ever know.

12

KAY

'Right, that's the bed made up for you,' I say, tucking the last corner of the duvet down tightly around the upholstered bed frame before turning around and doing a double-take as Ash walks back into the room holding baby George.

'Oh Ash! You look...' I stifle my giggle, despite myself. Not wanting to say the word 'ridiculous' but dressed in a pair of baggy floral tracksuit bottoms and a pink oversized t-shirt – the only clean clothes that I could find that would fit his tall, broad frame – ridiculous is exactly how the man looks right now.

It's Ash and Rosie's second shower of the day, because neither of them felt clean after so much time sleeping rough. Their clothes had been in an awful state too. Damp from the rain and soiled in places, I'd shoved the whole lot in the washing machine and washed the same load twice before shoving them on the airer in my kitchen.

'You look... better,' I lie. Pulling my gaze away from his, as I see the onset of irritation flash across his face, at the realisation that he has now become the butt of my humour. I've seen how quickly he can lose his temper and the last thing I want to do is rile him.

'Much better now that you've showered and changed. Your things should be dry by the morning. And if you want, I can pop down to the charity shop and see if they have anything suitable for you. One outfit isn't enough...'

For when you leave.

That's what I am about to say, only I stop myself. Stephanie had already made the same point at dinner and it hadn't gone well and the last thing I want to do is keep reminding these people that this arrangement is only temporary. I don't want to start stressing them out about that. I want them to relax and get some sleep tonight because they both look exhausted.

'Yeah, whatever,' Ash replies breaking his silence, his attention focused only on George, as he lays the tiny baby carefully down in the centre of the double bed.

'You're ready for your bed, aren't you, mate?' Ash says catching George's almighty yawn. 'At least this one doesn't care what he looks like,' Ash quips, tugging down the purple and yellow t-shirt that I had got from Stephanie for the child to wear. A crop top, apparently. The smallest item of clothing Stephanie had and yet the tiny garment still somehow manages to swamp him.

From here, I can just catch a glimpse of the pink skin of his arms and legs poking out from the material, glowing from where he's just been taken out of a nice warm bath. He has a fresh nappy on now too. The last of the small pack the couple had managed to salvage from the drenched tent.

I'll have to venture out early tomorrow and get him some more. And some Sudocrem to ease the red raw nappy rash that spans the tops of his legs and bottom. I shudder to think how long the poor mite had been made to sit in his wet, soiled nappies between changes, in order to make the nappies last. It wasn't entirely the young couple's fault, I know they'd done their best to keep him safe and warm. But without money their best just hadn't been good enough. Still, they're here now, and if I can help them out in any way, I will.

'Give him his medicine first, before you give him his milk, otherwise he won't take it,' Rosie informs Ash as she strolls into the room and I am startled by the girl's childlike appearance now that she is showered and fresh-faced.

Her wet hair is twisted tightly inside a towel that towers at the top of her head. A stricken look of anxiety fixed to her face as she watches Ash struggling to get the syringe of medicine into their son's mouth. George doesn't make it easy. Wriggling wildly around with frustration, he arches his back against the mattress, and starts kicking out.

'Stay still, little buddy,' Ash says, as his patience dwindles and he grabs at his son's face, a little rougher than George is used to. George lets out a loud howl, before the tears start coming once again and it's all too much for Rosie.

'Here, let me.' She steps forward with assertiveness but Ash refuses to back down and shakes his head.

'No. He's my son too, Rosie. I can do it.' His voice is firm. Authoritative. Controlling. As he holds George's chin with one hand, while administering the medicine with the other. Too fast this time, in his bid to prove his point. The liquid shoots into the baby's mouth and George begins to cough and splutter.

'Ash. He's choking.' This time, Rosie doesn't wait for permission. Ignoring Ash's request to leave him to it, she lifts her spluttering baby from the bed, before placing him upright against her chest and rhythmically tapping at his back.

'I had it,' Ash says sulkily.

I'm surprised at this. Instead of simply being relieved that his son is no longer choking, Ash is silently seething now. More concerned that Rosie has just undermined him in front of me. That Rosie didn't do as she was told.

'He'll be right as rain after his medicine and a good sleep,' I say, hoping to defuse the tension in the room. Only my words seem to have the opposite effect on Ash.

'Yeah, we could all do with that,' he says, glaring at me.

I am loitering, I realise. Stood gormlessly by the bedroom door while this family get settled for bed. I have outstayed my welcome.

'Right, sorry, yes. I'll leave you all to it. I hope you manage to get a decent night's sleep.'

Taking the hint, I make my way out through the door just as Stephanie comes through it.

'I'm just grabbing my Kindle. Can't sleep without it,' she says with a tight smile that doesn't reach her eyes, as she stomps across the room, grabbing the Kindle from where she's tucked it away inside the bedside drawer.

'Thanks again for letting us have your room for a few nights,' Rosie starts. Trying once more to reach out to Stephanie and form a friendship of sorts. 'We really do appreciate it. And the clothes—'

'I didn't have much choice. Besides, it's only two nights. You'll be gone after that,' Stephanie says, cutting the girl off mid-sentence. Clearly not interested in anything Rosie or Ash has to say to her. She turns and marches back out again. Still seething from earlier at dinner.

'She's going through a lot right now. She doesn't mean it. She's just not really coping,' I say softly, recognising the look of hurt on Rosie's face that Stephanie will not even entertain her attempt at an olive branch.

'Give her time. She'll come round eventually,' I say hoping that I'm right. Then out of loyalty for my granddaughter, I add, 'Besides, it's only for a few days, isn't it? It's not the end of the world if you have to step around each other. Now, get some sleep. I bet you could all do with some,' I say, stepping out of the room and closing the bedroom door behind me.

It's just a few days. The two of them could do this, couldn't they? Even Stephanie, if she just puts her mind to it.

13

ROSIE

Ash tightens his grip around my arm. His fingers twisting my skin and pinching hard at my flesh. His mouth moves in angry circles, as his face turns puce red. He's shouting. Only I can't hear the words he's saying because they are drowned out by the sound of blood whooshing loudly inside my ears.

I am staring down at her, transfixed on her lifeless form as she lays – dead – at my feet.

'*Run!*'

Ash's voice.

'*No!*'

Then my voice, panicked, slicing through the darkness like a sharp swipe of a metal blade.

I wake to find that I am covered in a thick film of sweat.

Breathe.

Relieved to find myself here, in Kay's spare room, I tell myself that it was just a bad dream. That I'm a million miles away from my haunting nightmares. That they can't hurt me here.

Only that isn't quite true. I am living them.

Pulling the duvet up tightly around me and curving my

body protectively around George like a shield, I reach out a hand and ensure the pillow that I'd placed against the mattress's edge earlier is still secure. That there's no chance of him falling out of the bed and hurting himself while I sleep.

When I sleep? If I sleep.

Sleep should come easier now we are here in the safety of Kay's house. Sleep should be restful, now that I am no longer on my guard at every sound that I hear. Now that I don't have to worry about anyone stealing our things. Or worse, lying awake gripped with constant fear that someone might try to hurt us. Or much, much worse than that, hurt George.

I don't have to constantly check that the mountain of blankets I've placed on top of my son to keep him warm haven't somehow been kicked off while he slept, exposing him to the freezing temperatures, or that he hasn't wriggled down and got tangled up beneath the layers.

Sleep *should* come easy, but tonight it's my demons that are making me restless. *We are safe here*, I remind myself. *For now, at least.*

Placing a hand on my son's tiny body, I relish the rhythmic movement of his ribcage beneath it, wonder of his tiny lungs filling with air, as George continues to sleep soundly and I am so grateful for that. Grateful that George is warm and fed and clean. More rested. That here, he will get better.

How this is all thanks to Kay.

I strain to see through the darkness, part of me still in disbelief that this is real, that we are really here in this room. In Kay's home. I still can't quite believe that there are really people like Kay out there. Genuinely good people. Kind and compassionate enough to allow two complete strangers into their home, without knowing a single thing about them.

Her one good deed, she'd called it. I smile at that.

Kay had been keen to know our reasons for being desperate enough to sleep outside in that tent in the woods. Prodding gently when she'd asked what had driven us to such a thing when we have such a young baby with us. Trying to extract what little information I will give her. I've given her none really. The bare minimum.

Yet still, she let us in.

Despite the fact that she is wary of Ash, having witnessed first-hand how volatile his temper can be. How stubborn and headstrong he is. There is so much that Kay doesn't know about us and part of me feels bad about that. So much she can never know about us. Because if she did, she would kick us back out onto the streets. Only here we are, hiding away in her house.

Her, harbouring criminals. Murderers.

Is that what we are?

I bristle at how that word sounds inside my head, before pushing the thought away, unwilling to accept that this is exactly who we are now. I can't think about any of that tonight, not if there's any chance of me getting back to sleep. I need to focus on the positives, right here in this moment. The three of us together, out of the cold, away from the storm, safe in the warm. In Kay's perfect home.

Well, almost perfect, I think, as I wrinkle my nose at the pungent, chemical smell filling the room that I can't quiet locate. I allow myself a small grin as I recognise the irony. At how quickly I've become accustomed to my new surroundings. How ungrateful I am, finding fault in something so insignificant as an overpowering air freshener. When less than twenty-four hours ago the three of us were all holed up inside a tiny, compact tent. The only smell that flooded our noses there was the stench of George's soiled nappies.

'You, okay?' Ash's voice comes from behind me. Pulling me out of my thoughts, I feel him as he rolls towards me in the bed, pressing his warm body up against mine.

'Sorry. I didn't mean to wake you. I had another bad dream. About her...'

'Shh! Don't Rosie...' He whispers firmly, silencing me.

Shutting me down, just like I knew he would. 'You can't keep doing this, Rosie. Please. It's done now. You need to forget about it.'

'Forget about it?' The words screech out of my mouth and it's all I can do to calm myself down. The last thing I want to do is wake George. 'How can I just forget something like that?' I hiss. Shrugging Ash off me, I shuffle a few inches away from him in the bed, purposely to make a point.

I know how stubborn he can be. That no matter what I say to him, he will not listen. He doesn't want to talk about this. Only it's all I want to talk about. It's all that I can think about. So much so, I feel as if it's driving me mad.

'Hey. Don't be like that.'

'Like what?' I ask.

'Pissed off with me.'

'I'm not pissed off, Ash. I'm scared. No. I not scared either. I am utterly, utterly terrified. What happened... What we did...' I falter when I say these words because we both know that this was never a case of '*we*'.

We didn't do anything.

But we'd both left her there afterwards, hadn't we?

We'd both ran.

Whether we like it or not, in the eyes of the law we're both as guilty as one another now.

'We can end this, Ash. There's still time. We can go to the police and explain everything. We can tell them it was an accident. That things just got out of hand, that we didn't mean...'

Ash shakes his head. Not wanting to even contemplate my suggestion.

'You know we can't do that. I'm not going to allow them to split our family up, Rosie. And that's what will happen if they find us. They'll take George away from us. I'll go to prison.'

'You won't go to prison...' I start, but I know it's no use

trying to persuade Ash otherwise. We've been over this same conversation a thousand times.

'Rosie, please, it's done. We can't take it back. There's no point in torturing yourself like this. We just need to figure out where to go from here. I'll fix this. I promise you that.' Ash tries again. Wrapping his arms around me, I feel the warmth of him. And despite myself I feel my body sinking back against his. Giving in to him once more, like always. Ash has a way about him. A hold over me. I can't explain it but it's heady and intoxicating and all consuming. Like some kind of magic spell.

'You need to stop arguing with Stephanie, Ash, or you're going to ruin this,' I whisper into the darkness eventually, taking my chance in broaching the subject of his argument with Stephanie at dinner earlier, now that I can feel how Ash has softened. That now I am pressed up against him, he'll be more likely to accept a truce tonight instead of another argument.

'Kay will ask us to leave if we cause any trouble.'

'Hey, don't blame me. It's Stephanie who has the problem,' Ash retorts stubbornly.

'Please, Ash, just try and keep the peace. If you can't be nice, then at least be civil.'

'Civil? Why should I? You heard her. Quizzing us and looking down her stuck-up nose at us, like we're some freeloaders when really she's no better. She's living off Kay too.'

'Ash, her mother died and Kay is her grandmother. It's hardly the same thing. Besides, you saw the girl tonight. She's grieving.'

I bristle at that last word. The realisation hitting me hard that perhaps I am grieving too.

For my old life.

For her.

I did it all wrong. I know that now. Keeping the news that I was pregnant from my mother. Hiding my changing body underneath oversized clothes in a bid to deceive her. To deceive the entire world. Even myself, really. Because I hadn't been ready or willing to accept that I was actually pregnant.

Even when the tight skin of my stomach softened and grew rounder. My breasts fuller and sore as they started to fill with milk. Still, I had hidden the fact that my mother was going to have a grandchild. When, if anything, she would have been the one person to have helped me.

I should have handled all of it so differently.

I can't cope.

The grief I'm experiencing is not leaving me numb and confused like I thought it would, it's making me unpredictable. Making me act differently from how I normally would. Completely out of character, making all these bad decisions. Making me go along with all of Ash's bad decisions.

'We just need to be careful, Ash. We're lucky Kay said we could stay for a few days, but there's nothing stopping her from asking us to leave before then if she wants.'

'I bet if Stephanie wasn't here, Kay would let us stay for longer than a few days. She likes you. And she loves George. Only well, let's face it, I don't think she's much of a fan of me...'

He says this last part with a small chuckle and I am glad that he at least sees this too. That he's aware how Kay hasn't warmed to him. That he's going to need to try much harder if he wants to win her over.

'Well in fairness to Kay, you didn't exactly give her the best first impression, did you?' I think about their first encounter, how Ash stood over Kay threateningly with a metal pole in his hand. 'She'd only wanted to give us some food and clean blankets, nothing worthy of getting her head caved in.'

'I wasn't going to use it, was I?' Ash declares, his voice cranking up a couple of notches, defensive now.

He would have, I think, if he'd had to.

Because that was Ash all over. Acting out impulsively without any thought of the consequences afterwards. Desperate to keep us all inside his protective bubble, in a bid to keep us safe. Sometimes that bubble felt airless and suffocating.

'There might be a way that we can stay longer, you know. Whether Stephanie likes it or not.' Ash keeps his voice low now, whispering into my ear.

'How?' I ask, instantly dreading Ash's answer. So far his grand plans hadn't boded well for us.

'We can pretend George is still ill...'

'No, Ash, we can't lie about that. We can't wish that upon our son.'

'When did you become so superstitious all of a sudden? We don't have to lie about anything. I can keep him in here most of the time, out of the way. We can just tell Kay that he's sleeping a lot. We don't even have to say it, just imply it. Nothing to make her worried enough to want us to call an ambulance or a doctor, or anything like that. Just don't let on that he's getting better.'

'I don't know, Ash...' I say, not wanting to even put the thought of George not getting better out there into the universe. Because right now, that would be just our luck.

'George will be okay, won't he?' I say after a brief pause, forcing the question from my mouth, half of me scared stiff to hear Ash's answer.

'Of course he'll be okay,' Ash says without skipping a beat and I am grateful for how certain he sounds. For his optimism. At least one of us has complete and utter faith in our child getting better. I just need to start believing in his recovery too. Because if anything happens to George, I know I'll never forgive myself.

'Kay's nice, isn't she?' I observe. 'There's not many people out there that would invite two teenagers and a baby into their home.'

'Yeah, she's all right.' I feel Ash's shoulders move as he offers a small shrug. 'A bit batshit though, don't you think? I mean, look at all the stuff she has everywhere. That isn't normal, is it? Collecting so much crap that you can barely see the wallpaper and carpet.' Ash wrinkles his nose, and I'm not sure if it's the potent air freshener lingering still, or the thought of all Kay's musty smelling boxes and bags that she has stacked up against almost every interior wall in the house, that is leaving a bad taste in Ash's mouth.

'Well, there's no harm in collecting stuff.' I shrug back, feeling defensive. Kay has helped us when we've needed it most. She's given George the best shot at getting better quickly. Who are we to judge the woman? Especially when Kay had made a point of not judging us.

'Collecting stuff? Oh, come on. Kay's got so many knick-knacks and old bits of tatt stacked up around here, it's practically holding the roof up.'

'Just because it looks like tatt to us, doesn't make it so. It's all Kay's things. They must all mean something to her. Just because she can't bear to throw some of it away, doesn't make her batshit! Maybe she's just, I don't know? Sentimental.'

'Just mental more like,' Ash mutters under his breath.

'Ash, Kay has offered us a lifeline. No one else would give us an opportunity like this. Can't you be a little nicer? Besides, we can't talk. Didn't we just set up home for the past two days in a grotty, stolen tent?'

As soon as I say the words, I regret them. Because I know that when Ash had stolen the tent and sleeping bags, he'd only been trying his best to make things better for us.

'Look, all I'm saying is there are worst conditions that Kay could be living in and being surrounded by "things" isn't one of them.'

'Yeah, I guess.' Ash nods his head in agreement, finally relenting for my sake if nothing else, before he purposely changes the subject.

'This place is all right though, isn't it? Here, can you

imagine if we had a place like this all to ourselves? Permanently. A proper home for the three of us. I mean, it would be nice, wouldn't it?' Ash says sounding suddenly upbeat for the first time in days and I can't help but get swept along by the thought of it. 'How cool would that be? Me and you, against the world. King and Queen of our castle. We could do a bedroom up for George. A nursery like you see in those baby magazines. Paint it blue and do, I don't know, some kind of zoo animal theme on the walls. Lions and tigers and zebras. He'd love that, wouldn't he?'

'Yeah, he would.' I grin as the imagery that Ash is describing plays out inside my head.

Our son deserves so much better than what we've managed to give him so far. He deserves a room all of his own. Painted with bold, bright colours. His own wooden cot dressed in matching blankets.

'I could make you dinner for when you finish work and then we could bath George before reading him a bedtime story. Then we could snuggle up together on the sofa and...' I look up at Ash, reminding myself how he isn't all bad. How he has tried his best to make this right. To keep us all together.

'And what?' Ash laughs, tightening his grip on me.

'Watch TV,' I say with a giggle, as Ash let out a playful laugh at my attempts at teasing him.

'One day,' Ash says, giving my hand a gentle squeeze.

Only I know different.

'I think we've ruined all chances of ever having a nice, normal life like this,' I whisper quietly, finally admitting what's eating me up inside. Waiting patiently for Ash to reassure me, to tell me that I am being stupid and overthinking again, only when he doesn't reply, I wonder if he's staying quiet because he is thinking this too. That we have ruined our lives. That we'll never be coming back from this.

'Ash?' I feel the heavy weight of Ash's arm, draped over me, sinking down against my flesh. His breath grows slow and laborious before he starts to snore loudly. Switching the bedside lamp off, I can't help but feel a tiny bit jealous of that. How all it takes for Ash to give in to sleep is for him to simply close his eyes.

Almost as if he hasn't got a conscience.

Unlike me, lying alone again in the darkness, riddled with guilt. Wide awake and full of anxiety as I relentlessly torment myself. Still convinced that we can end this now. That we should just confess. Because I'm not sure how long I can continue living like this.

Even if Ash is right and the worst does happen, even if we get into serious trouble – nothing can be worse than what we have endured the past few days. Exposing George to the elements and allowing him to get so sick. He deserves so much better than this and the longer we run from what we did, the worse things will be for us.

A faint noise outside our room catches my attention and I look towards the doorway, surprised to see that it's been edged open, just enough to allow a thin slither of light to slice through the gap.

Kay had closed it earlier, hadn't she?

I strain to listen, wondering if it was the sound of the duvet rustling as Ash moves beside me in his sleep. Or perhaps the wind whistling loudly down the chimney breast. Because every noise seems magnified now.

Only I hear it again.

The creak of floorboards just outside our room, just as a dark shadow of movement dances across the threshold under the doorway. I shiver, the sudden sense of unease prickles at my skin at the thought of someone purposely creeping around out there as they listen in to mine and Ash's private conversations.

My eyes remain fixed on the thin band of light for what feels like forever. Only it's so quiet now and there's no sound or movement at all. I start to doubt myself. Wondering if maybe my exhaustion from the past few days has caught up with me and is starting to make me imagine things that aren't really there. Perhaps Kay hadn't closed the bedroom door at all. Maybe she'd just pulled it to? I will not allow myself to start overthinking this. I need to get some sleep. I close my eyes, knowing that it's pointless really, there will be no relief.

Even if I do eventually drift off, my nightmares will come again for me.

14

STEPHANIE

The smell of sizzling bacon fills my nostrils, causing me to instantly salivate the second I wake.

Stretching my limbs out, like a cat limbering up upon awaking from its slumber, my feet hit the solid, tatty arm of the chair, and the sharp prong of metal spring that has been poking into the small of my back for most of the night reminds me that I'm not in my bed. I have woken up on Kay's ancient, uncomfortable sofa. Surprised that I've slept at all if I'm honest. The settee is so narrow that I'd been convinced I would roll off in the middle of the night and land with a thud, face down on the front room floor.

Now, sitting up. I unfold my body as if it's a crushed-up piece of paper. Compact and compressed and made smaller than it actually is so that it would fit in this tight, tiny space.

Part of me has always felt a bit like that.

I've grown used to making myself smaller so that I would fit in. Moulded myself into something I'm not so that I don't cause any fuss. Hadn't I slept in much worse places over the years?

Cuddled up behind my mother's frame on some stranger's sofa, the room full of loud, incessant chatter as pungent plumes from whatever they had all been smoking filled the air. Or once, on the cold tiles of someone's kitchen floor, with only the clothes I'd been wearing to keep me warm, and one of my mother's jumpers tucked beneath my head as a makeshift pillow.

I had slept last night. Though, I do not feel rested.

If anything, my attention fixates on the shrill noise coming from the kitchen. A commotion of cups clanging, chair legs screeching their way across the tiled kitchen floor. Bacon spitting in a pan. I feel instantly on edge and irritated once more.

At the sound of *them*.

I strain to listen in as the couple's animated voices fill my ears, only I am too far away to hear the exact words that are being spoken. But it sounds as if they are having a disagreement about something, and instantly I feel excluded. Like a spare part. Evicted from the spare bedroom and assigned to my new place, here on Kay's tatty, worn sofa. I'm on the outside again, desperately trying to look in.

I don't want them here.

That doesn't make me a monster or even a bad person, does it? Just because Kay wants to do a good deed by allowing these people in, doesn't mean that I have to feel the same way too.

I'm allowed to feel this way, aren't I? After all I have been through over the past few weeks. The shock of finding my mother in that awful state. The funeral. Then, finally moving in here. I hadn't wanted to say that last night, when I'd told Ash not to make his assumptions about me. I hadn't wanted to divulge all the details of how vulnerable I felt now that my whole entire world had imploded.

Now that nothing would ever be the same again.

The very last thing I need right now, or Kay needs, is a captive audience, closely watching our every move. Observing us while we're trying to put the fractured pieces of our lives back together. Especially after feeling the malice come off Ash in waves, taking offence at my line of questioning, I'd seen the flash of fury in his eyes and something far scarier than that. The desperation that he tried to hide too. I wonder what Rosie sees in him. She must see something, because she looks to him for his approval every time she goes to speak.

The fact that Kay has simply let this young couple into her home, without so much as a single question or explanation about why they'd been staying in a tent in the park in the first place is madness.

Madness, not kindness as Kay would have you believe.

Kay has put us both at risk. Surely I am not the only one who can see that? These people could be capable of just about anything, and because Kay doesn't want to rock the boat by quizzing them on their circumstances, because she doesn't want to make them feel uncomfortable or unwelcome, she simply expects me to follow suit. Well, I'm not playing. I don't have to tolerate them if I don't want to. And I don't want to. What harm would it cause to voice that? To make my concerns known to the couple? To remind them not to get too comfortable here? That this arrangement is only temporary.

Getting up from the chair, and pulling my sweatshirt on over my pyjamas, I head towards the kitchen to do just that. Though as I reach the kitchen door, I note how they've lowered their voices. The chatter inside the room has become quieter now. As if they don't want to be overheard. I stand deadly still and patiently listen in, only catching the muted blur of lowered voices. The odd inaudible word. A few murmured sounds.

Then something familiar.

'Kay might be easy to get around, but Stephanie won't be. As soon as the couple of days are up, she'll want us out. She made that clear last night.' Ash's voice. Low and hard as he practically spits out my name. 'We need to think of a plan B. A way to make them let us stay here longer. Kay will be easy to persuade, I reckon. A walk in the park.' He laughs at his lame attempt at a joke, and I immediately bristle, defensive at the way he's making fun of Kay. The way he thinks he can manipulate the woman when all she's done is show him nothing but kindness.

'Well, you can start by trying to be nicer to Stephanie. Befriend her? Try and keep her on side too. For now, at least.'

It's Rosie's voice now. Hanging on Ash's every word. Obedient, complicit Rosie acting every bit as cunning and conniving as Ash. The two of them working together, planning to squeeze every last drop of generosity out of Kay.

I'd been right about the two of them all along. These people are chancers, opportunists. Vultures. The kind of people who are never happy with the inch they are given, always demanding a mile and that's exactly what they were going to do to Kay if she wasn't careful.

My fists clench into tight balls at my sides, as I try my hardest to compose myself. It would be so easy just to storm in there right now and call them both out on their blatant audacity of standing in Kay's kitchen, cooking and eating her food, while conspiring so maliciously against her. They'd only been here one night but already they were both plotting and planning on outstaying their overly generous welcome.

Only I can't confront them. No. Not yet.

I'd already seen Kay's reaction to my many reservations that I had voiced last night at dinner. The way that she had sided with them. If I tell her what I've just heard, they'll only deny it and it will be my word against theirs. I'm not that certain I'll be the one Kay believes. I need to bide my time I decide as I push the door open, marching into the kitchen.

'Morning.' I compose myself, making sure that my expression stays neutral as their conversation abruptly stops.

Ash is sitting at the table, now fussing over baby George so that he looks as if he's busy, while Rosie gets to her feet and moves over towards the cooker. They both have guilt written all over their faces and I can't help but feel pleased at this reaction, that my sudden interruption managed to leave them speechless. Seeing the cautious look that they quickly exchange, how they are both wondering if I had overheard them. I try my hardest to suppress my smile.

'Oh, wow. You've both been busy...' I continue, not willing to give them the satisfaction of letting them know that I heard everything they both said.

Instead, my eyes sweep the state of the kitchen, momentarily floored at the unexpected amount of mess and chaos. I try my hardest not to react as I take in the sight of the sink, piled high with dirty bowls and plates or how half the contents of Kay's fridge are now strewn across all the kitchen worktops.

A loaf of bread sits on the edge, spilling out from its packaging. One slice, butter-side down is stuck to the tiled kitchen floor where it has landed. The lid is off the jar of jam and there are sticky red blobs slopped all over the counters.

'Oh, morning. I hope we didn't wake you.' Rosie greets me, brightly.

Too brightly, I think, for someone who just moments earlier was happy to sit here and plot against myself and Kay.

'Hungry, are you?' I say, wondering if this is really how they thought they were going to win us over. By helping themselves to stuff that doesn't belong to them and disrespecting Kay's home.

'Gordon Ramsey here thought she'd whip us all up a nice breakfast. Didn't you, Rosie? It'll be well worth all the mess.' Ash winks at me, and even from where he is sat at the kitchen table I see the challenging look lingering there in his eyes. As though he is silently goading me into saying something.

Only he knows that this isn't my house. That I am as much of a temporary guest here as they are.

'I just wanted to do something nice to thank Kay for letting us stay here...' Rosie beams, pushing the eggs and bacon around in a frying pan, oblivious to the destruction that has erupted all around her. The kitchen looks as if a bomb has just gone off.

A bomb that Rosie detonated no less.

'Not just for Kay,' Ash adds quickly. 'For you too. Think of it as a truce for last night. I was out of line, Stephanie. I'm sorry about that. Not making excuses but I think the last few days have caught up with me and I was just being a bit moody and tired.'

'Sweet...' I mutter with a nonchalant shrug of my shoulders, as if it was as easy as that. That one half-arsed sentence of apology from Ash, one greasy fry-up from Rosie, could fix everything.

'No hard feelings, then?'

'No hard feelings,' I reply, catching the steely gaze that Ash fixes on me. The way he's trying to suppress the corners of his mouth from turning up, as he speaks. The start of a smirk. He thinks he's so smooth, so clever, when in reality he's completely clueless that I'm on to him. I've met men like Ash a thousand times before.

'Do you fancy a cuppa?' I ask, making my way towards the kettle. My back to them, refusing to give either of them the satisfaction of seeing my anger.

'Oh, yes please. Two sugars and milk in both please. Ta love.' Rosie's answer is sickly sweet and it's all I can do not to bite back at the woman's complete ignorance to my dislike of her. My dislike of both of them.

Instead, I busy myself, mopping up the milk that has pooled out around the base of one of the cups. Another task already started but not finished. Wondering how much mess one person could make, as I wipe the tiny specks of white crystallised sugar that's been sprinkled all over the worktop like fine sparkling glitter, while I wait for the kettle to boil.

'How's George doing this morning?' I ask, focusing on a neutral choice of conversation, like the baby.

I'm grateful that for now the child's incessant crying has stopped. Yesterday, the sound – like a high-pitched drill screeching its way through metal – had wormed its way inside my head, inside my brain. Giving me an almighty headache. I wasn't sure if I could cope with that again today, especially at this early in the morning, before I'd even had a cup of tea.

'He seems a bit better...' I observe.

Only Ash is quick to put me right.

'He's not. He was up most of the night.' Ash pulls the blanket up protectively around his son now that he is finally sleeping. 'I'm surprised you didn't hear him crying. We were worried that he'd wake you.'

'No, I didn't hear a thing. I must have gone out like a light as soon as my head hit the pillow,' I say, not wanting to let Ash and his snide smirking face know how uncomfortable I'd been last night on that sofa. That I'd lain awake for hours, silently seething about our conversation over dinner, before sleep had finally taken me.

'Hopefully, he'll be better after a bit more rest,' I say as I plonk his cup of tea down in front of him at the kitchen table, knowing full well that Ash is lying. If George had been crying all night, I would have heard him, wouldn't I? His loud wailing cries carrying though the house. Especially seeing as their bedroom, my bedroom, is directly above the lounge.

'Yeah, hopefully. Thanks.'

'This is almost done.' Rosie flips the bacon and eggs in the pan before she turns the heat off and shoots Ash a smile, and I catch the look they both share. Pleased that Ash is playing nice this morning.

So, this is it. Their grand plan. Being nice to me.

'So, did you both go to Wild Park Manor, then?' I ask, trying to gauge Rosie's age by mentioning the local school that Kay mentions every time one of the students walk past the house dressed in its uniform.

'No. I went to Queen Mary's in Fulham.'

'Fulham? You're a bit far from home, aren't you?'

I watch as Rosie shoots Ash a nervous glance before giving me a half shrug in answer.

'I guess.'

'So, what year are you in? Only I'd guess you're the same as me? Year eleven?' I prod, wanting to take full advantage of the fact that the couple had secretly vowed to keep me onside. They could start by answering my many questions, I think to myself smugly.

Rosie nods.

'So you won't be sitting your exams, then?' I continue, well aware that Rosie could lie to me if she wanted to. She could spin me any story she liked and it would be down to me if I chose to believe it or not.

'No. I won't be sitting my exams.'

She is guarded, only divulging the shortest, vaguest answers, which leads me to believe that she is telling me the truth, she's just making sure that she only discloses the bare minimum.

'I've got enough to keep myself busy here.' Rosie nods down at her son, admitting that he is the reason she can't continue her studies. He is why she would be leaving school without any formal qualifications.

'You could go back. They'd help you, wouldn't they? Set something up for you so that you don't miss out?'

'Nah, school's not for me.'

She shrugs again, as Ash gets up from the table and starts rocking George in his arms as the baby starts to stir. Clearly not catching the warning look he shoots her before she continues. But I do.

'I tried to hide my pregnancy for as long as I could. Wearing big baggy blazers and coats over my uniform, but by about six months it looked as if I was smuggling a basketball under my jumper.' Rosie gives me a small smile. 'I couldn't hide it anymore. I had to tell my mum, and I'm not sure what I was expecting, but she went nuts. The school weren't overly happy about it either. They didn't officially kick me out, just "strongly encouraged" that going forward I should be home schooled. I was glad to leave to be honest.'

'And what about your mum? Did she come around to you having a baby in the end? Now that George is here?'

Rosie shakes her head and diverts her gaze to the floor.

'No. She wasn't happy about any of it, especially when I told her that I didn't want to be home schooled. I just wanted to concentrate on my baby. On being a good mum.'

Rosie clasps her hands, her fingers knotting together as she speaks. Uncomfortable at my line of questioning. Her eyes searching Ash's face in the desperate need of some moral support.

I keep pushing. Rosie is clearly willing to do and say anything she can so that she can stay here, including trying to gain my sympathy. I'm sure I'll find a crack in her story.

'Is that why you ran away from home?'

'She said that I ruined my life, that I've thrown everything away. Then she met Ash, and—'

'Christ. What is this? An interrogation?' Ash interrupts. A smile fixed to his face to try and show he's not rattled by Rosie's sudden influx of information, but I sense the undercurrent there. How clearly I have struck a nerve.

'Oh, shit. The bacon.' Rosie's voice is drowned out by the loud screech of the smoke alarm as it screams out across the kitchen, making me jump with fright, sending a splash of scalding hot tea all down my sweater.

The oil in the pan, heated beyond its smoking point, flares up dramatically into bright orange flames and the kitchen fills with black smoke. I place my cup down on the side and run to the window, cranking it open to let in some fresh air and hoping the black air disperses.

'I thought I turned the hob off,' Rosie screeches, grabbing the smoking frying pan and plunging it into the sink full of water as the burning oil spits and sizzles until finally the small fire is out.

The charred, cremated remnants of bacon and eggs float to the top, breaking up with the force of the water that spurts from the tap. Spraying the nearby walls and floor. The air is full of smoke now and I hear how Rosie splutters, as if her lungs are fighting for clean air. Grabbing a tea towel from nearby she flaps it wildly, in a bid to try and disperse the grey billowing smoke that lingers all around us. Only the cotton material whips at the cup that I set down on the side, sending it halfway across the kitchen before it crashes to the floor, breaking in several pieces against the ceramic tiles.

Rosie is down on her knees, picking up broken slithers of porcelain as she apologises profusely.

'Oh my God, I'm so sorry,' she mumbles through a stream of fresh tears.

What for? For the mess, and the burned bacon, for spilling her drink? For breaking the cup?

Or is she sorry for the tent in the wood? For George being sick? For their plan to stay here longer and manipulate Kay?

'For all of it. I'm sorry for all of it.' Rosie sobs uncontrollably, as if she's just read my mind.

The shrill sound of the smoke detector combined with his mother crying becomes too much for little George, who joins Rosie in unison. The two of them hysterically crying.

Ash continues to stand and rock George vigorously, desperate to soothe him but unable to calm him down. My eyes go to the cooker's hob behind him that glows red hot now. Turned up to its highest temperature.

Rosie had turned it off. Hadn't I seen her do it? Ash made

his way over there when I'd been questioning Rosie. Hovering there for a good few minutes under the guise of rocking George back to sleep. He had the perfect opportunity to turn the hob back on. To turn the temperature up.

'You did this.' The accusation shoots out from my mouth before I've even had time to process what I'm saying. 'You started the fire on purpose, didn't you?' My finger jabs out in Ash's direction, so angry now that I'm unable to control the shake of my hands.

'What the fuck are you talking about?' Ash glares at me, stepping closer. Doing his best to try and intimidate me.

He's good at that. Doing whatever he can to shut people down around him. Well, I'm not going to let him do that to me.

'Why would I do something as stupid as that? Rosie was making us all breakfast and I'm bloody starving. I'm hardly going to ruin it, am I?'

'You're a liar and I don't believe you. I saw your face when I was questioning Rosie. You didn't like it, did you? That's why you did this. You started a fire as a distraction.'

'You're bloody mental, you are,' he shouts, only I see it. The faintest flicker of something in his eyes almost as if he's the tiniest bit impressed that I've caught him out.

Though instead of any kind of admission, he covers it up, immediately getting defensive.

'You really are a horrible, conniving bitch, aren't you? Rosie was doing something nice for you and Kay, as a thank you. She burnt it by accident. She didn't mean it...' Ash raises his voice and I laugh despite myself.

'Oh, you're good, I'll give you that. Sticking up for your girl-friend now, are you? What a gentleman. Only we both know this has nothing to do with Rosie. This is all you, Ash.'

I am shouting now too. Determined to show Ash that he might intimidate his girlfriend, but he doesn't scare me.

'*She* didn't do it. Rosie isn't to blame here. I saw her turn the hob off. It was you. What was the matter Ash, didn't you like the way our conversation was going? You wanted to shut it down, didn't you? Stop Rosie from talking. Stop her from divulging all your secrets.'

'You have no idea what you're talking about. Nobody did this. It was an accident.'

'Please stop.' Rosie starts shouting then too.

All three of us, raising our voices, vying to be heard over the others as we make our point.

As George continues to scream.

Which is the exact moment that Kay decides to make an appearance. Fresh out of bed, woken by the noise no doubt, making her way into her kitchen in a trance, as if unable to believe what she is seeing. As pandemonium continues to break out all around her.

Immediately we fall silent at her presence, and I manage to catch her eye, unable to keep the I-told-you-so expression from my face because I am glad that Kay is here now. That she gets to witness this carnage for herself, first-hand. That these people are not the perfect house guests she thinks they are.

Far from it.

15

KAY

'Oh, Rosie. I thought you'd gone for a lie down?' I say, turning from where I'm stood switching the kettle on, ready to make myself a hot drink, only to see her standing behind me.

After hours of scrubbing the kitchen clean and getting rid of the stench of burned bacon and eggs that lingered in the room, I am exhausted. We all are.

Rosie had disappeared along with the others fifteen minutes or so ago and I had assumed that she'd gone off to get her head down for a few hours. Only she is back now, hovering in the kitchen as if she doesn't know what to do with herself.

'Ash and George are both fast asleep, so, I thought I'd leave them to it,' Rosie says, her eyes going to where the blackened scorch mark from the burning oil, spans its way up my cream floral tiles just behind the cooker and I sense she wants to talk.

'No amount of bleach or scrubbing would get it off. And believe me, I tried. To be honest with you, love, the tiles are looking quite dated now and the kitchen could do with a lick of fresh paint,' I quip, throwing my hand in the air to dismiss the damage and show Rosie there's really no hard feelings here.

'What's done is done. There's really no point in getting hung up about it.'

'I really am so sorry, Kay...' Rosie starts. 'All I wanted to do was thank you for being so kind and letting us come and stay for a few days. And I wanted to show you our appreciation for that delicious stew you made us last night. And well, just for being nice to me...' Rosie tails off at the word 'nice' as if it's a gesture just too much for her. Tears form in her eyes and despite my earlier annoyance, I see that the girl is genuinely sorry for what happened.

'Hey, don't cry. It was an accident. These things happen. It's no one's fault,' I insist, holding my hand up now, to stop Rosie from apologising yet again. 'Considering all the awful things that could have happened, a few scorched tiles and a broken mug really isn't the end of the world, is it?' I conclude, and I mean it. 'Me and Max can take a trip to the shop in a bit and stock up on some more food. You meant well, Rosie. Your heart was in the right place. That's all that matters as far as I'm concerned.'

The girl obviously only had good intentions. She'd been trying to do something nice. For me.

That didn't happen very often.

'Why don't you go and put your feet up in the lounge for a bit? Stick some telly on,' I suggest, seeing Rosie hovering by the kitchen table, still not sure what to say or do next. Only immediately she wrinkles her nose up at my suggestion and I sense a reluctance there.

Stephanie.

She's the reason for Rosie's hesitancy.

'It's probably best that I stay out of Stephanie's way for now. She was interrogating us earlier and then George started crying and I guess I must have got distracted...' Rosie admits. 'She thinks we did it on purpose. The fire. Well, she thinks Ash did it on purpose. But he didn't, I swear it, Kay. It was all my fault.'

'It wasn't anyone's fault. It's just one of those things.' I nod in understanding.

I'd heard Stephanie arguing with Ash earlier, when I'd walked into the kitchen. The two of them having a stand-off in each other's faces, shouting obscenities at one another. Stephanie accusing Ash of starting the fire on purpose. But that was ridiculous. Why would they jeopardise the opportunity I've given them to stay here?

Stephanie had tried to convince me though, when we'd been clearing up, but I'd taken little notice. She didn't have any evidence to back her theory up, and it was clear she didn't want them here. She was so set against it that it made me wonder... what wasn't she telling me? My mind spun with possibilities. Did she know Ash? Did she know Rosie? No, of course not. If they'd been in the hordes of homeless chancers Amanda entertained, Stephanie would have told me. I thought of all the time Stephanie spent in her room since she'd arrived here. How she was so against giving it up for these two. Was she hiding something in there? Was she doing something she didn't want me seeing?

No. I shook my paranoia away. That kind of catastrophising isn't going to help. Stephanie isn't Amanda. She wouldn't hide things from me. Would she?

'Ash wouldn't do that, Kay. Not after everything you're doing for us. If it was anyone's fault, it was mine. I got so caught up in trying to get everything just so, that instead of turning the pan off, I must have turned it up. It really was an accident.'

'Well, maybe we can tell Stephanie that. Put her straight,' I suggest, thinking that the two girls clearing the air while Ash is out of the way wouldn't be such a bad idea. If Stephanie gave Rosie a chance, she might actually find that she likes the girl. They'd get on, I think. Both so similar in age and overcoming their own challenges.

'No, honestly. I think it's better if I leave it. She's already made her mind up about us, nothing we say or do will change that now. She doesn't want us here,' Rosie says matter-of-factly, and I can't argue with that. Stephanie is stubborn and if the truce doesn't come from her, she'll only dig her heels in harder.

'Okay, so you're just going to hide away out here, in the kitchen with me, are you? Hoping to avoid her.'

'Am I that transparent?' Rosie offers a small smile in admission, before taking a seat at the kitchen table. I take two cups out of the cupboard and raise a questioning brow.

'Fancy one? I was just about to make myself a nice hot cup of Ovaltine.'

'Oh, I've not had Ovaltine before.'

'Well now. You don't know what you've been missing. There's not a problem in the world that Ovaltine can't fix.'

I busy myself pouring the boiling hot water into cups, thinking about the conversation I'd had with Stephanie this morning, convinced that my granddaughter had no reason to have any of her concerns. Though she is right about one thing. I have allowed Rosie and Ash into my home without knowing anything about either of them.

'They were talking about needing a plan B. They're trying to stay here longer,' Stephanie had warned me. 'They could be squatters, Kay. Once they're in here, they'll never leave. Haven't you seen people like them on TV? Bailiffs turning up at people's doorsteps wanting to move them on, only the new tenants refuse to leave and there is nothing you can do about it.'

'Having a plan B doesn't necessarily mean they're going to simply take over my house, Stephanie. I doubt very much that they're squatters,' I'd said, quickly realising that Stephanie could be right, yet here I was, blindly defending a couple that I knew nothing about. 'Plan B might mean they're planning what they're going to do once George is feeling better and it's time for them to move on. Or perhaps they just want an extra day or two here,' I say, unable to face the idea of sending sweet Rosie and

George back out there with Ash. At least until I know more about their situation.

Until I know that Rosie and George are really safe.

'What about Ash starting the fire? He did it on purpose. He's dangerous, Kay.'

I'd shook my head, still not sure what I should believe. 'But why would Ash risk damaging my property and me finding out? He'd lose his place here. Surely that defeats the object of them needing somewhere to stay.'

'I'm not sure he meant to start an actual fire,' Stephanie had informed me. 'I think he just wanted to create a distraction. He didn't like me asking Rosie so many questions and worse than that, he hated the fact that Rosie was actually answering them. I think Ash was worried about what Rosie might tell me. Because they're hiding something from us, Kay. Something big.'

I hadn't been able to argue with that, because the truth was I was starting to suspect as much myself.

Now that I have Rosie all alone, I wonder if I can persuade the girl to open up to me while Ash isn't around.

'You know, if there's anything you want to talk to me about, Rosie, any way I can help you at all, you have my complete confidence. It will just be between you and me,' I say, keeping my voice low. 'I won't say a word, not even to Ash.'

'Why would I be worried about you repeating anything to Ash?' Rosie bristles, and I curse myself for getting it so wrong. Rosie's eyes dart towards the kitchen door, checking there's no sign of him listening in nearby now that his name's been mentioned. And I can't help but wonder if she's scared of him.

'How's little George doing?' I note the visible relief on Rosie's face as soon as I change the subject. 'The poor little mite had worked himself up into such a state earlier.'

'He's better than he was, now that we're here in the warm. But he's still really poorly,' Rosie says wearily, and I hear it. How Rosie's tone is laced with guilt. A mother's guilt –

weighing down heavily on her, a feeling I know only too well. Because it's a lot to bear, the responsibility of these little lives on our shoulders, and it's all too easy to mess up. As I learned the hard way.

'It's not your fault, you know,' I reassure her, and I really do want to believe that Rosie really is trying. That none of this is her doing. 'You're doing your best by him. You didn't mean for him to get sick. You're a good mum.'

Only the girl is quiet then, her eyes fixed on the floor while she desperately tries to compose herself to stop herself from crying.

I see how hard living on the streets has been for her. How it's taking a toll on her too.

'Don't you have any family you can stay with? Your parents perhaps? I bet they'd want to know that you are okay, Rosie.'

'No. There's no one.' Rosie shakes her head. 'It's just me and George now. And Ash. We don't need anyone else.'

'And Ash doesn't have anyone either?' I continue, knowing that I'm treading a thin line. If you push people to open up when they're not ready, you only end up pushing them away. Though at the same time I know that right now, away from Ash, able to finally speak freely, this is my only opportunity to at least try and get through to the girl.

'No. He doesn't.' Rosie shakes her head sadly. 'His father died when he was seven, and his mum turned to drink after that. Ash has been forced to fend for himself from a young age. He doesn't have anyone else but me.'

Rosie doesn't offer anything more, and I know the conversation is over. That's all I am getting. It's her turn to shut me down.

'Well, I'm sure once the medicine kicks in and little George has had some proper sleep over the next day or two, he'll be right as rain. You'll probably feel a lot better too if you get some sleep. You're looking awfully pale,' I say gently.

I don't want to cross the line but I can see that Rosie needs to look after herself too. She's running on almost empty. She needs some proper rest.

'Pale is the very least of my problems,' she quips. 'I almost didn't recognise myself earlier when I looked in the bathroom mirror.'

I can envisage how pretty Rosie is, when her eyes are not dark and sunken from having little to no sleep the past few days, before her skin became sore and chapped from being outside in the freezing cold weather. Before her lip had become swollen and blistered with a newly formed cold sore.

'And, if I go to bed now, as shattered as I am, I probably won't be able to sleep. I've got too much going on inside my head.'

'Oh, I know all about that.' I hold up my cup up as if to offer a cheers in solidarity. 'Fellow insomniac at your service. I never really sleep, and well, I've been worse since Amanda.'

'Your daughter?'

'Yes.'

'It must be awful. Do you mind if I ask how she died?'

'It was an overdose. She was clean, or so we thought. She'd been prescribed methadone. Though we think she may have taken too much. The worst thing is, even when we get the post-mortem results back, the one thing they won't show is whether it was intentional or not.' I shake my head sadly. 'We'll never know if Amanda meant to do it, if she'd intentionally taken her own life or if it was just a cry for help that went wrong. The not knowing for sure makes it so much harder to accept. I think that's why Stephanie is struggling so much too. We don't have any real answers. We never will. Which is probably why Stephanie doesn't really seem herself at the moment...' I trail off, smiling then as something only just occurs to me.

'The truth is I don't really know Stephanie either. I only invited her to come and stay here the night Amanda died. I could hardly leave her there, in that flat, after discovering her mother's body. Amanda and I had what you might call "a volatile relationship". Amanda got pregnant and left home at sixteen and after she had Stephanie, she wouldn't allow me to have a relationship with either of them. She said that I was too controlling. Made up all sorts of accusations about me trying to split up her and her boyfriend.'

'And did you?'

I nod my head, my expression full of regret.

'I only did it for her though. He was no good you see. A drug dealer. He was the one who got Amanda hooked on the bloody stuff in the first place. I did what I had to do, only it was already too late. She was already sucked in by him, and by the lure of the crap he had her hooked on. She wouldn't listen to me. The last time we rowed, she'd come here asking me for money – for medicine for Stephanie in fact. Amanda told me that Stephanie wasn't well. Dragged the poor girl out in the pouring rain in a bid to prove to me that the money really was for her and not for drugs. Had her stood out on my doorstep like a drowned rat. I knew that Amanda was lying. I'd always been able to tell. She'd done it to me before. Begged for money for Stephanie from me, only to spend it on drugs and end up back in some rehab centre again. So, I told her no and I guess it was easier for her to cut me off after that. Because she knew I'd never give in to her demands.' I shrug, because in all these years I still haven't been able to make sense of how, in loving my daughter and only trying to do right by her, I'd ended up losing her for good.

After all this time, the pain still slashes at me like a knife.

I take a mouthful of my drink, relishing the burn in the back of my throat. The way the liquid scalds my tongue. Something, anything to get me back out of my head. Away from that awful, desolate feeling.

'Please don't breathe a word of this, I shouldn't really be

sharing any of this, but well, Stephanie was born an addict too. Somehow, for a little while at least, that had been enough of a reason for Amanda to feel guilty and change her ways. To get clean. Because she desperately wanted her baby back. Though part of me thinks she got clean to spite me too. Because she knew if she lost custody of Stephanie for good, I would have applied to adopt her and Amanda was just hell bent on punishing me.' Again, I shrug. 'So she got clean, got Stephanie back and then spent her entire life relapsing while doing her best to keep Stephanie away from me. Made up all sorts of accusations about me to anyone who would listen, so that anytime she slipped up and went back onto the drugs, I'd never be given any consideration for Stephanie's care. Amanda told the authorities that she'd rather put her daughter into foster care than send her here with me. Here, where I had a room, a bed. A loving home. I was her grandmother for Christ's sake. That's the lengths Amanda went to. And it worked. Stephanie and I are practically strangers, and it's difficult trying to get to know each other now, under the circumstances. While we're both grieving in our own separate ways. Both trying to navigate our way through it all. And no doubt Stephanie had her own reservations about me. She's probably trying to make sense of all the things her mother has said to her over the years, to poison her against me.'

Rosie nods her head as if she's finally understanding why Stephanie is so suspicious and cold towards them. Why she doesn't want them here. The truth is, she doesn't really want to be here herself.

'I just don't want you to misjudge her, that's all. She may come across as well, a bit difficult, but really, she's just going through a very tough time right now. The last couple of weeks have been a lot for her. Give her some time and I'm sure she'll come around.'

I watch as Rosie takes a big, thoughtful sip of her Ovaltine.

'How is it?' I ask, wanting to lighten the mood once more after that unexpected emotional confession.

Rosie doesn't need to answer. Her face twisting into an ugly grimace does that for her. Her expression full of disgust as she tries to force herself to swallow the mouthful of malty drink down, so that she doesn't offend me. Only I am not offended in the slightest, if anything I'm finding Rosie's exaggerated attempts a hiding it from me, extremely funny.

'Not a fan, I take it?' I grin, as Rosie tries to force herself to gulp the mouthful down, only to cough and splutter before dramatically spitting the brown watery liquid back into the cup.

'Eurgh! That is gross.' Her cheeks flare a bright red with embarrassment as she wipes the splatters of drink from her face and the kitchen table with the sleeve of her top. She shakes her head. 'That's a firm no from me.'

Getting up and taking the mug from her, I can't help but genuinely laugh.

'Do you want a normal cup of tea instead?'

I'm pleasantly surprised when Rosie says yes.

'Actually, Kay, you know you said that you'd help out in any way you can...'

Rosie glances over towards the kitchen door again, checking that they are still alone before she speaks again.

'There is something you could do for me.'

16

ROSIE

'Here you go. It's probably as ancient as the internet itself, mind. I don't know why I even bothered to get one, I've only used it half a dozen times.'

Kay places her old, bulky laptop down in front of me and begins wiping the thick film of dust that coats the entire lid with the bobbled sleeve of her jumper. I watch with fascination as she starts rummaging her way through all the kitchen drawers.

'The password is here somewhere, I'm sure...' she says, sifting through a huge stack of paperwork and bills until eventually she pulls out a torn, tatty bit of an envelope with a random, long series of letters and numbers scrawled on it, and waves it victoriously in my direction.

'Bingo.'

I smile despite myself, because it's a nice feeling knowing how much she wants to help me. I feel bad for giving her false hope. For allowing her to believe that I want to use her laptop so I can reach out to my family and let them know George is okay. I only said that so she'd let me use it. To stop her asking me all those questions.

'Families are complicated, and nothing ever appears as it

really is. But they'll be worried about you, Rosie. They'll be worried about little George. Wouldn't you feel the same way too, if it was George who had gone missing and you sat at home worrying where he was?'

In the end, I'd just gone along with it. Letting her believe she'd got through to me and that's exactly what I was doing now. Contacting a family member, when the truth is I have no intention of contacting anyone, because I know exactly what would happen if I did. Firing up the laptop, I push the guilt down that I feel at not wanting to disclose why I really want to get online.

'I'll give you some privacy. Make sure you're not disturbed.' Kay shoots me a conspiring wink before she heads towards the hallway, shutting the kitchen door behind her when she leaves.

She's being my lookout, I realise and I am grateful for that. I'd seen the way her gaze had followed mine. How she knows that I don't want Ash to know what I am doing, because I know that he won't approve.

Typing in the password that has been scrawled on the crinkled piece of paper Kay left on the side for me, I tap my fingers impatiently on the dining room table, while waiting for the WiFi to connect. I glance over my shoulder once more to double check that I am definitely alone now, before clicking on the internet browser as soon as it appears and tapping out my full name in the Google search bar. My heart sinks as the news articles fill the screen.

Police are concerned for the safety of young mother Rosie Enright and her newborn son, who were last seen three days ago in the North London area.

They are looking for me.
They are looking for George.
Of course they are. Ash warned me that they would be. It wasn't an empty threat or a way of getting me to do as I was

told. It was the truth. Though seeing the bright red 'Missing Person's' banner on the laptop screen, with my name printed boldly beneath it along with a photograph of me, suddenly makes it feel so much more real.

Max barks loudly from the hallway and makes me jump with fright. Instantly pulling me from the web of dark thoughts that have tangled inside my head. My hand hits the keyboard and the screen refreshes, revealing another post at the top of the search results – added only three minutes ago.

Abandoned blue tent discovered at Highgate Woods during search for missing Rosie and newborn George.

I eye the image of the crumpled, abandoned tent, that we left dumped in the woods and feel the swell of nausea rise up inside me at how close they are to finding us.

Too close.

SHIT.

Concerns are growing for a young mother and her newborn baby, who have been missing since Monday 28 January. It is thought that the mother and baby have been sleeping rough in Highgate Woods, North London, after police discovered a collapsed blue tent and cardboard box that is suspected to have been used as a makeshift cot.

Detective Superintendent Jonathan Franklin, who is leading the investigation, expressed his concern for the safety of the newborn baby, who he believes has been exposed to sub-freezing temperatures. While he urges the public to look out for the mother and baby, he would like to reassure the public that the police are doing a thorough search of the area, including making house-to-house enquires as well as trawling all available CCTV.

CCTV.

House-to-house searches.

I think about the car I'd broken into the night before, on this very street. How Ash had berated me, telling me that there might be images of me on one of the nearby cars' dash cams.

They are going to find us, and when they do they are going to take George away from me.

SHIT. SHIT. SHIT.

I shouldn't look further. I know that I shouldn't, but how can I not? When all the answers to my questions might be right here, just at the end of my fingertips and Ash is nowhere to be seen. I need to know, despite Ash's warnings.

I anxiously tap my fingers on table's edge, part of me willing myself to do it. To type in *her* name. To check what the internet is saying about *her*. Only there's a small part of me that can't bear to know what really happened. It will make it real, won't it? Seeing what happened spelled out in black and white on the screen. It will make it final.

If I don't go looking, maybe I can pretend for a little while longer that it didn't happen. That I'm not this terrible person I know deep down I've become. A bad daughter.

Only I need to know.

I type her name in, narrowing my eyes when nothing comes up. I tap it in again. Nothing. No crime reference. No police report of the incident. No articles in the newspapers. Nothing about the incident anywhere at all. I don't understand. Are the police keeping this information from the public domain on purpose, trying to lull us back home under the false pretence that we're not in any trouble? They can't falsify obituaries though, can they? If someone is announced as dead, it would be legally logged wouldn't it?

With shaking hands, I pull up the Official Register of Births and Deaths onto the screen and scroll down, searching for the date, just three days earlier before typing in her name once more.

Nothing.

Have they amended that too? Manipulated it perhaps? Delayed adding the entry?

Maybe she isn't dead.

I feel the tiniest glimmer of hope at that. Wondering if perhaps she was taken to a local hospital, if she's had treatment and somehow, she's alive. Only the image of her laying at Ash's feet. Lifeless, unmoving. All that blood. That would be impossible, wouldn't it? She must be dead, otherwise Ash's name would be plastered all over the news. There isn't any mention of him in any of the missing person articles either.

The police don't know that he exists.

A noise from the hallway startles me, pulling me away from the tangle of thoughts. A door opening. Footsteps. I quickly shut the laptop and shove it onto one of the dining chairs next to me, before tucking it neatly underneath the kitchen table.

'It's okay, Ash, I can grab a bottle for you.' Kay's voice. Louder and more exaggerated than usual, giving me a much-needed warning that Ash is coming.

I sit back in my seat and wrap my hands around my mug of now tepid milky tea that Kay had made for me earlier and stare purposely into space, just as the kitchen door bursts open.

'Rosie?' Ash stares at me mistrustfully. 'You okay? I woke up and you weren't there.'

I hear the suspicion in his voice and see the way his eyes dart around the kitchen.

'I'm fine.' I nod obediently in answer. Knowing full well that I can't tell him the truth. It will only lead to another argument and I haven't got the energy for that right now.

'I did check on you both, but you were fast asleep and I didn't want to disturb you, so Kay made me a drink.'

Ash, still unconvinced, turns and eyes Kay warily now as she stands directly behind him.

'I was just finishing my tea. Must have been miles away,' I say, though I can tell by the look on his face that he doesn't believe me. I see the way his eyes flicker from the kitchen table to the dining chair that conceals the laptop next to me. I hold my breath. Praying he doesn't pull the chair out and check whether I'm hiding something from him. Because I know that will not go well for me. He'd warned me already. Insisting that under no circumstances was I to go online and start looking things up.

'That's how people get caught, Rosie. Digging around for answers. You'll get careless and leave some kind of a trail. All it takes is one careless click on social media, and you'll end up drawing the wrong kind of attention to us both. They can find people now using IP addresses. It's not worth it.'

'Just sitting here drinking tea and daydreaming, were you?' Ash mutters, narrowing his eyes.

He is not stupid. Far from it. Shrewd and cunning, he knows as well as I do, that Kay purposely tried to keep him out of this room for a few seconds longer than he would have liked. That she'd raised her voice loud enough so that I could heed her warning. So that I could prepare myself.

I brace myself for him to interrogate me further, only he doesn't.

Though what he says next makes my blood run ice cold.

'You need to come, Rosie. It's George. He's not right.'

17

ROSIE

'George?' My voice trembles with fear as I rush into the bedroom, bracing myself for the state I am about to find my son in. My worst fears consume me as I ready myself for the harrowing sight of his tiny limp body. His breathing even more hollow and laboured.

Already, in a single heartbeat, I have made my mind up. We are going to have to give ourselves up, because George comes first and I need to get him to the hospital. Nothing is more important than getting my baby better. Nothing, and no one and that includes me and Ash.

Only now that I am here, back in the bedroom, the eerie silence that descends around the room is far more terrifying than the crying and whimpering I'd expected to hear from George. Ash closes the door behind us and doesn't move. My eyes go fleetingly to the bed, to where I know my son lays, cocooned inside a nest of pillows that Ash has stacked up around him. I look questioningly at Ash, who looks down at the floor and I feel my heart plummet inside me.

Why can't he look at me?

Full of panic I am outside of my body, floating. I move fast across the room, forcing myself to look. To go to my son. No matter how scared I feel right now in this moment, I have to.

I am his mother.

Peering down over the top of the pillows, an inaudible gasp leaves my mouth as I take in the sight of his tiny, still body. He is sprawled out in the middle of the cosy space. His eyes connect with mine and he kicks out his legs in a sudden, sharp movement, overcome with excitement at the recognition of seeing his mummy, as he coos loudly at me. His high-pitch, happy screech breaks me.

'Oh, thank God. Thank God. You're okay.' Relief floods its way through my entire body, like nothing I've ever experienced before. 'My darling boy. Mummy's here.'

I am crying now, as I pick George up and hold him tightly to me. Relishing the warmth of him, the solid weight of him in my arms. The thud of his tiny heart as it beats against my chest, and I am unable to contain the frantic sobs that escape my lips.

George is getting better.

He is.

He doesn't need to go to see a doctor or be admitted to the hospital. For now, we don't have to hand ourselves in. We can stay together as a family for just that little bit longer.

Ash moves behind me, reminding me that he is still in the room and my relief, short lived, is replaced with wild fury. Not wanting to upset George, I place him back down safely between the pillows before turning to Ash.

'You said that George had got worse... That he wasn't right... That I needed to come.' My whole body shakes incredulously, because I am so confused. 'Why would you say that to me? Why would you make me worry like that?'

'I'm sorry...' Ash says offering me a small grin and there's something about the smugness in his expression that ignites the fury in me further.

'You bastard.'

And I know why he lied. Because this is how low Ash is prepared to stoop in order to regain control of me. Using the insurmountable guilt I feel for making my son ill, against me. Manipulating me into thinking something is wrong with our boy. Ash knew that if he said that George was worse, I would have no choice but to leave whatever it was that I was doing in the kitchen and come back to this room with him. Immediately. No questions asked. No arguments. This was all part of his ploy to get me back here, all to himself.

'You lied to me, to get me here alone again, away from Kay. Just like you lied about me starting the fire too. I'd turned the hob off, Ash. I remember doing it. Only you turned it back on again, didn't you? I saw you standing there, with George. You deliberately burned the food and then you stood back and let me take the blame. Why Ash? Why are you doing all of this?'

I grit my teeth, my hands clenched at my side, and I resist the urge to run at him. To beat him with my fists. To scream and shout and cry.

'I HATE YOU,' I shout and, in this moment, right now, I'm not just saying it out of anger, I think I really do.

'I didn't mean to start a bloody fire. I just wanted to cause a distraction. To shut you up.'

'To shut me up. Wow. Are you for real?'

'Stephanie was asking too many questions, Rosie. Not out of kindness or genuine interest. She was digging around, looking for something to use against us and you were just handing it to her on a plate. Giving her more details to use against us when she's running her mouth—'

'You could have burned Kay's house down, Ash. We could have been thrown out. You risked everything.'

'You've risked everything too, Rosie. You've lied to me too,' Ash spits back, defensive now. Because he can see my angst. He can see the way he's just terrorised me and he knows he's crossed the line. Using George as a bargaining tool in his controlling game was a step too far. Somewhere, deep down inside him, he must have a conscience after all. Only he is trying to twist this all back onto me and make this all my fault.

'Do you think I'm stupid, Rosie? I saw it. You were using Kay's laptop. And don't lie to me, I saw the bloody charger still plugged into the wall behind you. You stashed it under the table, didn't you? Because you didn't want me to see. Didn't want me to know that you were digging around on the internet after I expressly told you not to. You know what will happen if they find us, Rosie. I told you not to go looking.' Ash raises his voice, intent on calling me out.

Nothing ever gets past him.

'And I suppose Kay's in on it now too, is she? Standing at the kitchen door keeping watch like a bloody bouncer. Ready to keep me out. What have you said to her? What does she know?'

'Nothing. She doesn't know anything.' I cry, only Ash shakes his head in disbelief. The sceptical look on his face telling me that he doesn't trust anything I say.

Suddenly I am the liar.

'I promise you, Ash. I haven't told Kay anything. She kept going on about me contacting a member of my family and letting them know that we're okay. I told her I would so she'd lend me her laptop. She believed that's what I was doing.' I pause, because I know how angry he will be with what I say next. 'I just wanted to look, Ash. To see what had been reported. What's being said about us. I wasn't on there for long. And I only hid it, because I knew you'd be like this. Because I know that you didn't want me looking, but I had to, Ash. Because I feel as if I'm going slowly mad.'

I pause, feeling the tears that I've been holding back fill my eyes.

'I can't stop thinking about her. About what happened. I just needed to see, to know... if she is really dead, Ash.' I cry, my whole body shaking now that I have finally said the words I've been dreading the most out loud.

Now we are finally talking about this. Up until now, Ash wouldn't entertain this conversation for so much as a second. He prefers denial. He believes that if we never talk about it, we can pretend it didn't happen and everything will eventually just go away. Only it's not going away, it's killing me. Killing us.

'It was all such a blur, everything happened so quickly, sometimes if feels as if it didn't really happen at all. And then we both just left her there. Bleeding out on the floor. And neither of us have spoken about it since. Not properly. And every time I try to, you shut me down,' I explain through my sobs, shrugging Ash's hand away when he reaches out to comfort me. 'But it did happen, didn't it?' I flinch as the image of her floods my mind again. 'Because there's nothing about it online. There's no mention of it anywhere. That doesn't make sense, does it? I searched the official Births and Deaths Register and it wasn't listed on there either. I even checked the local obituaries. There's no record of her death anywhere.'

'Maybe they haven't found her yet?' Ash offers, running his hands through his hair, agitated now. Because he knows it's strange too. 'Or maybe the records haven't been updated? Or I don't know, maybe the police are just trying to reel us in. Give us some false hope that we won't be in trouble so that we stupidly hand ourselves in. She's dead, Rosie. Christ, you saw her. She wasn't breathing.'

'I know. I know.' I shake my head. 'We should have tried to help her, Ash. We should have stayed and called an ambulance. They might have been able to save her. We could have explained everything. We could have told them that it was an accident. That we didn't mean it...'

'But we did mean it, Rosie. You heard what she said to me. The threats she made. She was pushed, and it was deliberate. It happened,' Ash says quietly, his voice almost a whisper, his words full of remorse as he regretfully assures me that this madness isn't all just in my head.

It did happen, whether we like it or not.

'The police have launched a missing person's appeal. They're looking for us, Ash, and they've found the tent. They're close...' I say now, pacing the room. Full of anxiety at what I've just read. 'I think we should hand ourselves in.'

'No, Rosie. We can't.'

'But Ash, the detective in charge of the case said he's going to make house-to-house enquires, they're going to trawl through all the local CCTV footage. They're going find us eventually.'

I recall again how Ash had been furious with me for breaking into one of the neighbours' cars and stealing the money. How he'd told me that there might be footage of me on a dash camera. Or one of the neighbours nearby might have a security camera or a ring doorbell. If the police do find us, he'll blame me.

'Handing ourselves in might make them go easier...'

'Easier on who, Rosie? On you? Because it won't make it easier on me. I'll do time for it.' Ash shakes his head venomously before adding, 'We ran, Rosie. Both of us. And by doing that we've made ourselves look even more guilty. It doesn't matter what we say to them, the second we hand ourselves in they'll take George away from us.'

'God, we should never have run. I should never have listened to you...' I place my hands over my ears and starts to hum loudly because I don't want to hear the sound of Ash's voice any more. Because I know that yet again, he is right. We have made everything ten times worse by running away.

My legs tremble beneath me and I sink down, perching on the edge of the bed as the stress of the past few days finally catches up with me. I feel bereft. Desolate. I've just had a baby for Christ's sake, and then all of this. Her, dead on the floor. Running away. I'm traumatised, in shock, and the last few days

I've been simply functioning, going through the motions. Trying to survive. I've stupidly listened to Ash and done what he said and look where we are now.

What a mess.

'What if the police knock here, Ash? They might ask Kay if she's seen us, and I don't think she'll lie if they do. Not when they tell her what we're running from.'

Ash closes his eyes, his face screwed up with pure frustration. Then, as if he's had an epiphany, his eyes flicker open.

'We can speak to Kay, Rosie. You can speak to her. I've seen the way she is with you and George. How she genuinely cares. What if you tell her what happened? She might help you.'

I shake my head, unconvinced.

'Even if we win Kay over, what about Stephanie? She doesn't want us here. If the police come and she speaks to them, it's all over for us. She's looking for any excuse to get rid of us.'

Defeated now, I rest my head in my hands and start to cry. Huge wracking sobs taking over my entire body, so loud that I don't hear the knock at the door.

Though I assume there was one.

Because when I look up again, I see Stephanie standing in the bedroom doorway.

'Stephanie,' Ash says, clearly as surprised to see her standing here as I am.

'I heard you both arguing. I wanted to make sure that you were all right.'

Stephanie doesn't look at Ash when she says this, she keeps her eyes focused only on me.

I look to Ash and wonder how long Stephanie's been stood there for.

And how much she's heard.

18

STEPHANIE

I knock on the bedroom door, only Rosie and Ash are so busy arguing with one another that they don't hear me come into the room.

I've only been standing here in the doorway for a little while now, but it's been long enough to hear Ash raise his voice and use that horrible vindictive tone of his when he's speaking to Rosie.

It's no wonder the poor girl is sat on the bed now, crying. I almost feel sorry for her. Almost. But then, no one is making her stay with this arsehole, are they? She's with him through choice and there's clearly no accounting for taste.

Hadn't my own mother had enough terrible men absently hanging around her over the years? A long list of narcissists, manipulators and gaslighters all parading around under the guise of being loving boyfriends and only having my mother's best interests at heart, all the while using her to get whatever it was that they wanted from her. A place to stay for a short while, money. Drugs. Or all of the above.

I should have hated my mother. For constantly making the same mistakes and inviting these people into our lives. Instead, I always felt sorry for her. Sorry that she couldn't see these people for what they really were. Sorry that she didn't have the strength to do it alone, just me and her.

Those were the times I longed for. Lived for in fact.

Those times it was just me and her.

I would try so hard to make her happy. To see her laugh. Telling her the same stupid jokes that she'd heard from me a thousand times before. Or I'd dance for her. Showing her my new twerking routine that I'd copied from a music video on TV.

'Stephanie love, there's nothing of you. You need a bum to twerk.' She'd laugh loudly through streams of tears as I bounced awkwardly around the room.

I wish my mother had been stronger. I wish she'd left those men or stood up to them. I wish she'd been the person she was when we were alone.

Not all abusive men use physical violence as their form of attack. Coercive control is much more subtle than that, much more sinister. So much easier to hide. That's how these men manage to get inside your head. How they twist things around and manipulate you into believing that everything is really all your fault.

Like Ash is doing now. Using emotional blackmail to keep Rosie compliant, so that she will stay silent and submissive and do as she is told, when whatever it is they are running from clearly isn't even her fault. I know this, because I just heard Ash tell Rosie that if the police catch up with them, it will be him who they'll be sending to prison. He is blackmailing her into staying quiet and keeping his secret.

In the meantime, it is Rosie and George being made to suffer. For him. Protecting Ash means that they are being forced to live this half-life. Sleeping rough in shop doorways and tents in the woods and here in Kay's home.

'Are you all right, Rosie?' I make a point of looking only at her.

'I'm fine,' she lies, nodding back at me, covering up for Ash just as she is expected to. Quickly dismissing my concerns as she wipes her tears away. It's too late for her to compose herself now.

'Are you sure? Kay mentioned that Ash came and got you, because George is really sick? Is he worse?'

'George is sleeping. He'll be fine after he's slept,' Ash interrupts me, but I continue regardless, as if I haven't heard him.

'You don't look okay, Rosie, and I heard you both arguing.' I persevere, letting her know that she doesn't need to keep covering up for him. That I heard and saw all of their conversation. Only, I didn't actually hear all of it. I caught the tail end of what they were saying, but they don't need to know that.

Let them sweat. Let Ash sweat.

'You don't have to put up with being spoken to like that,' I say, ignoring Ash's steely glare as it burns into the side of my head. I'm determined not to give him so much as a second of my precious attention, which only seems to antagonise him more.

Even from over here in the doorway, I can feel it. The rage radiating from him at my blatant audacity of coming in here and poking my nose into 'his business'. For daring to ask Rosie how she is. Last time I tried asking questions that Ash didn't like, he'd almost set fire to Kay's kitchen to stop me. Well, good. Let him be mad. Let him be furious. I'm not scared of him and I am about to say as much when a loud, happy squeal sounds out from the centre of the bed.

Ash steps forward at the same time as I do, in a pathetic attempt to intimidate me as he blocks my view. Undeterred, I step around him, peering over the small tower of pillows that are built up on the bed, to where George is cocooned. He smiles brightly up at me. His nose crusty with dried snot and his skin is still pale, but his eyes sparkle brightly and he's kicking his arms and legs wildly, while cooing to himself loudly.

'He doesn't look like he's got worse,' I say, surprised, before catching the shared shifty look that passes between Rosie and Ash.

Quickly I realise exactly what has been going on here.

'Oh, wow! You've both been lying about George still being sick, haven't you? Lying about him getting worse? Why? So you can deliberately prolong your stay here?' I shake my head, disgusted by the guilty look on Rosie's face as she diverts her eyes away from mine, giving me my answer. I am sickened. This is exactly what is going on here.

'Oh my God. I'm right, aren't I? Wow, this is a whole other level of low, even for you two.'

Suddenly I see it all so clearly now. Why Ash keeps George cradled in his arms with a blanket covering him at all times. Never letting him down. Never letting him out of his sight. Why he'd refused to let Kay hold him at dinner the other night. How Ash barely leaves this bedroom, constantly hiding himself and George away in here. Under the guise of George needing more sleep. All so Ash can cover up the fact that George is clearly already over the worst.

If George is almost better that means they'll have to leave soon, and they know this. Kay is good and kind and only wants to help, and while she believes George is sick, she won't kick them out. Only, instead of being grateful to her for that, they are taking complete advantage of her kindness.

'I want you to leave,' I say, my voice is quiet but the words shake with my fury as I say them.

'We're not going anywhere. Kay said we can stay,' Ash shoots back.

'She said you could stay for a few days. Until George is better. He's better now,' I say more sternly. 'Besides, things are different now...'

I turn to face him dead in his eyes, showing him that he might frighten Rosie, but he doesn't scare me.

'I know what you did.'

And it's not a complete lie, is it? I heard enough to know that whatever they did was enough to see Ash go to prison. And Rosie doesn't want to be here. Not really. She wants to tell the police before they find them. She wants to face the consequences. Try and get back some kind of normality in their lives.

Only Ash won't let her.

'Oh! Don't tell me you've been snooping down Kay's laptop too?' Ash spits back, instantly rattled at my comment. I have no idea what he's referring to, but I'm determined to hold my ground.

'The police are looking for you.' I repeat what I'd heard them arguing about, pulling my mobile phone out of my pocket.

'This is you two, isn't it? Breaking into one of the neighbours' cars? Stealing that money. Is this what you do? Go around breaking into people's cars? Worming your way into people's homes? Stealing their things?' I tap at the screen, before playing the footage I recorded the other night of the neighbour's car being broken into. Pointing at the two dark figures. The unmistakable silhouettes of Rosie and Ash.

The first is small and petite, just like Rosie, the second is tall and broad just like Ash. The taller of the two figures is holding a heavy object in their arms. I had thought at the time it was a bag. Only now I realise that it was a baby.

'What are you going on about? You can barely see anything? That could be anyone,' Ash shoots back, visibly irritated by my attempts at rattling him.

He's right. The footage is so dark and grainy that it's difficult to clearly make out, but I'm certain it's them. Because what are the chances? They've been camped up in the park behind the house. They have no money and until Kay invited them here, they had nowhere to go. They are the obvious suspects.

'Maybe, but I'm sure the police would be interested in seeing it, regardless. Especially as they're making house-to-house enquiries and searching through all the nearby recent

CCTV,' I say, again repeating what I'd just heard Rosie tell Ash.

'You think the police give a shit about a few pound coins nicked from the front seat of a car?' Ash cuts in, laughing nastily at my expense and I feel wrong-footed.

This is not the reaction he was supposed to have. I wanted to show him that I had something on him. Proof of him committing a crime. But clearly whatever it is they are both running from is way bigger than this because the police wouldn't make all this fuss over one car break-in. These people must be repeat offenders.

Chancers, opportunists, thieves.

'It was me. I did it. I had to get George some medicine,' Rosie starts to explain. Once again, happy to take the blame so that Ash doesn't have to.

'Rosie. You don't have to explain yourself to her,' Ash cuts in, silencing Rosie once again. 'Who cares what she thinks?'

'I care. Because I think you're both taking advantage of Kay's generous nature. You've seen an opportunity to worm your way in here and you're not going to leave. Not if you don't have to. But the police are looking for you and it's only going to be a matter of time before they find you. Less time, if I send them this.' I tap my phone again, smugly now. Finally I see a flicker of something that resembles fear on Ash's face as they both shift uncomfortably.

He knows that I'm not bluffing. That I'll do it if I have to.

'What do you want from us?' Ash says finally.

'I want you to leave,' I say matter-of-factly, getting straight to the point. 'I want you to pack your things and go back to whatever rock you both crawled out from. I want you to leave Kay alone. She doesn't deserve the trouble that you're going to bring to her door with the police turning up, upsetting her, after everything she's gone through the past few weeks.'

I watch as Rosie nods obediently, before she looks over at

Ash, who doesn't speak. He can't, because his temper has already got the better of him at the audacity of me coming in here and holding them to ransom like this. Blackmailing them into doing what I want.

'Okay.' Finally breaking the long, stilted silence, Ash nods his head slowly in agreement.

'Kay said a couple of days so it's time to move on soon anyway. One more night?' Ash cocks his head, his eyes boring into mine, willing me to say yes.

'Please? Let George have one more night here. We'll leave tomorrow,' Rosie begs me, and I see the desperation in her eyes.

I look down at George on the bed and know that as much as I don't want these people here, I don't want to simply throw them out on the street this late in the day, when I know they have nowhere else to go. They can leave first thing in the morning.

'One more night,' I say, proving to them both that I'm not a complete heartless cow. 'But then I want you gone. You say thank you to Kay for the few nights that she gave you here but tell her it's time for you to move on. No drama. No sob stories. No letting on that I had anything to do with his. Tell Kay that your friends are back from their holiday and you're going there. So that she doesn't worry. Agreed?'

Those are my terms. Take it or leave it, I think, as I wait in silence while Ash and Rosie exchange another of their muted, shared looks.

They're both well aware now of the power that I hold. That this isn't some empty, half-arsed threat. That if they don't leave, I will call the police and hand them in myself.

'Agreed.'

19

ROSIE

I clasp the shiny gold locket and its long, thick chain tightly in my hand for a few seconds, relishing the weight of it. It's heavy and we'll probably stand to get a decent sum of money when we pawn it, I think, as I carefully slip it into the pocket of my jeans, making sure that Kay doesn't see.

'I really don't know how you managed to talk me into doing this,' Kay says, distracted now, her tone full of regret at the thought of parting with her beloved things. She stares down at the three giant heaps of her belongings that we've spread out across her bedroom floor.

'It's bad for you, Kay. Mess and chaos that clutters up a home, can clutter up your mind too. It's called being a hoarder,' I say. Just like Ash had instructed me to. 'All this random stuff you've got laying around the house can have a really negative effect on your health. It can disturb your sleep patterns and well, you said that you never sleep...'

'I've never slept. Even before I started to collect all these things. I think I've been worse lately though, since losing Amanda.'

I nod my head to show my understanding but, really, Kay has all the excuses in the world to keep me from going through her things and I equally have all the reasons that I need to convince her otherwise. I've been insistent because I have no other choice but to go along with another of Ash's brainwaves: stealing some of the more valuable things that Kay is hoarding and selling them on for cash.

I was sceptical at first, full of guilt for even thinking about stealing anything from Kay, especially when she'd shown us nothing but kindness. Only now I am starting to think that Ash might be right.

'Kay probably doesn't even know what she's got in most of these bags and boxes,' Ash had said, when he'd tried to persuade me, and he'd been right. What harm is it really if Kay can't even remember what's lurking in these piles? She's hardly going to notice if some of it goes missing.

So far, I've managed to pocket a beautiful gold locket and chain, an old Nokia phone and a fifty-pound gift voucher, all without her noticing a thing. None of which will amount to a fortune when we sell it on, but Stephanie insisting that we need to leave in the morning means that we need money and quickly. Otherwise, we'll end up back on the streets. Sleeping in some piss-stinking shop doorway or alleyway somewhere and I just can't do it.

I can't put George through all of that again.

That's the only reason I'm going along with it, because I know whatever we get for selling this stuff will be enough to give us a head start. Instead of going back out onto London's streets, we might have enough to pay for a hostel for a night or two while we figure out what to do next.

'Well, maybe we could just do this room for now, and see how I get on,' Kay offers half-heartedly, staring around her bedroom while trying to contain the stress she feels at having to finally clear out some of her things. It's making her anxious and twitchy, and I don't want to push her too hard, because I know that this is difficult for her.

'Yeah, we can just stick to your bedroom. It's a good start. It doesn't have to be as daunting as you think. We won't throw a single thing away. Yet. We'll just go through it. Sort it into piles. "Keep. Throw. Donate." Baby steps. Oh, now this has got to be a keeper.' I grin, trying to make light of the situation and cheer Kay up, I place a huge floppy straw hat with fluffy pink pom-poms hanging from its brim on my head, before spinning around and giving Kay a twirl.

'How do I look?'

'Oh, you really don't want me to answer that,' Kay quips, laughing at the sight of how ridiculous I must look.

'I take it we are "throwing", then?' I dangle the hat over the pile nearest to her, waiting patiently for Kay to give me permission to add it with the rest of the items that she's reluctantly agreed to 'throw' away.

Kay nods her head even though we both know that she doesn't really mean it. The second my back is turned she'll be scavenging around to retrieve it. I've seen her do this to a few things now, move things out of the 'throw' pile and back into the 'keep'. Trying to salvage whatever she can when she thinks I'm not looking. I'm not really convinced that the woman has any intention of actually throwing or donating any of her stuff. She can't, she's too attached to it all. Too emotionally invested in the loss of 'her things'.

I have a sneaky feeling that the only reason Kay is up here right now, agreeing to go along with my idea of sorting through all her things and clearing out all the clutter, is so that she can take the rare opportunity at having some time alone with me. Because, like Stephanie, I know that Kay would have also heard me and Ash arguing earlier.

'I'm glad we've got some time on our own actually,' Kay says, taking a seat on the end of her bed next to me, as if she's just read my thoughts. 'There's something I wanted to speak to you about.' She pauses, taking her time now. As if carefully selecting her words.

'Is this about me and Ash arguing earlier? I'm sorry, Kay, I didn't mean to bring our dramas to your door. Things have been tough lately.'

I look over towards Kay's bedroom door, double-checking that Stephanie isn't loitering there listening. She seems to have a habit of doing that. Lingering in dark corners and listening in to our conversations. Using whatever information she can get against us.

'You're not bringing dramas. I'm just worried about you, Rosie. I meant it earlier, that you can talk to me anytime. If you're worried or scared, or if you need help with anything. Anything at all. I heard Ash shouting at you earlier and then you crying and well, I know how he has a temper.'

Kay has allowed her gaze to follow mine. She thinks I'm looking out for Ash, that I am making sure that he can't overhear us. That I'm scared of him.

'I know you're wary of Ash, Kay,' I say, recalling how he'd almost hit her with the tent pole the first time they'd met. How he'd given her such a bad first impression. 'But you've got him all wrong...' I say, though I silently curse myself as the words come out too quickly, for me sounding too defensive.

Because I can see by the expression on her face that she doesn't believe me.

'He drives me mad sometimes. And yes, he's got a temper, but he doesn't mean it though, not really, at least not in a nasty way. He just sometimes acts before he thinks.'

'Rosie, you have to stop making excuses for him,' Kay continues, only I have to stop her there.

'I'm not making excuses for him. I promise you. Ash is just really protective of me and George, that's all. He loves us so much. He just wants to keep us safe.'

She doesn't believe me. So, I take a deep breath and decide that I am going to take my chances and tell her what's really going on. Because really, what have I got left to lose?

'It's not Ash I'm worried about, Kay. It's Stephanie.'

'Stephanie? Why on earth would you be worried about Stephanie?' Kay asks, resigned to already hearing the worst about her granddaughter, because so far the girl had made her feelings perfectly clear about us staying here.

'She's asked us to leave…' I start. 'No that's not quite true. She's *told* us to leave. First thing tomorrow morning. She filmed us breaking into your neighbour's car the other morning and stealing that money.'

'That was you?'

'I was desperate, Kay. George needed some medicine and I didn't have any money and now Stephanie is saying that if we don't go of our own accord tomorrow, she's going to give the police the recording.'

'She's blackmailing you over that? I mean, gosh, I don't condone what you did. But it's hardly the crime of the century.' Kay eyes me warily. 'It's not about the car, is it? What aren't you telling me? There's more to this, isn't there? Why are you both running, Rosie? You can tell me.'

'I wish I could, Kay, but I can't. I promised Ash that I wouldn't say anything…' I nod and start to cry wanting to tell Kay everything. To confide in the woman, to finally unburden myself. Only I know that I can't.

Ash has warned me what would happen if I told. How once what we did was out there, there would be no taking it back. Kay won't want us here in this house. She'll throw us out, just like Stephanie wants to do. Ash will go to prison. We both will. They'll take George. I can't risk it.

'We did something bad…' I pause, wanting to say so much more than I can. 'Something unforgivable. Please don't ask me what, because I can't tell you. But we're in big trouble, Kay, and if Stephanie turns us into the police, they'll take George away from me for good. They'll never give him back. I can't lose my son, Kay.'

I wait for my words to sink in, for Kay to berate me or question me further, only she does neither of those things. Instead, she places her arm around me and allows me to sink into her. I relish her warmth and the comfort she offers.

'There there,' she says, rubbing my back and it's all I can do not to break down and tell her everything. About what happened to make us run. As much as I want to confess, Ash's words spin around in my head and I know that I can't. That I mustn't say anything. Not now. Not yet.

'I don't know what you did, Rosie, and quite frankly it's none of my business. But what I do know is that it's none of Stephanie's business either and it's certainly not her place to tell you and Ash to leave. This is my house and she is as much as a guest here as you both are. She'll do well to remember that.'

It's the first time that I've heard Kay sound angry and part of me is grateful she cares about me enough that it has evoked some emotion inside her, that she's clearly on my side.

'The girl is bluffing. It's an empty threat. Mark my words, the last thing Stephanie wants is the police here again. She's had enough of them to last a lifetime. She won't be calling anyone, I can promise you that. No one's going to take George from you. Not while you're here, under my roof. I'll make sure of that.' Kay gently strokes my hair as she speaks and I don't know why, but I believe her.

I trust her. I know she means it when she says that she'll do right by me and George.

'I'll speak with Stephanie. You leave her to me,' Kay says resolutely, before pausing and lowering her voice. 'We all have secrets, Rosie. Even Stephanie. Let's see how she likes a taste of her own medicine.'

I am about to try and probe Kay further and ask her what she means, but she changes the subject.

'You, Ash and George can stay for as long as you need to. It's no trouble. Stephanie will have to get over that.'

'We can stay. You really mean it?' I say, suddenly feeling a mixture of immense relief that we don't have to leave straight away, and monstrous guilt about the things I've stolen from Kay that now feel as if they are burning a hole in my pocket.

'Not forever, of course.' Kay laughs. 'But a few more days won't hurt. Besides, I'm not going to be able to sort all this stuff out on my own, am I? I'm going to need your help.'

She nods down to the piles of things on the floor and I grin wildly, as I spot something familiar staring up at me.

'Er, that's the keep pile,' I say, spotting the hat with the pom-poms has moved to the mound of things nearest to us.

'Well, I was always very fond of that hat,' Kay quips, getting up from the bed and placing it on her head, giving me a little twirl as she stifles a small laugh. Letting me know under no circumstances was she going to make helping her clear this house easy for me.

20

STEPHANIE

I found it.

Kay's laptop. Stashed away on one of Kay's dining chairs. A crumpled piece of paper, scribbled with a password flattened beneath it.

'Oh! Don't tell me you've been snooping down Kay's laptop too?'

Ash's words still spin inside my head. This laptop is how he thinks I found out all their secrets. I'd heard Kay and Rosie earlier, while pretending to be engrossed in watching the TV. I'd taken in every word of their pathetic little heart to heart. Good old Saint Kay, persuading Rosie to do the right thing. Begging her to reach out and let a family member know that she and George are okay.

'Your family will be worried about you, Rosie. How would you feel if it was George out there missing?'

Kay had harped on so much that finally, reluctantly, Rosie had no choice but to give in and Kay had practically fallen over herself to get her laptop after that. Before going on to rip the entire house apart looking for the password.

Only there was something in Ash's sarcasm earlier and the

way he shot an angry look at Rosie that made me doubt what she'd used the laptop for.

I eye the black charger cable that twists its way up the wall, still plugged into the socket. I'm guessing that if Rosie didn't have time to unplug the thing, then the chances were, she hadn't shut it down properly either.

So it's not really snooping, is it? I tell myself as I take a seat, and fire the laptop up, quickly tapping in the password when prompted. Not when it's all been left out for me. I am simply looking out for Kay, I justify to myself silently. Because unlike her, I don't take people at face value and my gut is telling me that we shouldn't trust these people. They aren't who they claim to be. They are hiding something more than just the car being broken into.

Something way bigger than that.

But if I'm going to persuade Kay of any of this, I'm going to need solid proof. It hurts that she won't take my word for it. It feels almost as if she's taken theirs over mine. Only wanting to see the good in them, yet in doing so she only sees the bad in me. She thinks I am selfish and jealous. That I don't like them and I want them gone. She thinks that's my motive for not wanting them here.

Only it isn't that at all.

I have a bad feeling about them. An instinctive gut feeling that something is off with Rosie and Ash, and I don't want them to take advantage of Kay's generous nature. Pretending their baby is still sick so they can stay here longer than Kay agreed has already proved I was right. I don't want them bringing any police attention here to Kay's house, either. Not after everything that happened with my mother.

And maybe a selfish part of me wants my bedroom back, so I can grieve in peace without an audience. Maybe I do want time with Kay alone...

That doesn't make me a bad person though, does it?

The screen lights up and my eyes widen, pleased to see that my suspicions are right. Rosie has left multiple tabs open on the screen, allowing me to scan the numerous web pages that she had been looking at earlier.

Silly, silly girl, I think as I realise Rosie hasn't cleared her browsing history either. That was foolish of her. Careless even. Costly. Rosie's error is now in my favour, as I begin my search through every link.

I very quickly learn that Rosie is a liar. There are no emails or private messages reaching out to any family members for help like she had promised Kay. By the looks of it, the only thing that Rosie has spent all of her time on here doing, is googling her own name. I shake my head, unable to believe what I am seeing as I click on the first purple coloured highlighted link. I follow the trail of the links Rosie has already clicked on. The articles and posts that I know she's already seen.

'Missing Person's Appeal'

This article was posted by the Metropolitan Police, expressing their growing concerns for a runaway mother and her newborn baby.

Rosie! This article is about Rosie.

I was right all along. These people are running from something. The question is, what?

The next link reveals a photo of a tent discovered abandoned in Highgate Woods. Damaged beyond repair from the treacherous rainfall and gale force winds of Storm Kathleen. The little that was left rendered it unfit for purpose, which is why Kay had offered Rosie and Ash somewhere to sleep for a few nights in the first place. She'd felt sorry for them, stuck out there with nowhere else to go.

The police are appealing to the public to remain vigilant.
They suspect that the mother and her baby may have been
using the tent as shelter for the past couple of nights.

I think about the tatty, old cardboard box that Kay had
told me they'd been using as a cot. That must be how the
police know that the occupants of the tent had a baby. In their
haste to accept Kay's offer of a roof over their heads, they'd
left it behind as a clue. Another careless mistake they've
made.

They've made?

There is no mention of Ash. At least not in any of these articles. There is no mention of his name, anywhere. Not in the
missing person's report or any of the other articles online. They
are only about Rosie and George.

It's almost as if Ash doesn't exist.

Which doesn't make any sense.

The police will be conducting a house-to-house investigation
in the local area, to gather information and intelligence
regarding Rosie and George's whereabouts.

I close my eyes, a sinking feeling in the pit of my stomach
now that I know for certain what I'd overheard Rosie telling
Ash was true. The police might come here.

Shit.

I'd only been bluffing when I'd threatened to go to them.
Using the little information I had managed to dig up on them
both, to use against them to get them to leave. The last thing me
and Kay need is the police here, digging around for answers
about Rosie and George. They might start asking other questions about our business too.

I can't cope with that. Not again.

Feeling sick with anxiety, I am just about to shut the laptop back down when I see it. One final open tab, dragged to the top corner of the screen. I'd almost missed it.

The Official Register of Births and Deaths.

Deaths precisely, I conclude, as I scroll down list of the recently deceased names that run in neat columns across the screen. My heartbeat thudding rapidly inside my chest, my mouth is suddenly dry, and I try and fight the rising burn of nausea that threatens at the back of my throat as I recall how Kay told them about my mother's sudden death last night at dinner and I had tried to shut her down.

Had Rosie been looking for my mother's name?

That is my first thought as I search. Making my way down the list, once. Twice. Three times. Just to be certain that she's not there.

Had I given myself away by being so defensive?

Because Ash had caught it, hadn't he? He'd picked up that something was off between me and Kay, because of the way I'd reacted when he'd asked about my mother. Had that been enough to rouse his suspicions, that I was hiding something too? Is that why they've gone looking?

Or had Kay said more to them after I left the room? No. She promised she'd never tell another living soul and I need to believe her. Besides, Rosie's search for my mother's name doesn't add up, because looking at the dates she's entered, she's got the timeline all wrong. My mother died fourteen days ago, Rosie's search only goes back four. The same four days that the missing person article claims Rosie and George went missing too.

I sit back in my chair, staring hard at the screen, as if the important missing piece of the puzzle is just going to jump right out at me.

I don't think Rosie was looking up my mother's death at all. I wonder if it's something else, something more personal. Has she lost someone recently too? I guess that would make her behaviour make a lot more sense. Rosie seems nervous and jittery and on edge all of the time, reminding me of a rabbit caught in the glare of oncoming headlights of a fast-moving car, resigned for the next impact to strike her. Like it's only a matter of time.

I'd thought it was Ash that she was scared of, and maybe to some extent it is, because I've seen how controlling he is. The way that he constantly watches Rosie, as if he can't bear to let her out of his sight. I think of the fire he'd started in the kitchen to stop me asking her all those questions. Almost like he was frightened of what she might say. He doesn't trust her to protect their secrets. Or his secrets. He thinks she'll talk. Only now that I really think about it, it might be grief that I've been watching play out in Rosie.

Because I know grief intimately too. I am living it, night and day. One minute I am drowning in sadness, adrift without my anchor to keep me secure, the next I feel nothing at all. Only a distorted kind of numbness that makes me feel completely detached from the rest of the world.

I am lost without my mother. That's the truth. For all of her faults, all of her mistakes, I am completely and utterly lost without her. The two weeks since her death have felt like forever and no time at all, and still, I can barely function, my loss so raw and painful I am convinced that part of me died that day with her.

If Rosie's grief is only four days in, the likelihood is she is still in shock. Still coming to terms with whatever terrible ordeal has happened. The worst is yet to come for her.

Shit. How had I missed that?

It makes sense though. What else could have been so terrible that she'd been forced to run? That she had no other choice but be driven to sleeping in a tent in the woods with her young baby. What was it that made them want to stay here, hiding away in Kay's house?

My mind goes back to the obituary and a sudden random thought forms inside my head. Has Ash killed someone? Is that what Ash is scared Rosie will give away? Is my grandmother harbouring a murderer inside her house?

Murderer.

For Christ's sake, I'm such a bloody hypocrite.

The guilt and shame wash over me once more, as I knew it would.

The police can't come here. I can't allow it. It's too much of a risk. If they come here looking for Rosie and Ash, digging around in order to unearth their secrets. They might dig up some of mine too.

21

ROSIE

'Sorry, it's not much,' I declare, emptying my pockets out onto the bed and watching the look of disappointment flash across Ash's face as he sifts through the few items that I managed to steal from Kay when the woman wasn't looking.

'Not much? This lot will amount to pennies, Rosie. To nothing. We'll be lucky if we can afford to buy ourselves something to eat with the money from this lot, let alone pay for a bed somewhere for the night. Fuck, man. We need more time.' Frustrated now, Ash runs his fingers through his hair, and I know just the thing to cheer him up.

'Well, it's funny you should say that.' I shoot him a small, conspiratory smile. 'Kay knows about Stephanie. She said she'll speak with her. That we don't need to leave, not yet, we can stay a few more days longer.'

'You're kidding me?' Ash's disheartened expression turns into a small triumphant smile that mirrors my own. Only it doesn't last. His expression wilts and he shakes his head. 'You heard her though, Rosie. Stephanie seems pretty set on getting rid of us. What if Kay can't stop her?'

It's my turn to shake my head then.

'She seems to think that she can.' I shrug. 'I don't know what she has on her, but Stephanie's hiding something too, Ash. Kay pretty much said as much to me,' I say, now that I've fully digested the very little that Kay did say to me earlier.

'Hiding what?'

'That's just it, I don't actually know what. Kay was being cryptic. She said something about us all having secrets. Even Stephanie. She said that Stephanie won't want the police here poking around.'

'Why would she say that?'

'I don't know. But she seemed pretty angry about Stephanie asking us to leave without consulting her first. And when I told her about the footage on her phone and that she was black-mailing us with it, she said something about Stephanie needing a taste of own medicine.'

'So, what? Kay is going to blackmail Stephanie now?' Ash laughs, clearly impressed at Kay's new show of hand. 'I wonder what she has on her?'

I bite my lip. Unsure if I should voice my theories on that, because really that's all that I have. Theories. Minuscule snippets of information Kay has let on to me.

Nothing concrete, no proof.

'I think it's got something to do with Amanda, Kay's daughter,' I say carefully. 'You remember the other night at dinner when Stephanie said she'd been living here with Kay for the past two months? That she'd discovered her mother's body one night when she'd been visiting her. Only Kay slipped up. She said that she'd invited Stephanie to come and stay the night of Amanda's death. She said that she could hardly leave her there, in that flat, after discovering her mother's body. Which means Stephanie only moved in two weeks ago.'

'Right?' Ash stares at me blankly, not sure where I am going with this, and I doubt myself once more. 'So Stephanie lied about how long she's lived here for. So what? I don't get it?'

I shrug, because really, I don't get it either. It's just a feeling a have. A hunch.

'Why would Stephanie want us to believe, and more importantly, want the police to believe, that she wasn't there the time her mother died?'

I pause, hoping that the penny would finally drop, only still Ash stares at me blankly, as if I'm talking in a completely different language to him.

'Perhaps that's her alibi. Maybe she wasn't just there when her mother died. *Maybe* she was responsible.'

'Why would Kay cover that up though? I mean, Stephanie might be her granddaughter, but Amanda was her daughter. If she suspected Stephanie of doing something dodgy, she's hardly going to invite her to move in and start playing happy families with her, is she?'

I shrug again, because I've been thinking the very same thing.

'Perhaps Kay offered her an alibi?'

'But why would she need an alibi…?' Ash trails off, as though actually considering it for the first time. 'You really think Stephanie had something to do with it? Her mother's death? I thought the woman was an addict though. That she died of an overdose.'

I shrug again, because I don't have all the answers.

'They're still waiting for the autopsy results apparently. All I know is that Kay doesn't really know Stephanie that well either. She told me they have no real relationship. They're practically strangers too. I think she's having a hard time getting the girl to open up to her…'

'And meanwhile, Kay is making new best friends with you.' Ash laughs and shakes his head. 'I bet that's half that bitch Stephanie's problem. I bet she can see how close you and Kay are and she doesn't like it. That's why she doesn't want us here. She's jealous of you.'

'Maybe...' I say, not convinced.

Stephanie hadn't warmed to me that's true, but from the minute she'd met us her main problem seemed to be with Ash. She'd taken an instant dislike to him and as usual, Ash seemed completely oblivious to that fact. Oblivious that he seemed to rub so many people up the wrong way.

'You never know, Rosie. If you get into Kay's good graces, it might be Stephanie who ends up getting turfed out and not us.'

'Well, either way, we don't need to leave just yet. Kay said we can stay, and well, it's her house.' I grin, glad that we don't have to worry about going back out onto the streets first thing tomorrow morning. We can stay here for a few more days at least.

'In the meantime, I'm going to keep on doing my best to persuade her to let me sort through the rest of her things.'

Ash nods with approval.

'Good, the more stuff we can stash away, the more we'll have to flog when we leave. I just hope you're right about Stephanie, because she can still call the police you know. Kay won't even need to know that it came from her. One anonymous tip-off to the cops and it'll be all over for us.'

'Kay won't let that happen,' I say with enough certainty that Ash must believe me, because he nods too and hides our stolen stash underneath the mattress. He stands up and says, 'Good. Because if Kay doesn't deal with her, I might have to. I won't let anyone hurt my family.'

22

KAY

I can't sleep again.

Tonight though, it's the conversation that I'd had with Rosie earlier that is keeping me awake. How she'd called me a hoarder. Only she'd made it sound as if it was something negative. As if I had some kind of a condition. It has bothered me enough that now, picking up my phone from where it sits on my bedside table, I tap the word into the search bar, to look up its definition.

Hoarder: A person who acquires an excessive number of items and stores them in a chaotic manner, usually resulting in unmanageable amounts of clutter. Hoarding can be a symptom of an underlying mental health condition.

My hands shake and I feel suddenly nauseous. I *am* suffering from a mental health condition. I read on.

Mental health disorders relating to hoarding can include Obsessive Compulsive Disorder. OCD-related hoarding is generally an unwanted response to obsessive thoughts and anxiety.

Am I mental? I think I might be, because every time I close my eyes and try to sleep, all I see is her. My beautiful Amanda. Writhing around inside that coffin, her long nails clawing against the grain of the wood as she screams wildly at me to get her out. The image of her like that, back inside my head once more now that I'm fully awake is utterly terrifying, causing me to sit bolt upright on the bed and switch the light on.

Needing a distraction, I stare around the room and take in the sight of all the boxes and bags scattered across the carpet. Each one bulging with my much-loved belongings. Stacks of worn musty books that I've collected over the years, that I haven't had time to read, tatty lampshades that come without the plugs or bases. Biscuit tins full of hundreds of mismatched buttons. Chipped, chintzy china ornaments and figurines and threadbare cushions.

My much-loved belongings? Who the hell have I been kidding?

These are all *just* things. Pointless clutter, I know that deep down. That none of it holds any real sentimental value to me. Most of it doesn't hold any value at all. It's all just junk. Items that I have accumulated and stored 'in a chaotic manner'. *Shit.*

This is how I am dealing with my constant, torturous anxiety, isn't it? Purposely collecting all this stuff to fill the empty void in my sad pathetic life, after Amanda had cut me out all those years ago.

The worst thing about Amanda severing our relationship for good was that it had been all my fault. I am the one who destroyed it. It's a heavy cross to bear. Too heavy for me to carry alone, so instead of dealing with the consequences, instead of moving forward, I'd spent the many years since putting up walls. Thick ones, lined with piles of boxes of things, and stuff, and junk. Locking myself away alone in my home, unable to take the painful rejection of being disowned by my one and only child. Shutting the whole world out. Convincing myself that all this stuff would make up for the enormous loss I'd encountered. That these things would give me stability, because they were mine and no one could take them from me.

It's the definition of crazy. The way I have lived. Allowing my home to become a dumping ground for everyone else's junk and rubbish. Even madder is the fact that I don't own any of it. This stuff owns me. I know this for a fact, because earlier, even the thought of having to place my belongings into bin liners as Rosie had suggested and give them away – *'Keep, donate, throw'* – had stirred up such a sense of dread. Such a sense of overwhelming terror in me that I hadn't been able to do it.

Rosie is right. I am a hoarder.

I am mental.

God! How have I allowed this to happen? The walls of my house to close in on me under the weight of all this pointless clutter. The space inside each room of this house so narrow that most days, I can barely breathe.

I'd only really noticed how untidy and cluttered the house is since Stephanie came to stay. Then Rosie, Ash and George. How cramped and claustrophobic the place started to feel now that all five of us are squashed inside it. Surrounded by all this crap. I'd been lonely, I reason, trying to be kind to myself. Because loneliness makes people do desperate, awful things sometimes.

I should know.

I think of how I'd watched as Stephanie had stood over her mother's grave, riddled with her own secrets and guilt from what happened that night.

Then of Rosie and Ash sleeping outside in that tent, purposely dodging the police at the expense of their defenceless, tiny baby.

We've all done bad things, haven't we? We've all made mistakes. We're all bad people deep down. I am not perfect either. Not by a long shot. Good, kind, generous Kay. Allowing these strangers into my home. That's what they all think of me, only I'm not any of those things.

Amanda is the only one who knew it.

She saw the real me in all my selfish glory and she had hated me for it. That's the ugly truth. I am nothing more than a pathetic, lonely old lady, happy to use people as much as they are using me. That's why I've invited these people into my home. For my own benefit, not theirs. Because I simply can't bear it. The thought of having to rattle around inside this big old, cluttered house, for one more day with only my little Max for company.

Amanda's sudden death had triggered that. The realisation that I only have one life and I've been wasting it, rotting away inside this house all on my own.

I thought having Stephanie here would help me to fill the void, but I now see it. How Amanda's death has left us both constantly treading water, trying not to drown in the river of guilt we both feel for her last, final moments.

Stephanie is guarded with me. All the lies and poison Amanda fed her with for all these years have made her wary of me. She wants to believe that I am a good person now, that I learned my lesson and I have changed. Only still, she doesn't quite trust me. Too much time has passed between us, too much distance. We are strangers and I do feel awful about that. After everything it took to get us both finally here together.

Whereas with Rosie it is different.

I enjoy her company and dare I say it, I have more of a bond with her than I do Stephanie. Rosie is loyal to a fault. Her fault being Ash. Despite the way the man behaves, Rosie still insists on sticking up for him at every given opportunity, and as much as I wish she'd see him for what he is, there is integrity to her actions.

With her and baby George here in the house, it feels as if I've been given a second chance to make amends for not being present in Amanda's and Stephanie's lives.

Having Rosie and George here is like a revelation. As though a thick, white veil has been suddenly lifted from my face, allowing me to see so much clearer now. For the first time in forever, I can finally envisage this new life of mine. I have a purpose again and it makes me sad that Stephanie had almost sabotaged that by asking Rosie and Ash to leave without even consulting me first.

She has good intentions really, I know that deep down. She is just looking out for me and making sure that Rosie and Ash don't outstay their welcome. That they don't take advantage of me. But they are not taking advantage of me. If anything, it's me taking advantage of them, because for the first time in ages my house feels as if it's come alive. Full of noisy conversations and genuine laughter. Cups clattering, doors slamming, the sound of running water, and that makes me feel alive too.

It's time to start living. Time to finally move on from my hurts of the past. Besides, Rosie needs my help. I've seen the way Ash is with her. The way he controls everything she does and says. The longer Rosie stays here, the more chance I'll have at making her see that Ash is no good for her and George. That she can get away from him if she wants to.

Though I know from bitter experience that I can't push these things. If my eternal rift with Amanda has taught me anything it's that. Warning my daughter that her boyfriend was no good had not served me well and even when she'd finally seen it with her own eyes, she'd blamed me. Shooting the messenger and all that.

Rosie needs to see Ash for who he is for herself and I believe that in time, she will.

My mind is made up. Tomorrow I will speak to Stephanie just like I promised Rosie I would. I'll make it clear to her that the last thing I want is for Rosie and Ash to feel as if they have to leave. Not yet. That she can't go making accusations and threatening people with the police. Not unless she wants them crawling all around the place, asking questions that I know she won't want them asking. That should do it. A veiled threat. A gentle warning. Enough to make the girl keep quiet.

There. It's decided. First thing tomorrow I'll get back to sorting out these mountains of junk. Only this time no tricks. I'm finally going to get this place clean again. I am done with pretending that all this junk is enough for me any more. I am going to surround myself with people instead of things from here on in. I am not going to be mental any more.

Turning off the bedside lamp, I close my eyes and miraculously, for the first time in years, I immediately fall straight to sleep.

23

STEPHANIE

The blinding white light of the early morning sky sweeps in through Kay's lounge window, abruptly pulling me from my deep trance-like sleep. Not ready to get up and face yet another day roaming around Kay's house like a spare part, I close my eyes tighter and try my hardest to block it out.

Only a sudden cough from behind me makes me turn abruptly. Careful not to fall from the narrow sofa where I lay, I see that it's Kay. She has drawn back the curtains. The over-powering sickly smell of malty Ovaltine floats from the mug that she's holding in her hand.

'We need to have a little chat,' she says, taking a seat in the armchair opposite me before sipping her hot drink.

Now? She wants to have a 'little chat' with me, right now?

Wiping the clumps of sleep in the corner of my eyes with my fingertips, I reluctantly sit up, trying to quickly compose myself for what's to come. Because everything about Kay's abrupt awaking, the tone of her voice, her body language tells me something is wrong.

'Is this about Rosie and Ash?' I ask, already knowing that's exactly what this is about. I've underestimated them. Instead of fearing me, they've called my bluff. Taking their chances with giving Kay their own version of events, no doubt. *Shit.* I should have seen that coming. They've probably told her about the threats I made too. How I'd asked them to leave. Demanded that they leave, in fact.

'I know it wasn't my place, Kay, but please just hear me out. Ash started that fire in the kitchen yesterday morning on purpose—'

'Stephanie. Stop. We've already been over this. It was an accident. Rosie has already said as much. She thought she turned the pan off, only instead she'd turned it up.'

'No, that isn't what happened. I was there, Kay, I saw it. Ash did it because he didn't want Rosie talking to me. Answering all my questions. Besides, Rosie will stick up for him, no matter what. Can't you see that? She's scared of him, Kay. Please, you need to listen to me. George isn't sick. At least, he's not *as* sick as they're making out.'

I try to find the right words, because I only have one shot at making Kay really listen to me. I can't mess this up.

'They're keeping him in that bedroom, out of the way, because they want you to think he's getting worse – so you'll let them stay here longer. They think while George is poorly, you won't make them move on. They're trying to manipulate you, Kay. And there's something else. The police are looking for them.'

This is my trump card. The thing I really need Kay to hear.

Even better, I think, she can see it herself. Reaching for my phone that I had tucked under one of the cushions of the sofa last night. I decide that I'll show her. I'll type Rosie's name into the search bar and let Kay read all the articles herself. Only as I sweep my hand several times beneath the fabric, I know my phone is not there. I reach down further, patting frantically around on the carpet in case it's fallen and slipped underneath the chair somehow. There's no sign of it there either.

'If this is about the car, they explained all of that. Rosie needed medicine for George. He *is* poorly, Stephanie. I saw him with my own eyes, they are not making that up. Rosie was desperate. The police aren't going to lock her up for something like that,' Kay retorts as if I am an idiot and I know that even before I have begun convincing her, I am already losing her.

I give up on looking on my phone for now, Kay needs my full attention. I have a long list of well-rehearsed evidence against Rosie and Ash ready and now she has no other choice but to hear me out.

'The police are making house-to-house enquiries, Kay. They don't just do that for a random car break-in. There's something else going on here. Something much bigger than that.'

'Like what?' she says, and I hear the disbelief in her voice.

'I'm not sure.' Kay lets out a low, sad laugh at this and I ignore it, determined to persevere.

'Kay, they're not who you think. They are not good people.'

'They're not good people? And what are we, then? Are we good people, Stephanie?' Kay says quietly, but there's an unmistakable edge to her voice that I've not heard her use before now, and her comment completely floors me.

I know exactly what she is referring to. The night she died. This is the first time since my mother's death that Kay has made any reference to the events of that night. Whereas I have thought about nothing else since.

My mother's sudden, tragic death has all but destroyed me. Without her I am lost and consumed with overbearing grief. But much worse than that, it's the guilt that's eating me up inside. Knowing how it is all my fault. I didn't just fail to save my mother. I am the reason why she's dead. I killed her. How does someone live with that?

'It was an accident. You know that... That doesn't make me a bad person,' I stutter, my voice so small now that even I can barely hear it.

But Kay does.

'An accident that we covered it up, Stephanie. We pretended that you weren't there, remember. I offered you an alibi by letting you come and stay here with me. So that the police wouldn't probe into who was with your mother that night. So they wouldn't ask any questions about who else could have given her that last, fatal shot of methadone. That makes us bad people too.' She pauses, and I see her try to compose herself. And I remind myself that she is grieving too. That she has lost her daughter.

'Christ, Stephanie, we haven't even had the results from her autopsy yet and you're really willing to risk the police coming here to the house? Because they won't just ask questions about Ash and Rosie, you know that don't you? Not all the while your mother's cause of death hasn't been officially announced. You'll be putting yourself on their radar too. You need to drop it. Whatever Rosie and Ash have done, it's none of our business.'

She's blackmailing me.

That is my first thought, because there's something about Kay's tone and her demeanour that has set me on edge. If I keep Rosie and Ash's secrets, she'll keep mine too. Is that what she is really saying here? Her words an indirect warning.

Christ, no. What am I thinking? Of course Kay isn't blackmailing me. Kay is the one who helped me throughout all of this. She was the first and only person I'd called to the house when I'd found my mother in that awful state. Watery vacant eyes. Tinged blue lips. Foaming at the mouth.

I hadn't known that she'd already exceeded her daily dose of methadone. I'd thought she was clucking. That she was going to give in to the pull of it and end up back on heroin. I thought I was helping. Only she'd had a seizure and by the time Kay arrived she was laying lifeless on the floor.

Dead.

Kay had taken control. Staying calm and composed, as she'd

ushered me away from my mother's body that I'd been hysterically clutching. Ordering me to pack a bag. Telling me that I
could stay here at her house. That we'd tell the police I'd been
living here for a while, so they'd have no reason to suspect that I
was at the house at the time of my mother's death. The fridge,
empty of its contents as usual, barely contained enough food for
one person, let alone two. Our possessions and clothes were so
minimal, they'd have no reason to suspect that they didn't all
belong to my mother.

That made it easy for me.

To make it look like I hadn't been there that night. To make
it look like I hadn't ever lived there at all.

It wasn't as if the neighbours would give me away. It was
surprising how invisible you could feel, living in a bustling
tower block in London. Full of so many people, yet with no
sense of community, there was little daily interaction. Despite
the constant stream of noise that penetrated in through every
direction of the flat's paper-thin walls and ceiling, at all hours of
the day and night. The loud arguments, the slamming of doors.
The noisy sound of sex. It was the kind of place where you felt
alone and isolated. We barely saw each other, let alone ever
spoke.

Besides, my mother had so many visitors coming and going
all of the time, that I doubt if anyone even noticed that I'd lived
there. 'This doesn't have to ruin your life too, Stephanie,' Kay
had said. And even though I knew it was wrong, I knew that we
should have called an ambulance and the police. That I should
have told them what I'd done. I'd been too shocked to think
straight. In a trance-like state, I'd happily let Kay take the lead.

My mother's room, still remaining just the way she'd left it
when she had been my age, meant that if the police did come
snooping around and asking any unwanted questions, it would
look as if I'd lived here with Kay all my life.

That my mother's room had always been mine.

'We can take this opportunity to finally get to know each other properly. To build a relationship. A fresh start,' Kay had said, and I had clung to those words.

A fresh start. My God, I had needed that. I didn't want to accept the reality that I'd lost the only person in the whole world that I'd loved. That I had no one else now. That this lonely, sad old woman was my only living relative. A poor substitute for all that I lost. So here we are. Both of us dancing around one another, trying to make this all make sense.

Kay is only trying to help me. I know this really. Despite the things that my mother told me about her, despite all their differences, Kay has only ever shown me love and kindness. Which is why we're in this situation in the first place. Arguing about random strangers in her home.

'Promise me that you'll drop it, Stephanie,' Kay says again and this time her words come lighter, and I wonder if I'd imagined the hardness there before.

'For you. I'll do it for you,' I say finally. Reluctantly. Because really what other choice do I have?

I owe her, don't I?

For helping me in my hour of need.

For killing her daughter.

24

STEPHANIE

Someone has taken my phone.

I know this, because I've spent the entire day searching Kay's house, to no avail. If it was simply lost or misplaced, I would have found it by now, wouldn't I? Tucked underneath a chair where it had accidently slipped down or buried beneath a pile of clothing. It's gone. Nowhere to be seen. Vanished like a puff of smoke into thin air and I am willing to give one good guess at who has taken it.

Ash.

I stare at Ash and Rosie's bedroom door, slightly ajar like an invitation to lure me inside. Should I? They've all finished dinner now, so if I do this, I don't have much time. The smell of the hot, delicious food that wafted up the stairs earlier, when Kay had dished up, still lingers. Making my stomach growl with a hunger that I'd told Kay I no longer feel.

'I've lost my appetite,' I'd lied, wanting her to know my rage. To know how I refuse to sit with those people and entertain them for a second longer.

I had told her that my phone is missing. I told her it must have been Ash or Rosie who had taken it, that they were trying to ensure I don't share the footage of them breaking into the neighbour's car with the police.

'Oh, Stephanie. Please. You said you would drop this vendetta you have against them. If anything, it's probably been accidently buried under a pile of the things that myself and Rosie have been sorting through. I'm sure it'll turn up eventually,' Kay had said sternly, rolling her eyes despairingly at me, and in that moment I knew that I had lost her.

Kay thinks I have a personal grudge against Ash and Rosie and that I will do anything in my power to cause trouble for them. She seriously thinks I am the one who is being unreasonable here. All the while Ash and Rosie have been busy worming their way into Kay's good books. Spending the best part of their day sorting through all of Kay's things, helping her to decide what to keep and what to throw away.

Even Ash has made himself useful. Lifting and carrying anything heavy that Kay reluctantly agreed to throw away into one of the bins outside. Clearly intent on proving to her how helpful they both are. How useful they could be.

I'm the only one who sees it. How fake they are. How this is all just another part of their act. They are only doing all of this to win Kay around and to push me out and the worrying thing is, it's actually working. Kay is sucked in by the both of them and I'm the one who looks like the bad person here. I'm the argumentative, difficult one.

I hear the gentle splash of water coming from the bathroom down the hallway, and Ash's husky voice sings out as he coos and laughs with George while he bathes him.

Downstairs, the sound of crockery being stacked away in cupboards. The rush of running water gushing from the kitchen tap and I imagine Kay and Rosie tidying up the kitchen.

I seize my opportunity. Tiptoeing carefully into my old bedroom, I stare around the room. I'm unsure where to start first, but I know that I must be quick. If I was Ash, where would I hide my phone?

I start with the small chest of drawers next to the head of the bed. Rummaging my way through the small pile of my mother's old books inside.

When I moved in, I didn't bring much with me, because the truth is, I don't have much. I'd turned up here with just a carrier bag of clothes, some toiletries and make-up and my Kindle.

There's no sign of my phone.

I close the drawer and get up, thumbing my way through the sparse contents of George's baby changing bag that sits open on the chair nearby. A few nappies, a pot of Sudocrem that Kay had bought them earlier and a couple of old muslin cloths. There's nothing of any interest in there.

I stare at the bed, a feeling of unease fizzing inside me as I make my way over and crouch down on the floor. I allow my gaze to sweep the narrow space that's under the bed, checking that my phone hasn't been shoved under there.

Nothing.

Pulling myself up onto my knees, I skim my hands beneath the slither of the gap that runs between the mattress and the carefully tucked in fitted sheet. My fingers glide across the cotton, about to give up. Because so far the search is useless. Only my hand hits something cool and hard. I feel around, noting how there are several objects tucked under here, all different shapes and materials. Metal, plastic. And something made of card.

I lift the mattress up so I can get a better look at what they have stashed there and eye the mobile phone. An ancient old Nokia that isn't mine. A gift voucher for a jewellery shop. A pile of loose change and a gold locket and chain. Why have they hidden their things here? Are they frightened that Kay or I would steal them?

I pick up the locket and click the clasp open, and stare at the familiar photos inside. A woman and a young girl on one side. A tiny baby on the other. I've seen these photos before, I realise. Displayed on Kay's mantelpiece. Only these are much smaller versions. Kay and my mother, when she'd been a young girl. Me as a tiny baby. The only photo Kay has of me, she said.

This is Kay's locket. Ash and Rosie are stealing from her. That's why all these things are stashed here. Hidden out of sight. Ash and Rosie are not helping Kay organise all of her stuff, they are stealing from her. Right under her nose, under the guise of being good, as Kay watches on obliviously.

I feel sick to my stomach and my blood boils with rage, as I vow to myself that I won't let them do this. I guarantee that they've taken my phone too, only they've hidden it somewhere else. They might even have it on them.

I slip the locket into my pocket, my proof to show Kay that Ash and Rosie can't be trusted.

This time she can't ignore me.

25

ROSIE

The sudden, repeated thud startles me. It sounds like something smacking hard against every step of the staircase.

That was loud.

I think of Ash. Upstairs bathing George, after spending much of the day sifting through the remains of Kay's endless boxes and bags. Seeing if there's anything worth salvaging for us to sell on among all the random stuff that she keeps. It had taken us the entire day to sort through her bedroom alone. The rest of the house was going to take forever. Ash seems happy about that. He said that if we pace ourselves and take our time, we'll be able to stay here for at least another couple of weeks.

Had Ash finished bathing George and started moving things again? Had he just dropped something heavy down the stairs?

It had sounded too loud to be just a random object from one of the bags or boxes. The fact that I had heard it from all the way back here too, at the rear of the house, in the kitchen, means it couldn't have been something small. Especially with the hot tap running at full force, the water noisily gushing out as I rinse George's bottles.

Perhaps he dropped an entire box.

I turn the tap off and stand deadly still. Listening intently though the house sits in an eerie silence.

Kay's house is an accident waiting to happen.

Hadn't Ash said this himself, only earlier today, while stacking up the numerous boxes and bags and piles of random stuff that Kay had built up in every corner of her bedroom. Ash had moved everything out to the hallway and the top of the staircase, ready to carry them downstairs. He was right, it was only a matter of time before someone tripped or fell.

Fell.

An awful thought hits me. What if Ash was carrying George down the stairs, checking where I have got to with his milk? Had the thudding sound that I'd heard been accompanied by muffled scream? I think it might have. Or am I overthinking this? Allowing my wild, exaggerated imagination to take over, playing out my worst fears. Something in my gut is telling me that something bad has just happened. That someone has just fallen.

'George?'

I run from the room, out through the hallway, yanking the lounge door open, only to let out a huge chilling scream at the sight that awaits me. Someone *has* fallen. There's a body splayed out at the foot of the stairs. The crumpled shape of a person, sprawled out on the ground, limbs twisted awkwardly.

'Oh my God. Stephanie? Are you all right? What happened?'

The words leave my mouth in a tangled, panicked screech and before I have time to call out to him, Ash is hurtling down the stairs towards me. His feet pounding with urgency.

'Shit. Did she fall?' Ash's words are vague and stilted as if they are coming from somewhere far off in the distance.

All I can do is nod in reply, because I am unable to speak now, which is just as well because Ash does not wait for my response. He's on his knees, crouching over Stephanie as he checks for any sign of life.

'Fuck,' he mutters shaking his head. Letting me know that there are none. She is still. Too still.

I watch as Ash, panicking now, feels for the pressure point on her neck, his fingers pressing firmly just below her ear. Nothing. He moves down towards one of Stephanie's wrists. Clasping her limp hand in his as he checks for her pulse. For some kind of movement.

I've gone into shock. The sight of Stephanie's lifeless body at Ash's feet triggers something visceral inside me. And I am back there again, staring down at my mother.

Vacant eyes staring ahead at nothing. Not breathing. Dead.
Another dead body.

'Rosie?'

I hear Ash's voice, but my brain can't seem to compute with my mouth. My mother is dead. That's all I can think as I stand there gormlessly watching the scene unfolding before me. I am useless in situations like this. Unlike Ash, who is always so good in times of crisis and panic. An expert at staying calm and keeping his cool.

He'd done it that night too. Taken control of the situation, after the brutal shove had lifted my mother from her feet, launching her backward in slow motion. I recall how her skull cracked loudly against the edge of the coffee table. All that blood. Ruining the new carpet. It's funny that had been the first thought that had entered my head, on seeing the spray of dark red splattered across my mother's expensive new carpet. Especially when the carpet was so easily replaced.

My mother is dead! My mother is dead!

I've been blocking it out. The trauma of the past few days. What happened to my mother, our lives living on the streets, George being so sick. A strange noise echoes loudly inside my head, like that of an injured or dying animal, groaning in agony.

It takes a few seconds for me to realise that the sound is not inside my head at all. It's coming from me. I am wailing.

'Rosie.' Ash raises his voice again, trying his hardest to make me snap out of it only the sound doesn't stop. Still it pours out from me, as I stand there staring down at Stephanie. Dumbstruck.

Unable to move, to think straight. To speak coherently.

Ash had shouted at me that night too, at my mother's house. Ordering me to calm down when I'd started to become hysterical. Grabbing the phone from my hand, forbidding me from calling the police.

'It was an accident, Rosie. Please. Don't call them. Don't tell the police. We'll lose everything.'

We.

He spoke as if we were one, the same person, the same entity. As if we would both be punished for what happened.

As if both of us did it. 'They'll take George.'

That had been the way he'd stopped me from telling the police in the end. I couldn't risk them taking my baby from me.

'Rosie.'

My cries have subsided, I realise. I am hyperventilating now, struggling for air. A panic attack.

BREATHE!

You're okay. You're in Kay's house. You're safe.

Only I am not okay. Somehow it's happening all over again. I stare down at Stephanie's broken, awkward body and wonder how death seems to follow us wherever we go.

'Stephanie, can you hear me?'

Ash has given up on me, he is focusing his attention back on Stephanie now, desperate to get her to respond to his voice.

'You're going to be okay. You had a bad fall.'

Has she had a fall?

Is that what this is? Just a bit of bad luck? One of those unfortunate freak accidents that simply happen sometimes? I'm desperate to believe that it's the truth, only I can't shake the feeling of foreboding that this has nothing to do with being bad luck at all. Every sense in my body now feels heightened and there's a heaviness inside my chest telling me that something isn't right here. That this was not a random accident. Ash's words the night before come back to me.

If Kay doesn't deal with her, I might have to. I won't let anyone hurt my family.

Is this Ash's way of dealing with her? Of making sure she didn't chance her luck when Kay wasn't around and make a call to the police. Because Ash doesn't trust her. He's made that perfectly clear and Stephanie's fall seems orchestrated. A grasped opportunity.

'Did you push her?' The accusation leaves my mouth in an urgent whisper, as if even I don't want to hear it. Because once this question is spoken out loud, it makes it real. And this is all real. This *is* happening. Stephanie is laying unresponsive at the bottom of the stairs less than a day after she'd blackmailed us to leave.

That can't just be a coincidence.

'What?' Ash replies, vaguely, as if he hasn't heard me.

'Did. You. Push. Her,' I repeat louder. Forcing Ash to answer me.

'Of course I didn't push her...' Ash starts, but we are both distracted then by the movement on the floor at our feet, as Stephanie's eyes flicker open and she stares straight up at us. A strange, twisted look of confusion on her face as she tries to work out where she is.

'She's not dead,' I mutter manically on repeat. 'Oh, thank God. She's not dead.'

'It's okay, Stephanie, you had a nasty fall. But you're going to be okay.' Ash bends down and places a hand reassuringly on Stephanie's arm.

'What on earth?'

I look up and see Kay, standing at the top of the stairs trying to make sense of the scene that is unravelling before her.

'Stephanie? What happened? Is she okay?'

'She had a nasty fall. I think she must have tripped up on some of those boxes we moved earlier.'

The boxes that Ash moved. Had he left them there on purpose, a safety hazard at the top of the stairs that someone could easily trip over? He is pointing fingers. Making Kay feel bad. Because it's her stuff that's piled up high everywhere. Her stuff he moved to the top of the staircase. Ash is good at that. Redirecting everyone's focus away from him.

'I think she's going to be okay. Maybe a bit of mild concussion, but other than that she's fine,' Ash continues.

'She doesn't look fine,' I say, taking in the bulbous, egg-shape bump in the middle of her forehead and the blood trickling from the jagged cut above her brow bone.

'You're okay aren't you, Stephanie?' Ash says, as if to prove his point and to my surprise Stephanie obediently nods her head, the confused look on her face telling me that she isn't completely coherent. She probably doesn't know exactly what it is she is agreeing with him about.

'I'll call an ambulance.' I grab the house phone from the hallway's dresser. Determined that this time, no matter what Ash says. I am going to call for help, because I will not have this on my conscience too.

'NO! Don't call anyone.'

The order is short and sharp. Delivered with so much force that it stops me in my tracks.

It's Kay's voice. Not Ash's.

'Don't call an ambulance, Rosie. If you do, they might have to notify the police...'

'But look at her...' I start, knowing Kay is only saying this for our benefit. Because she knows involving the emergency services might mean that Stephanie will get a chance to speak to them alone. She might tell them that Kay is harbouring criminals here. That we are wanted by the police. Especially if Stephanie is coherent enough to know she hadn't fallen at all, Ash had pushed her. Because despite his denial, I know this is all down to him.

'Kay's right, Stephanie doesn't need an ambulance, she'll be fine.' Ash stares at me. Willing me to do as they both say and put down the phone.

'Bring her up to my room, Ash, Stephanie can get some proper rest up here. She can have my bed,' Kay says.

It's a compromise, but it's better than nothing. If Kay seems convinced Stephanie will be okay and she doesn't need medical help, then that's good enough for me. Reluctantly I put down the phone.

'She's got a huge bump on her head though,' I state, not sure if putting Stephanie to bed is the wisest of moves. 'She was out cold when we first got here. So, she must have blacked out. What if she's concussed? Letting her sleep might not be the best idea right now.'

'She's had a shock, Rosie. That's all. Let her lie down for bit and recover,' Kay says with a finality that tells me that this conversation is over. She is Stephanie's grandmother. This is her house. Her decision.

And she is right.

Though as Ash wraps his arm tightly around Stephanie and helps her to her feet, I wonder if Kay is suspicious of Ash's actions too. If she blames him for Stephanie's fall and she's eager to get her granddaughter away from him.

Standing finally, Stephanie moves slowly, wincing in pain with each step as she struggles to put her weight on one of her ankles.

'Come on, Stephanie, you're okay. I've got you,' Ash says, jovially. Playing it down as he tries to encourage Stephanie up the stairs towards Kay's bedroom.

'Get off me,' Stephanie mutters, trying to shake Ash's hand away from her arm, only he holds on to her tighter.

'Hey, it's okay. I'm not going to hurt you. I'm only trying to help,' Ash says, feeding her with this new narrative in the hope that she'll believe him.

'Ash is helping you up to bed, Stephanie. Where you can rest for a bit,' I chime in for good measure, out of habit. Always backing him up. Wanting people to only see the good in him.

Only when Stephanie turns to me and meets my gaze, I finally see it. How there is something so much worse than just pain shining out from Stephanie's eyes.

Genuine fear.

She knows it too, I think.

Stephanie didn't fall. She was pushed.

26

STEPHANIE

I wake.

My eyes strain through the darkness of this unfamiliar room. Catching the small slither of light that seeps in from the narrow gap beneath the bedroom door. I am in Kay's bedroom. In Kay's bed. At the very top of the house, which explains why there's such an absence of noise. Unsure how long I've been asleep for, I guess that it must be some time because it's pitch black and the middle of the night. Everyone else in the house will be asleep now.

I try to move, to sit up, only an agonising burning pain shoots from my ankle up the entire length of my body. It's broken. I don't need a doctor to confirm that. It's battered like the rest of me. Every part of my body feels tender and sore as if I've just been beaten up. My body used as a punchbag, rained upon with endless sharp kicks and savage punches. I close my eyes and try to envisage how I've ended up here.

Then I remember the fall.

Me, standing at the top landing, about to take the stairs. A strong shove of a hand in the small of my back.

I was pushed.

My body propelling forward, the unexpected loss of balance making my head whip backward. My feet left the ground, suddenly weightless, I was flying. Gathering momentum, falling fast. Then crashing down. My head and torso repeatedly smacking against each step, until finally an explosion at the back of my skull as my body finally slammed to a stop on the ground.

Oblivion came after that.

Then Rosie and Ash's blurred faces. They'd been the first things I'd seen when I'd finally come around. Stood over me, speaking in hushed whispers, oblivious to the fact that I'd regained consciousness.

You pushed her. Rosie's words.

Talking about me as if I wasn't even there. Then minutes later.

Thank God. She's not dead. She's not dead.

That had galled me. How Rosie had started mumbling incoherently, as if she was the one in shock. Her, not me, the one who had actually just seen my whole life flash before my eyes.

They tried to kill me.

Ash had tried to kill me.

He had pushed me down the stairs in a bid to silence me after the threats I'd made earlier.

One more night. But then I want you gone.

The cocky bravado I'd displayed had been foolish. I see that now. I should never have agreed to let them stay here for just one more night. The extra time I'd given them had bought them more time to make a plan to shut me up for good. Luckily for me, this time, Ash hadn't succeeded.

My phone.

I'll call the police now, tell them that I am in danger. That Kay is in danger. Ash has already tried to kill me once. I'm not going to give him the opportunity of attempting to do it again. I feel around under the duvet, frantically patting at my tracksuit bottoms to no avail. My heart sinks as I realise my pockets are empty. Remembering now that my phone is missing.

'Oh, there she is. Sleeping Beauty. You lost something?' A voice cuts through the darkness startling me and my blood runs cold.

It's Ash's voice.

I hadn't realised there was anyone else here in the room with me.

My vision adjusts to the darkness now and I'm just about able to make out the shadowy outline of his figure, sat on the chair at the foot of Kay's bed.

How long had he been sat there, watching me?

'That was a nasty fall you had.'

I hear it, the mocking tone to his words. The way Ash tries to mask his sarcasm with concern. Only I am not buying it.

'Do you remember how it happened?'

He is testing me. Trying to find out how much of the incident I can recall. Whether or not I know that he was the one who had pushed me. If I am going to be brave enough, or stupid enough, to say it.

'I fell. I think...' I say vaguely, playing along. I attempt to shake my head, only the movement causes a shooting pain inside my skull, so severe that it makes me feel sick. 'I don't really remember.'

'Yeah, that's right. You did. You fell down the stairs. Rosie's been worrying that you might have concussion, so we've all decided to take turns in sitting with you. Just in case.'

'In case of what?' I manage to mutter, my mouth going dry, causing my words to croak as they leave my mouth.

In case I remember what really happened?

In case I try to get help or try to run?

'I don't know.' Ash gives a small chuckle. 'Rosie seems to be convinced that concussion can have delayed complications. She said she saw it once on some TV show. If you sleep for too long, or too deeply, after a bang like you had to your head, it could be fatal.'

Fatal.

The word hangs in the air between us causing me to shift awkwardly in the bed. I'd only just woken up, hadn't I? And I feel like I might have been asleep for a while. Is that what Ash was hoping, that something fatal would happen to me on his watch, and he could blame it on my concussion?

I try to move my legs only they feel heavy and weighted and I realise that I am trapped. If I need to scream out for help, to alert anyone that I am in trouble, no one would be able to hear me call out from up here.

I can't run either, I can't get away. Not with my ankle hurt so badly, and I know it's bad. Because even with my leg stretched out on the bed and the support of the mattress beneath it, an almighty pain radiates from it. I'll be lucky if I can even stand and put my full weight on it, let alone try and make any attempt at a getaway.

'Listen, Stephanie, I've been thinking. I know we didn't get off to the best start.' Ash keeps his voice slow and controlled as if he is making a real effort to carefully select his words before he says them. 'But it looks like myself and Rosie are going to be sticking around for a little bit longer now. You know, to help Kay sort through all her things and well, to look after you...' Ash pauses, clearly wanting a reaction from me, and despite the way my body tenses, my hands balling into tight fists at my sides, I refuse to give him the satisfaction of one.

Looking after me? The audacity of him. He almost killed me.

'I guess, what I'm trying to say is, why don't you and I put our differences aside for a bit? Call it a truce of sorts.'

I imagine his shark-like smile, the shiftiness of his eyes as he speaks. This is not a question. We both know that Ash does not require an answer from me.

'Rosie and I won't be going anywhere, anytime soon, Stephanie, so you may as well just accept that,' Ash says, and I hear the underlying threat in his tone. He is letting me know in no uncertain terms that he has won. That there's nothing I can do about any of this. Not yet, anyway.

'My head hurts,' I say finally, changing the subject because I have no intention of agreeing to a truce with this man. Nor do I want an argument.

'Here. Kay left some painkillers and water out for you. Let me give you a hand.'

Before I can refuse, Ash is standing at my side. Peeling back the aluminium foil from the plastic, before dispensing two tablets from the blister pack that Kay has left on the side for me. Then, holding a glass of water to my lips, I obediently drink the tablets down.

'Get some more rest,' Ash says, placing the glass back down and returning to his seat.

Ready to sit there in the darkness and watch me some more.

I close my eyes. Not to sleep, because I won't sleep now. But to shut him out. I know that the only chance I really have at getting away from him is if I keep my cool and not let on that I know I'm in any real danger. I'm going to have to bide my time and wait it out until the morning. I can get Kay on her own then.

I'll tell her that it was Ash who pushed me. She'll listen this time. She has to. These people are not messing around. They are unhinged and I am genuinely scared for my life. Scared for both our lives. I made an awful mistake by underestimating the lengths that these people are prepared to go in a bid to keep their freedom. To stay here in Kay's house. For now, I am going to have to go along with Ash's sick, twisted game. His pretence of a truce.

Because I'm not going anywhere, anytime soon.

I am at these people's mercy now.

27

ROSIE

'Good morning,' I say, as Stephanie finally stirs.

I've sat and waited patiently for hours for Stephanie to wake and now that she has, I am shocked at the sight of her.

'Oh, you're looking a lot better today,' I lie, because I don't want to cause her any more added distress than she's already gone through. Only the truth is she looks awful. The skin around her eye is worse now, reminding me of a fallen, bruised apple. Shades of brown and purple just beneath its flesh, as it starts to turn soft and mushy and rotten.

'Ouch!' She winces, as she shifts awkwardly on the bed, trying to sit up.

'How are you feeling?' I say, knowing that it's a stupid question, but I don't know what else to say as I offer out my hand so that I can help her to manoeuvre herself into an upright position. Stephanie shrugs my hand away.

'I don't want your help.'

'I just want to try and make you more comfortable,' I say, vowing silently to myself not to take Stephanie's reaction to me so personally. Reminding myself how she's in a lot of pain. She's banged her head hard and she's groggy. Probably severely concussed. She's not herself right now.

So instead of being offended, I focus on rearranging and plumping up the pillows behind her, so that when she finally sits back against them, she'll feel a little more comfortable. Anything to make myself useful. Anything to show her that I genuinely feel awful about the state she's in.

'Where's Ash?' Stephanie hisses Ash's name with so much venom that it frightens me. I wonder how much Stephanie remembers about yesterday.

'I took over from Ash a few hours ago,' I say, letting her know that she hasn't been left alone. That I am doing my bit too. That nothing else untoward will happen to her now I am watching over her.

She is safe here.

Because despite the tension that has been building between us all before this, I'm not completely heartless.

'Kay?'

I follow Stephanie's gaze towards the bedroom door, as she shouts out, looking expectantly at the doorway as if willing Kay to come through it.

'You just missed your nan actually. She's just popped out.'

'You're lying. I can hear her,' Stephanie says defiantly before calling out.

'Kay? Kay?'

'I promise you, Stephanie, she's not here. She's taken Max out for his walk. Look, are you sure you're okay? Maybe that bang to your head has you hearing things, because all I can hear is the TV.'

I watch as Stephanie sinks back down into the bed, no longer shouting out her nan's name. But the expression on her face tells me that she doesn't believe Kay has left the house. She thinks I'm lying, that I'm keeping her away from her. Only she is exhausted and doesn't have the energy in her to fight me on it.

'Kay did pop in to see how you were doing before she left. About ten minutes ago. She made you this. It should still be warm. It smells good.' I nod to the tray of food that has been placed next to the bed, before picking it up and placing it gently on Stephanie's lap.

'I don't want it,' Stephanie says, though we both know by the loud rumble of her stomach at the smell of the warm, syrupy porridge, that she is lying.

'You should eat something, Stephanie. You need to get your strength up and get better.' I try again and that seems to do the trick, because Stephanie picks up her spoon, and starts devouring the porridge in huge, greedy mouthfuls. As if purposely forcing it down, not caring about the taste at all. She just wants to get better again. She just wants to be out of this bed.

'Right. That's the last of them. It's all clear out there now.'

Ash stands in the bedroom doorway, carrying the last of the boxes from Kay's bedroom, his sudden presence startles us both and I watch with fascination as his eyes rest on Stephanie, as if he too is assessing the damage that's been caused. Then clearing his throat, his awkward cough turns into a choke, as if he is trying to push his next words back down instead of saying them out loud.

'I've cleared the landing,' he says finally, his eyes not leaving Stephanie and I know he is thinking how awful she looks. Broken and battered as she lay in Kay's bed. An abnormally huge lump protruding from her head.

'There shouldn't be any more accidents,' he says, in his pathetic attempt at offering Stephanie some kind of reassurance, only I hear the mockery in his voice, and while I'm certain that Stephanie must hear it too, she doesn't give him the satisfaction of any kind of reaction.

'Are you all right up here?' Ash finally turns his attention back to me and I nod my head.

'Good. Well... I'll go and make a start downstairs in the kitchen, then.'

'Okay. Great.' I wait for Ash to leave before turning my attention back to Stephanie.

She has stopped eating. Setting her spoon down on the edge of her bowl as if she's unwilling to pick it up again, I see that she can't, because her hands are violently shaking.

'Are you okay, Stephanie?' I ask, keeping my voice low, in case Ash is still hovering just outside the doorway, listening in.

Because there's a strong chance that right now, he might be doing that. He's got form for it. Sneaking around and staying under the radar, while listening in on people's whispered conversations. He's admitted as much to me before. That knowledge is power. Ash had used that tactic many times over the years. He'd had to. Using things against people like a weapon to get what he wanted was a form of survival to Ash. He did what he had to, to get by. He'd blackmailed a friend's dad once, he'd told me. Caught him red-handed, having an affair and threatened to tell unless he was paid off.

I'd seen the way he'd manipulated the homeless man in the shop doorway too, the night he'd stolen his tent and sleeping bag. Befriending him, until he thought he could trust him. He'd gone off to have a wash in the local leisure centre toilets, only to come back and find all his things gone.

Though, naively, I hadn't realised that one day he might use these tactics on me. It isn't just Stephanie Ash doesn't trust; he doesn't trust me either. I've seen the way he watches me lately, the way he follows me around, constantly checking that I'm not saying anything that might incriminate us both.

'I'm fine.' Stephanie pushes her bowl towards me, letting me know she's lost her appetite now.

'Are you sure you don't want any more?' I try, but Stephanie refuses, shaking her head.

'That's the only good thing that's come from any of this.' I nod my head in the direction of the doorway where Ash had just been stood, happy to change the subject. 'Your nan must have woken up with an epiphany this morning. She finally agreed to get rid of all of her stuff. All of it. She means it too. We've spent hours already this morning sorting through all her things ready for the clearance company she hired to come and pick it all up. You must have given her quite a scare. She's blaming herself, of course. Even though I've told her that it wasn't her fault. She couldn't have predicted that you would have...'

I stop talking.

Kay couldn't have predicted that Stephanie would have, what?

Fallen? Tripped? Been pushed?

'Do you have any memory of what happened? Any recollection at all?' I ask, trying to make my questions sound casual. To not let on that despite Kay's acceptance of it being some kind of freak accident, I have my own suspicions about what's gone on.

'I'm not sure, I can't remember,' Stephanie says, though I'm not sure that I believe her. She won't confide in me, of course she won't and why would she? She knows my loyalties lie with Ash.

'I hit my head and I think my ankle is broken.' Moving her feet in the bed, as if to demonstrate what she's saying is true, she cries out in pain, clearly uncomfortable. Frustrated too, because she wants to get up, to go downstairs. Only Stephanie isn't going anywhere for a while yet.

'Kay said that you need to stay in bed, Stephanie. You need to rest.'

'You're not listening to me. I've broken my ankle. What I need is a fucking doctor.'

And I nod, because I know she is right.

'I wanted to call an ambulance, but your nan said not to.

She said that she'll take you to A&E later on today. When things have calmed down a bit.'

Things calming down being Stephanie, I think. Though I don't dare say as much, instead I let that sentence hang in the air between us and wonder if Stephanie is capable of reading between the lines.

'It's weird though, because at first I thought that Kay doesn't want to risk you talking to the paramedics, or asking for the police, because she thinks you might still try and cause trouble for me and Ash.'

Stephanie has secrets too. Aren't they Kay's exact words she had said to me the day before?

'But it's not me and Ash that Kay is trying to protect here, is it? She's trying to protect you from something too, isn't she?'

I pause, willing myself to say what I am thinking.

'Is it something to do with your mother's death?'

I am overstepping the line, I know that, but I need to at least try and make some sense of this all. Because I'm almost certain now that it isn't just me and Ash that are hiding something, Kay and Stephanie are hiding something bad too.

'What did Kay tell you?' Stephanie asks, her piercing blue eyes boring intently into mine and just like that, unwittingly she's given me my answer.

I knew it.

She and Kay *are* hiding something.

'She didn't tell me anything. Not really,' I say honestly. 'Only your stories about how long you've been living here with Kay don't match up. At dinner the other night, you said that you moved in a couple of months ago. But yesterday, Kay told me that you've been estranged. She said she barely knows you. That you only moved in with her the night that your mum died,' I say, trying to read the look on Stephanie's face, only the girl, staring blankly ahead, is determined not to give anything away.

She's trying too hard not to react, I decide. Which tells me that I might be on the right track.

I push harder.

'She said you called her that night in hysterics begging her to come to your house, but by the time she'd got there, your mother was already dead. You weren't living here for months, were you? You only came back here that night. Why would you lie about that? Did Kay give you an alibi so the police wouldn't find out that you were there when your mother died?'

Stephanie shifts awkwardly in the bed and still she doesn't look at me.

'Why would Kay refuse an ambulance? What could be so bad that she would rather take her chances and risk your health like that?'

I see it, how tense her jaw is set, how her tear-filled eyes are fixed on the wall so that she doesn't have to look at me.

Because she can't. She knows if she does, I'll see the truth. She won't be able to lie any more.

'You did something to your mum, didn't you? You had something to do with her death. And Kay is doing everything in her power to help you cover it up. She's even protecting you from yourself, isn't she? Stopping the police from coming here in case you end up saying something you shouldn't and getting yourself in trouble.'

I pause giving Stephanie a chance to deny my allegations but she doesn't, so I know I am onto something here.

'I've been through a lot the past few days myself, Stephanie,' I say, honestly. Not sure why I'm telling her this, only that perhaps, if I do confess, if I open up to her, she'll see that I mean her no harm. That she really can trust me.

'We've probably got more in common than we'd both care to admit.' I push, knowing how much we had both been through the past few weeks.

I suddenly feel protective of her and wonder if perhaps we

can help each other. Maybe we could look out for one another, now that I know exactly what Ash is capable of. The lengths he'll go to, to make sure that the police don't come with all their long list of questions.

Despite myself, I want her to know that she can trust me.

'Look, whatever happened, Stephanie, whatever you did... We all make mistakes.'

Suddenly I want to say it. I want to confess to Stephanie what Ash and I are running away from. Because she might understand it too. She has also lost her mother. Only just before I go to speak, Stephanie lets out a small bitter cackle, stopping me before I've even formed my next sentence.

'You and me are nothing alike, Rosie. You don't know *anything* about me. You don't know anything about what happened that night. But I know all about you,' she starts. 'I know that you put yourself and Ash before the health of your own baby, it's your fault he got sick. And you're taking advantage of Kay's good nature. You're not helping her sort through her things, you are both stealing from her. You are both liars and thieves and *you* are a bad mother.'

I am about to deny everything that Stephanie accuses me of being, only the words bad mother hit me like a punch to my gut.

Am I a bad mother?

We did put George's life in danger to try and save our own. And we are thieves. I think of the tent and the sleeping bag that Ash stole. The car window I broke in order to steal the pile of lose change. Kay's belongings stashed beneath our bed. Only they are not stashed there any more I realise, as Stephanie reaches into her jogging bottom pockets and retrieves the gold locket and chain that I had found in Kay's bedroom the previous day.

'I found this and some of Kay's other belongings stashed underneath *my* bed.'

I think about lying. About pretending she is wrong, that the necklace is mine, only as Stephanie holds the chain up, the locket hangs open. A photograph of an unmistakable, younger looking Kay stares back at me, her arms wrapped around a little girl. Amanda, Kay's daughter I assume. A photo of a tiny baby occupies the second space. Stephanie.

'I know you've taken my phone too.'

'I didn't take your phone,' I say, knowing that in the scheme of things, it really doesn't matter what else we've taken. She has called us out now.

'We're not thieves...' I say weakly, because even as I say it, I have nothing to add that will offer me a worthy defence. Stephanie is right.

A liar, a thief and a bad mother is exactly what I've become.

How have I allowed myself to sink so low? When did I stop being Rosie and become this person I no longer recognise instead?

'You gave us an ultimatum and told us to leave, Stephanie. You backed us into a corner. What other choice do you think we had? We needed money, especially if we're going back out onto the streets again.'

'If,' Stephanie says, her voice shaking with anger now. 'That's just it, Rosie. "If" wasn't part of the plan. You had no intention of actually going, did you? That's why you both told Kay about me threatening to call the police, that's why you took my phone with the footage of you breaking into that car. And that's why Ash tried to kill me by pushing me down the stairs.'

There. She finally said it.

Ash did push her.

I had suspected as much, but part of me hadn't wanted to believe that Ash could be capable of doing something so cruel. He'd lied to me.

'I want to be left alone,' Stephanie finally says, closing her eyes for a few seconds as if she suddenly has trouble keeping them open and I realise this is too much for her. All these questions and accusations. She's not ready for intense conversations like this yet.

'I can't just leave you,' I begin, only Stephanie shuts me down.

'Yes you can. I don't need you sitting here watching over me. Babysitting me. Pretending that you actually give a shit when you and your psycho of a boyfriend are the reason I'm here like this in the first place. So you can go. Go on, fuck off. Leave me alone.'

She shoves the tray in my direction and I feel fresh tears form in my eyes. Not wanting to let her see me cry, I get up and leave the room, knowing full well, that everything she sees in me is true.

I am a liar. A thief. A bad mother. And so much worse than that.

I can't stay here. I need to take George as far away as possible, from this house and all its madness. I need to get far away from Ash, because I have no idea what he is capable of doing next.

28

STEPHANIE

My breath is shallow and no matter how hard I try to suck the air down into my lungs, I can't seem to breathe.

How I managed to hide this from Rosie, to hold it all in, until she'd finally left the room, I'll never know. Only I'd been so determined not to give the girl the satisfaction of knowing that Kay breaking my trust by saying anything to Rosie at all has affected me this badly.

I thought I could trust her.

Manoeuvring myself into a sitting up position on the edge of the bed, I let my legs hang over the side. Wincing, I stare down at my swollen ankle, twice the size of my other one. It's broken, the bone sticking out in at an abnormal angle beneath the skin, making it appear deformed and I know without even trying that I won't be able to walk on it.

I feel sick and dizzy and at first, as the room starts to spin wildly, I convince myself that it's because of the pain. That it's my body's natural response to the agony that is radiating all the way through me. Only it goes on for so long, my sickness not subsiding even when the pain does, that I am forced to rest my head in my hands. Because without the support, I can barely keep my head upright.

I am weak now and can barely open my eyes and I know that something is very, very wrong. Or perhaps I'm being irrational. Am I? Perhaps I'm not in danger in this moment at all. Despite the overwhelming sense of terror that I feel, the rational part of my brain is trying to tell me that what I am experiencing right now, is just another panic attack.

If I stay calm, I can breathe my way through it.

I will be fine.

I know this, because I've done it before. My last attack had been the night my mother died, only like much of that evening, I'd blocked it out. This is the first attack I've had since then, and I brace myself because, my God, that last one had floored me. So much so, that I had erased it from my mind completely, refusing to allow myself to think of anything at all that had happened that evening. It was all too painful, it's all too painful even now for me to comprehend.

My mum laying unresponsive on the floor, staring into space at nothing. Her eyes blank and vacant as she muttered incoherently how she couldn't do this any more. This life. She'd begged me for something to help her take the edge off her horrendous meltdown. Begged me. And I had seen my mother's darkest, bleakest of days, many times before this, but this was something else completely. A whole other lever of sheer and utter desperation. My mother was reduced to nothing more than a crying, screaming mess. Scratching out huge gouges in her skin and tearing out clumps of her long red hair.

Please, Stephanie. I'll never ask you for anything again. I promise.

I was terrified at what my mother might do to herself if I didn't give in to her demands and comply. Unable to face the thought of her being carted off again to some secure institution, and me where would I go? Another children's home or foster family. I am sixteen now, who would want me?

Please, Stephanie. Help me, baby. One last time. I'll never ask you for anything ever again. If you love me...

And I did love her. My God, I did love her.

So much so that part of me still can't believe she has gone from this world. That I'll never, ever see that vibrant smile of hers again. I'll never feel her arms around me. Holding me tight, telling me how much she loved me. Because despite everything, she had loved me and she was a good mother.

A strained sob escapes my mouth as a wave of almighty grief all but floors me.

That last dose of methadone I'd given her had been enough to push her over the edge. I believed her when she'd told me how an extra dose wouldn't affect her badly, that she'd been on the stuff for so long, she was practically immune to its benefits now. Which was why she was clucking so badly that night. It wasn't strong enough, she'd needed more. And I, scared that she'd go back on something worse if I didn't give in to her demands, stupidly, foolishly believed her. Serving her up that final dose of poison.

My mother had kept her final promise to me, she hadn't lied. She really would never ask anything of me ever again.

I killed her.

I hadn't meant to. Of course I hadn't. I'd loved my mother dearly. Despite her erratic, chaotic lifestyle and the way she'd chosen to bring me up. She'd always tried her best. Done her very best.

Only the night she'd died, she'd been so wrapped up in her addiction and her need for oblivion, that was all that seemed to matter to her. As soon as I gave it to her, I knew by her reaction that it was too much. Instantly incoherent, foaming at the mouth, her eyes rolling in the back of her head.

I had panicked, taking the number from my mother's phone,

I had called the only person in the world that I could think to call. My estranged grandmother, Kay. My only other living relative I knew of.

And Kay had come. She had shown up for me. Despite the horrific circumstances that she'd walked into, despite the tragic loss of her one and only daughter. She'd calmly taken control of the situation, stopping me from calling the police and handing myself in and ruining the rest of my life. Because she was right, wasn't she? My mother's death wasn't my fault, what was the point in both of us losing our lives? There was a way out of this, she had told me. A way to salvage something from this catastrophic mess. A chance to finally build our own relationship.

If I left with her that night, Kay would be my alibi.

We concocted a story, both of us saying that I had lived with Kay for the past two months. That I wasn't there that night the night my mother died. I wasn't the one who had found her.

My mother was a known user, she'd had many relapses over the years. It's not as if the authorities would class her death as suspicious. They wouldn't go looking. All I had to do was lay low at Kay's until it all blew over. The autopsy would come back stating an accidental overdose and we could all go back to normal.

A new normal, because our lives would never be the same.

Kay was right though, her way meant that there would be no fuss, that no one would need to know the truth.

Only by telling Rosie that I'd come here the night of my mother's death, Kay had jeopardised all of that. Rosie was now suspicious, and she would use it against me. Rosie and Ash both would, if they had to.

I think about Ash sitting at the end of my bed this morning when I woke. The veiled threat he'd made about how they intended to stay here for much longer now and how there was nothing that I could do about it. If I call the police, they will use this new information that Kay has given them against me. I am certain of that. They will stop at nothing.

Breathe, Stephanie, breathe.

I need to stop thinking about them. About my mother too. Reliving those tragic, painful moments in my head, because it's making my panic attack worse. This time it's so severe that I really do think I might die. My heart is pounding like a drum inside my chest and no amount of steady breathing is helping me.

They will stop at nothing.

The words spin inside my head, as I feel the constriction start in the back of my throat. Like it's gradually closing up. My tongue expanding, filling my mouth. An awful, terrifying revelation hits me. This is not a panic attack at all.

I'm having some kind of reaction. How? I stare at the half-empty bowl of porridge that sits on the side. Covered in a thick layer of honey. Sickly sweet. To mask the taste of anything bitter that it had been laced with.

Have they drugged me?

Rosie told me Kay had made it and I'd only had her word for that, but I'd naively believed her. And hadn't Ash come and stood in the doorway, watching me intently? Was he making sure that I'd finished it?

Was it him, or was Rosie in on this too? Because I had heard Kay downstairs, I'm sure of it. Rosie had lied to me, telling me that Kay had gone out with Max. She'd tried to convince me that I am hearing things. That the voices inside my head are not real, they are part of the concussion.

I think of the tablets Ash had fed me earlier too. He'd told me that Kay had left them out for me.

Painkillers.

Though all I have done since the moment they've brought me in this room is sleep.

'If you sleep for too long, or too deeply, after a bang like you had to your head, it could be fatal.'

Ash's words when I'd finally gained consciousness.

This is why they are the only ones taking it in turns to look after me. This is all part of their plan. Ash and Rosie are deceiving Kay by making out that they are caring for me, all the while they are trying to kill me off slowly with a painful overdose.

My chest is tight, and I am wheezing now.

Getting up from the bed, I try and stand but the searing agony that shoots up from my ankle makes me bite down with excruciating pain. I taste the blood from where my tooth has penetrated my lip. Grimacing, I hobble awkwardly forward. Despite the fact that I can barely put any weight on that foot now, I know I have no other choice but to move.

I need to get to Kay. She's my only chance.

If I stay here much longer, I know that I'll die.

29

STEPHANIE

Hobbling, trying so hard to keep the weight off my broken ankle, I'm not sure how I've managed to make it down the stairs. I feel the sweat prickle across my hairline, my face contorted with pain as I scan the rooms for signs of Ash and Rosie.

They are nowhere to be seen.

A noise outside makes me move unsteadily towards the window and as I peer out I see them loading bags and boxes onto the back of a van. All of Kay's things. I wonder how much they have stashed away in their bedroom now, how much they've stolen from her without her noticing.

'Kay?' I call out, but there's no answer, then as an afterthought I call out for Max. When he doesn't come either I wonder if Rosie hadn't been lying to me after all. Had Kay taken him out on a walk?

I make my way to the kitchen, the sheer force of will to find Kay masking the acute pain that shoots up my leg, every time my foot makes contact with the floor beneath me. I check for Max's lead on the hook behind the door and see that it's gone. I start to question myself about if Rosie was really telling me the truth. She said that I was hearing things, that it might be the concussion.

My head is banging, and my brain does feel foggy. I feel like I'm in a trance. Like I keep forgetting things. What did I come down here for? My phone. No, it's missing. I came here for Kay, but she is gone too.

About to leave the kitchen, I remember the laptop. Stashed away still beneath the chair. Maybe I can use that, I can send a message to the police that way. Grabbing it, I use the password from the crumpled piece of paper still concealed beneath it. Only there's no internet or at least the laptop won't connect, because nothing is happening. In my panic to get online quickly, before Ash and Rosie come back in, I am obviously doing something wrong. Tapping in the wrong letters and numbers into the password. Or in my confusion, I'm hitting the wrong key.

I don't have time for this.

Pushing it across the table with frustration, I am about to go back into the lounge to check the internet connection when I see them. The packet of tablets like the ones I have upstairs. Empty now, shoved behind the saucepan that's lined with the congealed contents of the porridge that Kay had apparently made for me. I pick it up and examine it properly. Sleeping tablets, not pain killers at all.

And I know then that it's all Ash and Rosie's doing. They have laced my food with sleeping tablets. Along with the ones they fed me while I was in the bedroom, I'm not sure how many I've had, but it explains the way that I feel right now, and I wonder if it might be enough to kill me.

Because I feel as if I might die.

I shove the packet inside my pocket, as more proof to present to Kay when I finally reveal to her who these people really are. What they are capable of doing.

My stomach is cramping, and my vision is blurry and it's all

I can do not to lie down on the floor and close my eyes. Only I know that I must stay awake. If I sleep now, I may never wake up again.

I need help.

I need to see a doctor.

Going into the lounge, I crouch down on the floor checking the internet hub beneath the TV stand. All the lights are off. And when I check the plug, I see that the cable that connects it all has been severed.

Someone has cut the wire on purpose.

Ash and Rosie.

First they took my phone. Now they're stopping me from getting any help at all. Blocking me from all contact with the outside world, any way they can.

If I die, Kay would be none the wiser. Because they'll lie to her, won't they? They'll say that I died because of the injury to my head. That I misplaced my phone, that the internet is down. They are full of excuses.

My eyes feel so heavy now. My body sinking into the carpet.

I must get up. I must.

But maybe if I close my eyes for a few seconds. A minute or two. Just to gather up some energy.

Just a little sleep.

My vision blurs into darkness and I give in to it.

30

KAY

I'm only just in through the backdoor for a few seconds, busy taking Max's lead off, when I hear the strange wheezing noise coming from the lounge.

'Rosie? Is that you love? Is everything okay with George?' I call out, thinking the worst. That Ash wasn't exaggerating about George getting worse, he really is going downhill fast. Especially if I can hear his wheezy breathing from all the way out here in the kitchen.

'Rosie?' I call out again, only when I get no reply, I make my way into the lounge to investigate for myself.

Taking a quick glance around the empty room, I start to convince myself that perhaps I am mistaken, perhaps I am hearing things that aren't really there, because I do that sometimes. Allow myself to imagine voices calling out to me from other rooms in the house.

I know it sounds strange, but it's a comfort thing mostly, pretending the voices are real so that I don't feel so completely and utterly alone all the time. Maybe that's what happening now I think, about to turn and go into the kitchen and make myself a nice hot drink. Then I see her. Stephanie, sprawled out on the living room floor.

'Stephanie?' I shout, rushing over to where my grand-daughter lay unresponsive on the carpet next to the television unit.

Is she dead?

'Stephanie? Can you hear me, Stephanie, are you okay?' I crouch at her side, sighing with relief as I see the slight rise and fall of her chest with every slow, laboured breath she takes. Her eyes flicker open, and she catches my gaze, only to close them again as she fails to fight off how exhausted she is. Her ankle is twisted at a strange angle, and I realise how it must have taken her all of her energy and effort to get down here. The pain she's in must be excruciating.

'Oh, Stephanie my darling. I think you've passed out from the pain. You shouldn't be down here. Not after the fall you had, you should be in bed. Look at the state of you, my love. You look exhausted.'

Rosie had warned me how battered and bruised Stephanie was, only I hadn't expected her to be quite so horrendous to look at. I am shocked at the sight of her. Her face and body are peppered black and blue with so many bruises, as if she's been beaten up. She looks almost unrecognisable. Up until now, I had only peered in from the bedroom doorway and checked on Stephanie from a distance, because this whole ordeal, so soon after Amanda's passing was just too much for me.

I didn't feel able for it.

So Rosie and Ash had kindly offered to take over. Volun-teering to make use of themselves and take it in turns to keep an eye on Stephanie for me, and I really appreciate that. The effort they are both going to, to make this arrangement work. To show me that this is doable. The five of us, together in this house.

Stephanie has done nothing but sleep, they've told me, and

I've been witness to that. Every time I've gone and stood in the doorway, to see how she is, she's been cocooned in the duvet. Her face partly concealed by the pillow and blankets as she slept.

Now though, as Stephanie's eyelids fight to stay open, it isn't just the huge, deformed protruding lump from the middle of her forehead that gives me a pause for concern. It's the crazed look in her eyes as she tries to focus, her eyes wide with fear, darting rapidly around the room. Reminding me of a frightened animal caught in a well-placed snare. Prey about to be hunted.

'Whatever is the matter, Stephanie?' I ask trying to calm her, only she looks past me as if she is trying to look for someone else. As if she is scared that someone else might be here in the room with me.

'You don't look well at all, love, come on, let's get you back to bed. You should be resting. Here, let me help you.' I hold out my arm for Stephanie to take, only she bats it away aggressively.

'I need an ambulance, Kay. I need help.'

At least that's what I think Stephanie is trying to say, only she's slurring her words now. Barely capable of stringing so much as a sentence together. If I didn't know any better, I'd think she was drunk.

'They're kill... trying to...'

Stephanie is panting now, her words are all jumbled.

'I can't understand what you're saying...'

'They. Are. Trying. To. Kill. Me.'

Stephanie grits her teeth, forcing her words out and I hear her clearly now.

'What in the world? Who?' I shake my head, a confused look spreading across my face. Convinced I must have misheard the girl. Only I know that I haven't when she speaks again, this time she takes her time, using every ounce of energy she has inside her. Purposely pronouncing her words more slowly.

'I didn't fall down the stairs,' Stephanie says, between long slow breaths. 'I was pushed. Ash pushed me. They've been giving me tablets, Kay. Sleeping pills. I think they've crushed some up and put them in the porridge you made for me.' She pauses again, impatiently sucking in air to her lungs.

'What porridge? I haven't made any porridge, Stephanie love. I've been out with Max,' I say. 'Listen love, you're not making much sense. You've had a really nasty bang to the head, and I think you're a bit confused. Rosie and Ash are trying to help you get better. They've spent hours upstairs in that room at your bedside, making sure that you don't slip unconscious again. They're only trying to help.'

I want Stephanie to know that so far Rosie and Ash have done nothing but show kindness in this situation. Both of them offering to sit in with her and keep an eye on her as she slept, so that I wouldn't have to. Because I'd been through enough the past few weeks, they'd both insisted and I hadn't bothered to argue. It was so nice to have someone finally looking out for me. Someone showing me that they care. That I matter too.

'Rosie told me you were in a bad way. She said you were a bit confused. Said that you were hearing voices.'

'Oh, I bet she did.' Stephanie laughs manically. 'This is what they want, Kay. They want you to think I'm crazy. Delirious. That I don't know what I'm saying, after the fall. But I do know what I'm saying, Kay. Please, you have to believe me.'

'Oh, Stephanie love. I know that it feels like what you're saying is true, but trust me, concussion can take hours to properly set in, days sometimes and unfortunately confusion and hallucinations are all part of it. Which is why you need to rest. Come on, let me take you back to bed.' I try once more, holding out my arm and willing Stephanie to take it, only still she refuses. Too fired up. Too desperate.

'Kay. You need to listen to me. We're not safe here. Ash threatened me. He told me that he and Rosie wouldn't be moving on and that there's nothing I can do about it. He told me that I have no choice but to accept it. And I heard them the other night, talking in whispers about staying here in this house. They were both talking as if this place might one day be purely theirs.'

I stay quiet, not wanting to antagonise the girl further. 'They're going to try and take your house, Kay. First, they're going to get rid of me and then it will be you next.' Stephanie raises her voice, her hand reaching for her forehead to stifle her obvious pain.

'Stephanie, darling. Ash isn't calling the shots around here, I am. Ash and Rosie are staying here longer, because I asked them to. Not for any other reason than that. They are helping me clear all my stuff out. Because I need to get rid of all of this junk and make this house safer. Rosie hasn't poisoned you or drugged you.'

I let out a small chuckle unable to hide my feelings that what Stephanie is saying is pure madness.

'The girl doesn't have it in her, Stephanie. Rosie is a good girl, she means well. I really don't think you've given either of them a chance...'

'Why won't you fucking listen to me? Ash pushed me. Then threatened me. Then this morning they put something in my food. They've drugged me, Kay. I can't fucking breathe. I can't fucking think straight. I need help.'

Unable to stand because of the pain in her ankle and the way that her whole body is shaking now, Stephanie doubles over as she says this, crawling across the floor. She wretches loudly, emptying the contents of her stomach out all over the carpet. Exhausted, drained of all her energy, she looks genuinely sick. As if any minute now, she is going to pass out. Yet still she moves, determined.

'Stephanie, darling. Please stop this. Stop this right now. You're scaring me.'

'Look,' Stephanie says, after dragging herself on all fours that last few inches over to where the landline and internet are plugged into the wall beneath the TV and holds up the purposely severed cable of the internet for me to see. 'My phone's gone missing and now the internet has been cut.'

'Cut? Are you sure? Only it might be mice?' I offer, only to see Stephanie close her eyes with frustration. 'Well, we get them sometimes coming in from the woodland. They've chewed through wires here before. I had an infestation under the floorboards a few years ago...' I trail off, because I know what she's thinking. That I'm still making excuses for these people, despite all her evidence against them that says otherwise.

'Why won't you believe that there's something sinister going on here? They are trying to kill me.'

I stay quiet, knowing anything I say will antagonise her further, because the truth is I don't believe her. I know Ash and Rosie haven't done the things she's accusing them of, only Stephanie is on a tangent now. Working herself up into a frenzied state, meanwhile her skin is getting paler. A film of sweat is forming across the surface and her lips are starting to turn a tinge of grey. 'It's like you're choosing not to see the bad in them. Like you just don't want to. But someone has deliberately cut the internet cable, Kay. It's been purposely sabotaged so we can't get online. They're cutting us off, Kay. They're trying to prevent us having any contact with the outside world. So that we can't ask anyone for help.' Stephanie is really panicking now, I can hear it in her voice.

'Don't you think it's strange how they're both desperate enough that they'll sleep in a tent with a baby? They'll break into cars to steal money. Yet when you offered to help them, to put them in touch with a charity that could offer them some temporary accommodation they refused. And instead of taking George to see a doctor, they've hidden him away in their room. He's not sick like they're trying to lead you to believe. He's better. They're telling you he's not so that you don't throw them out. They've been buying themselves more time. Ash pushed me down the stairs and now they're drugging me. We're not safe here, Kay. You know that, don't you? You invited them in. They want your house, Kay. They want this life. They don't want to leave.'

Stephanie stutters. All her energy exhausted now that she has tried to make me listen to her warped, exaggerated theories. She wobbles unsteadily before passing out.

31

ROSIE

'Do you think she's going to be okay?' I ask Kay, as we both stand at Stephanie's bedside silently staring down at the girl as Ash places her safely back into Kay's bed.

Stephanie looks awful, a sheen of sweat covering her skin like a plastic film and her mouth is slack, hanging open.

'She needs a doctor, Kay,' I say, unable to hide my concern as Stephanie remains unconscious.

Nothing seems to be able to wake her. Not even Ash, scooping her up into his arms and carrying her up three flights of stairs.

'She'll be fine. She just needs to sleep it off,' Kay says.

But Kay is wrong this time, Stephanie doesn't need more rest, she needs help.

'We should call an ambulance, or a doctor and get her looked at properly. Make sure she hasn't done any serious damage to herself. She took a real bang to her head, Kay.' Unable to hide the panic in my voice, I watch Ash position Stephanie's arms and legs in the bed, so that she'll be more comfortable.

Her body limp, a deadweight now. She doesn't move and I am genuinely scared for Stephanie's wellbeing.

As much as I am grateful that Kay wants to protect me and Ash, that she won't allow anyone to take George away from us, I know she's trying to protect Stephanie too. Only this isn't the way to do it, if Stephanie doesn't get urgent medical care soon, she might die. Yet still Kay refuses to acknowledge the gravity of the situation.

'She's showing all the signs of severe concussion,' I persevere, when Kay doesn't reply.

'It's not concussion,' Ash says dismissing the seriousness of Stephanie's injuries as he places the duvet around her.

'These were in her pocket.' He holds up an empty blister packet of pills before handing them to Kay.

'Oh God. I knew it,' Kay says sadly, shifting awkwardly in her seat as she inspects the medication, and I catch the edge to her voice that tells me I am clearly missing something glaringly obvious.

'You knew what? What are they?'

'Sleeping tablets,' Kay says, shaking her head sadly, as if her worst fears have just come true. 'They're mine. They went missing from the shelf in my lounge the first night she arrived here. Ash, love. Could you do me a favour and get me a glass of water? Actually, no scrap that. I'm going to need something stronger. Could you make me a mug of Ovaltine and stick an extra sugar in there for me?'

Seeing how Kay's complexion has paled, how the visible angst shines through the newly formed tears in her eyes, Ash does as he is asked without question. Leaving me and Kay alone in the room.

'Stephanie wasn't making much sense before she passed out, she was talking in riddles. Confused about what was going on around her.' It's a few moments before Kay speaks again and when she does she pauses as if she carefully selecting her next words. 'She made a couple of accusations against you and Ash. She claimed you both tried to drug her.'

Stephanie's allegations hang in the air like a question between us and I see the way Kay's eyes bore into mine as if she is searching them for my answer.

'Drug her? What? No, we didn't, Kay. I promise you. We wouldn't do that.' I shake my head refutably, only Kay continues.

'She thinks Ash pushed her down the stairs. She thinks you're both trying to kill her. That Ash is trying to kill her.'

I don't speak. I can't. Because part of me believes that Ash might have pushed Stephanie too. He's more than capable of it. He'd said as much himself. He'd do whatever it took to keep us together and protect his family. Was Ash drugging her too? Only if he was, why would he hand the empty packet of pills to Kay? Surely it would have been better for him to blame her rapid downhill decline on the injuries she's sustained from falling down the stairs.

Unless Ash's conscience had finally got the better of him. Stephanie looks really bad this time and whatever she has taken might actually kill her. Perhaps Ash, by giving Kay the tablets and letting her know exactly what it is that Stephanie has taken, is trying to unburden himself of his guilt? So if anything does happen to her now, this won't be all on him.

'I promise you, Kay. I haven't. I couldn't...'

'Of course you didn't, dear.' Kay squeezes my hand reassuringly, though she doesn't say the same about Ash and I wonder if she thinks it too.

'I don't know! Maybe it's me? Refusing to see what's been going on right in front of my own eyes. I should have read the signs, because they were all there. The erratic mood swings, the way she refuses to interact, preferring to shut herself away in her room than spend any time with me. The way she doesn't want either of you here.' Kay shakes her head, annoyed that it had taken her so long to see what was going on right before her eyes.

'She's been taking them since she got here, I had my suspicions about that. Only, I hadn't realised how dependent she's become on them. I guess being an addict is learned behaviour. And unfortunately Stephanie learned from the best of them. I've noticed the rapid decline to her mental health since she's been here. How her mother's death has brought so much trauma. I just thought she'd be okay in time,' Kay continues.

'As much as Stephanie's life was hard with her mother, Amanda was all she had. She was dependent on her and I think coming here, she had hoped for a similar relationship with me. Only she's too closed off to let me in. And then, well, when you came along, I think Stephanie was a little jealous of that. Of you.'

'Jealous of me? Why? I don't understand.'

'You and I, we have a bond, Rosie. Without even trying, we just naturally hit it off. And, well, I don't mean to sound mean but with Stephanie the bond just isn't there. No matter how hard we've tried. The empty years between us have severed that. Amanda's poison that she spoon-fed her has seeped into my granddaughter and brainwashed her against me.'

I hear a tremble of emotion in Kay's voice. I see the way her eyes turn watery.

'I see so much of Amanda in the girl. All the good parts. And all her bad bits too, you know. How Stephanie can be so negative and hostile. It's hard to get close to someone who's so shut off like that. Stephanie's broken. Traumatised by the life she's lived, guarded and untrusting.'

'But like you said yourself, you don't know each other properly yet. You don't know each other at all. Not in two weeks. Not after all she's been through. She lost her mother in tragic circumstances and she's grieving. You're grieving too. Maybe in time things will be different,' I say, feeling uneasy about hearing Kay talking about Stephanie in such a negative light.

Part of me is still convinced that this has nothing to do with the girl not coping and everything to do with Ash.

'Perhaps you're right.' Kay shrugs, looking back at Stephanie once more before she continues. 'Even if it was concussion, I can't call an ambulance because they'll call the police. Especially with all the crazy things Stephanie is saying and I can't risk that. Them coming here and asking more questions.'

'Because of Stephanie's secret?' I ask and Kay simply nods.

'It's not just that, Rosie. She'll tell them all of her crazy theories. Ash pushing her, Ash drugging her. The police won't take allegations like that lightly and if they're already looking for you...'

Kay looks at me intently.

'Stephanie said what you were looking at on the laptop. At the obituaries. I may be a dithering, old lady, but I'm not stupid. I know there's something, Rosie. You don't sleep out in a tent with a tiny baby if you're not running or hiding from something. What is it you're not telling me?' Kay says, squeezing my hand once more. Letting me know that I can confide in her. Whatever it is we can work through it.

I stare at Stephanie, her body so limp in the bed that it looks as though she is melting into the mattress. Stephanie having a head injury from the fall is triggering for me. I'm worried that the concussion might lead to her having a bleed on the brain or more permanent damage. It's making me think about my mother. About what we did.

I can't do this.

I can't have another death on my conscience. It's all going to come out soon anyway, and I don't want to run any more.

'Let them come, Kay. Let them ask their questions. I really don't care. I'm just exhausted from it all. We can't keep running. It isn't fair on George living like this. I just want this all to be over. We'll have to face up to what we've done eventually.'

'Tell me, Rosie. Let me help you,' Kays says gently.

And that's all it takes for me to confess about my pregnancy. How I'd kept it hidden for as long as I could. When my mother finally found out, I'd kept who the father was a secret because I knew she wouldn't approve.

'I thought once George was here, my mum would be okay about it. She'd see that we loved each other, how much of a good father Ash was going to be. Only when Ash came to the house to meet his son, she went mental. I may be sixteen now but I was only fifteen when I'd got pregnant and Ash had just turned eighteen. My mother started saying crazy things like Ash would be arrested for rape. Can you believe that? He didn't rape me. We love each other. But she said that the police would class it as that. They'd say he took advantage of a minor. George was proof of that.

'The whole thing just got way out of hand, my mother was in Ash's face, screaming at him how he's ruined my life. That he'll never get access to George once she was finished with him. Everyone would know what he was. He'd be put on a sex offender's list.'

I'm crying now. Hot tears streaming down my face as I relive those last harrowing moments inside my head.

'I don't even know how it happened but one minute she was shouting and screaming and shoving him hard in the chest. It was over in seconds. One push. One hard shove and she flew through the air backward, her head slamming down hard on the coffee table's edge. There was so much blood, and she wasn't moving, and I think I started to scream. But Ash stayed calm. Grabbing me by my arm he forced me to move, to pack a bag. Told me we needed to leave. That the police would call this murder. That's why they're looking for us, Kay. Because we'll go down for my mother's murder. We both knew it happened and we both ran. We'll both be found guilty. And George will be taken away from us and I just can't let that happen.'

'I won't let it happen either, Rosie.' Kay wraps her arms around me and pulls me close. Allowing me to lean into her as my sobs take over. 'I'll help you, Rosie, because this isn't your fault. Ash did this. Forcing you to run. Forcing you to keep this all a secret to protect *him*. Manipulating you into staying silent about it ever since. He needs to face the consequences of his actions.'

'No.' I shake my head and pull away from Kay. 'It's not like that. Ash only ever tried to keep us all together. He's only ever wanted to make this all right. He's trying to fix this.'

'He's manipulating you, Rosie. That's what he wants you to believe, the only person Ash is interested in protecting is himself.'

'No.' I shake my head again, because Kay really doesn't understand. 'Ash didn't do it. He didn't push her, Kay. It was me. I pushed my mother and then I left her there for dead.'

32

STEPHANIE

I am awake.

Only I won't let Kay and Rosie know that. Instead, I lie here with my eyes shut. Taking it all in.

The bond that is evident between Kay and Rosie as they keep vigil together at my bedside. I try to concentrate on the words that are being spoken just a few feet away from me, only I still feel groggy and confused. The poison from all the tablets Ash fed me, still lingering inside my system, though it's lessened now since I've been sick. I'd be dead now, I think, if I hadn't emptied the contents of my stomach on the floor of Kay's lounge. That's all that saved me.

Chance, luck. Fate. Call it what you will.

I've heard it all. Rosie telling Kay what happened. That she had run after killing her mother. I think of my mum laying there on the floor, unresponsive and there's something, teetering just on the edge of my memory that I cannot reach. Some tiny detail that every time I try to home in on and catch, my brain purposely blocks it out. My head throbs and I lose my concentration.

Focus, Stephanie.

I focus on the conversation, Kay telling Rosie about me taking the pills. I didn't think she'd noticed. She tells Rosie how she thinks me and my mother are one of the same, but I am not like her. I'm nothing like her in fact. The tablets were to help me cope with the guilt, with the grief. With not being able to sleep. I'd only taken a few.

They were just a vice, something to get me through my darkest days since my mother's death. I may have been born with an addiction because of my mother using while she was pregnant with me. But I am nothing like her. I can stop taking the pills at any time. Surely Kay must know this. Why is she saying all this about me? She knows the state I've been in. She knows what I've gone through. She said she'd help me. She's the one that covered up my mother's death.

Come and stay here with me. We can say you moved in weeks ago, months ago, that you left your mother to it.

Bringing me back here to her home meant that Kay had given me an alibi.

Good, kind Kay.

Though my mother had always warned me that wasn't what Kay was at all. Kay wasn't a good person.

As a child, she'd controlled my mother. Deciding what she ate, what she wore, what she could watch on TV, even when she'd been my age, sixteen. When my mother had tried to get away from her, staying longer at school, to get some space from her, Kay had controlled that too, insisting my mother was sick when she wasn't, and purposely keeping her off.

People can change though. They live and learn and maybe Kay is different now. I think of everything she has done for me. Only when she starts to say that I'm jealous of Rosie, I hear an edge to her voice. She's lying. I am not jealous of Rosie, and she knows it. I don't trust the girl and after what I've just heard, I have good reason not to.

So why is Kay saying all of this?

I hear her telling Rosie how broken I am. Traumatised by the life I have lived, guarded and untrusting. How she makes out that I'm closed off. That I don't have anything to offer her. That the bond she'd hoped we'd have just isn't there. No matter how hard we try. The empty years between us severed any hope of that.

Have they?

She tells Rosie how she's worried that my mother's bitter poisonous hatred of Kay had seeped into me, making me cold and untrusting too. Maybe Kay's right. Maybe I am all of those things. Broken and traumatised and riddled with guilt at what I've done. Yet here Kay is, sitting and bonding with the girl that seems to be able to do anything she likes and get away with it. Shit, Rosie has just admitted to murder and still Kay is offering to stand by her.

She is taking Rosie's side in this, and I don't stand a chance. Nothing I say now will convince Kay to believe me. I know Kay. Despite the distance she claims has stretched out between us. The woman will want to protect Rosie at all costs. Just like she had once told me she would protect me too.

Only now Kay is acting as if I am the one who has become a liability. Me, not them. She is not going to help me which means I am at these people's mercy.

Ash did push me. I am not imagining that. He drugged me too. Both of those things are a fact. I am not crazy or concussed. Why is that so hard for Kay to believe? It's almost like Rosie and Ash have somehow managed to brainwash her against me, while convincing her that they can do no wrong.

Does Kay blame me for my mother's death, deep down? Is this her way at getting back at me?

I keep my eyes tightly shut and wait for Kay and Rosie to leave the room and I know exactly what I need to do. If Kay won't listen, then it's down to me now. I need to go to the police with everything I know about Rosie's mother.

I need to get us help.
But first I need to escape from this house.

33

ROSIE

I shouldn't have told Kay.

That's all I can think as I pace the bedroom, now that I've come to my senses again. Triggered by Stephanie's fall down the stairs, and full of fear that Ash had something to do with it, I'd been at breaking point. All Kay had to do was gently prod to carefully coax the truth out of me as to why we are really here. I'd stupidly let my guard down. I've said it now. I can't take it back. I need to tell Ash. I make my way down the hallway and knock on the bathroom door

'Yeah?'

'It's me Rosie. Can I come in?'

Ash unbolts the door, and steps back to let me in. Fresh out of the shower, with a towel wrapped around his waist, I'm unable to hide my guilt from him. He sees it immediately.

'Rosie? What's happened? What's the matter?' he asks, his voice full of concern.

'I've done something bad. No. Something stupid. I'm sorry, Ash. I know I shouldn't have, but it just came out.'

'What came out?' Ash asks, eyeing me suspiciously.

'I've told Kay what I did,' I say, my voice trembling as the words pour out. 'I know you told me not to, but I trust her, Ash. And I'm scared. We can't keep living like this. It's not fair on George.'

I see the look of anger flash across his face. Anger directed at me now and I shiver.

'What did you tell her? How much of it does she know?'

'All of it, Ash. The truth. She said she'd help me. Help us.'

'God, Rosie. You're an idiot. You really think she means it? With everything she told us that Stephanie had been spewing about us before she'd passed out. All those accusations she'd made. Kay was probably testing you. Seeing if you would confess to any of it.' He shakes his head, furious now. 'And you just played right into her hands. You've let her know that we're capable of doing all of those things.'

'Are we?' I glare back at Ash. 'I can take responsibility for what I did. But what about you?' I allow my eyes to fix on him for a few moments longer than feel comfortable for us both.

'What about me? All I've done is try to protect you, Rosie. To keep you and George safe. To keep the three of us together.'

'Stephanie's convinced it was you who pushed her down the stairs, she told Kay you were drugging her too.'

'Oh come on, Rosie. Stephanie has no idea what she's saying. You can't really believe I had anything to do with that? You saw the state she was in. She was out of it. I found the pills in her pocket, and I gave them to Kay. If I was drugging her, why would I do that? I would have kept my mouth shut and made out it was the concussion making her act so crazy,' Ash says and I can't argue with that, because I'd seen the state of Stephanie for myself.

He is right. Why would Ash give Kay the pills if he had used them to drug Stephanie? Why would he place himself in the firing line like that?

'I'm sorry... I'm so confused, I don't know what to think,' I start, realising how stupid I have been. Only Ash doesn't want an apology from me.

'Fuck, Rosie. I can't believe you told her. They'll call the police now. You know that, don't you? They'll take George off us. We'll go to prison.'

Ash storms out of the bathroom.

'I'm sorry...' I say, following him into the bedroom, where he quickly gets dressed, angry now. Fuming in fact.

'We can't stay here now. You know that don't you? Because of you running your mouth. Get your stuff together. We need to leave.'

I shake my head, still in two minds at what to do now. Maybe Ash is right. Maybe Kay was testing me to get to the truth. Perhaps she will tell the police what she knows now.

All I do know is that I'm sick of running.

'I'm not going anywhere, Ash,' I say, feeling braver than I have in days. I'm sick of Ash calling the shots, telling me what I can and can't do. I'm a grown woman, a mother. I'm capable of making my own decisions, despite Ash thinking that I can't.

I think of the words he'd used just the previous night. How he'd do anything for his family. Anything at all if it means he keeps us all together. I think of the way he'd held the tent pole up above Kay's head that first day we'd met her. The fire he'd started in the kitchen to stop Stephanie from asking any more questions. He's more than capable of pushing Stephanie down the stairs. He's capable of drugging her too.

And he's capable of lying. I know that, because it's all we've done for days. I don't want to do it any more.

'I'm not going. Not with you.'

There. I've said it. Deep down, I don't believe him.

'I said I'd take the blame for what you did, Rosie. That if we got caught, I'd tell the police it was me who pushed your mother. I'd say I was the one who killed her. So you wouldn't be taken away from George. I did all of this,' Ash opens his arms wide, his face turning an angry red puce as he raises his voice, 'for you. To protect you. Running. Taking the tent and sleeping rough in that fucking park. All of it to help you and this is how you repay me. You believe the first bad thing that's said about me? I love you, Rosie, you know that. I'll do anything for you and George.'

'Anything?' I say sadly. 'Including hurting Stephanie?'

'We don't have time for this bullshit, Rosie,' Ash says, knowing that he's not going to win this argument, though still he's determined to stay in control. 'Get your things together.'

My things. One small carrier bag of clothes, and George. That's all I have in the world right now. Nothing and everything all at once, I think as I stare over towards the bed, to the mound of pillows which surround my son while he sleeps.

George means everything to me and I owe it to him to keep him warm and safe. I can't take him back out there onto London's streets. I won't. But what if Ash is right? What if by confessing to Kay about what I've done means that I'll lose him for good? The police may already be on their way. A flurry of panic spreads through me at what I've said. What I've done. And I too feel the sudden need to leave.

I fling myself across the bed, moving the pillows, ready to scoop George up in my arms and do just that: run fast, protect my child. Keep us all together, no matter what the cost.

The space between the pillows sits empty.

'Where is he?' I cry out, turning and glaring at Ash.

Confused at what he's done with our son. Only Ash looks as shocked as me to see the empty bed. Immediately agitated, he runs his fingers through his hair and stares over at the bedroom door, thinking the same thing that I am. While we were in the bathroom, someone came into our room.

Someone has taken our son.

A loud scream floats up the stairs, followed by the sound of George crying.

34

STEPHANIE

I descend the stairs as fast as I can, gripping the handrail so tightly with one hand that my knuckles turn white and bloodless. Hobbling, I try not to apply too much pressure to the fractured bone in my ankle. Though the agony radiates up from my foot regardless, and is excruciating, causing me to wince in pain with every step that I take.

I can't stop. Not now.

I'm almost there.

The front door is just up ahead of me. A few more steps and I'll be able to undo the latch and I'll finally be free from this house. Free from them. I'll take my chances out there, hiding in the shadows, protected under the blanket of a black, star-filled sky as I make my way to the police station. That's my plan. To tell everything I know about Ash and Rosie to the first police officer I see. I'll get Kay help.

Steadying myself as I reach the last step, I balance George in the crook of my other arm as he starts to stir, fractious now, no longer sleeping peacefully like I'd found him.

'It's okay, sweetie,' I say, in a bid to try and soothe him as he looks up at me, his big brown eyes widening with something that looks like fear and I wonder if he can feel the waves of panic spreading through me like wildfire, or the drum-like thud of my rapidly beating heart inside my chest. The quickening of my pulse taking over as I try to make my escape.

I hadn't planned on taking him, I'd heard the running water when I'd passed the bathroom. Along with the sound of Rosie and Ash's angry, raised voices. Relief spreading through me that they were both preoccupied in the midst of yet another argument. That they wouldn't hear me leave.

I don't know what possessed me to peer into their bedroom, perhaps I just wanted reassurance that it was empty. There really was no one here to stop me. That's when I saw him. Little George, splayed out in the centre of the bed, sleeping so peacefully. My insurance policy. To keep Ash and Rosie both here while I go and get the police. Because there's nothing else to keep them here otherwise. Once they work out where I've gone, they'll go on the run again, I'm sure of it. There's no way that they'll stick around waiting for the calvary to turn up and take George from them.

Though the child, whimpering now, has no idea he is being saved. That I am not stealing him away from his good, loving parents, I am rescuing him from a life of living with these selfish, untrustworthy people. The boy deserves so much better than this. Better than them.

Liars. Manipulators. Murderers.

As I reach the bottom step, I am already rehearsing my lines at what I'm going to tell the first officer who greets me at the police station. All about how Rosie killed her mother. How Ash tried to kill me too. Twice. They will take them away.

I think of George's fate and a flicker of regret flutters through me at the idea of him being placed in foster care. I shudder at the thought of all the memories I have as a child of being passed from one stranger's house to another. The constant feelings of pain and rejection that have plagued me for most of my life, at losing my place in the world.

No. This is not the same. George is a baby, he doesn't know anything else. It will be different for him, I tell myself as I lunge towards the door. My fingers clasping at the latch, only my broken ankle twists awkwardly beneath me as I step forward, sending a jolt of pain shooting up my leg like a bolt of electricity conducting right through me. I scream out in agony. So loud that I'm sure I've just alerted the whole house as to where I am. Footsteps pound across the carpet above me. Quickly, I fumble at the lock, releasing the latch. I pull the door handle, but the door doesn't open.

Shit.

It's been double locked. To stop me from getting out.

'Stephanie,' Ash's voice calls out. The footsteps, belonging to him, getting louder as he takes the stairs. Gaining traction, he is closing in.

'Where do you think you're going with my son?'

I hear the rage in his voice, even before I turn and see the menacing look on his face. His skin puce red with rage. Spittle at the edge of his lips. His fists clenched at his side that I have no doubt he would use on me if he thought he had to. If it meant he'd get his son back.

I'm in real danger now. The first grave mistake I've made tonight is thinking I could take his child from him. The second, is believing that I could somehow get away with it. Believing I could get away at all.

35

KAY

I hear the noise before I see what the commotion is. Loud voices shouting. George crying hysterically. It's coming from the kitchen I realise, getting off my chair and homing in on the loud boom of Ash's voice. Deep and full of rage as it echoes off my kitchen walls.

My first thought is Rosie. Full of fear that she has confessed to him, that she's admitted to telling me their secret. That Ash has gone on the rampage, attacking the girl. I move fast on my feet, rushing into the kitchen to defend her. Only as I slip in through the kitchen door and see Ash with his back to me, it's Stephanie who is standing there in front of him. Rosie rushes in behind me, and we both stare at the carnage that's unfolding in front of us.

'Give George to me, Stephanie. You're frightening him,' Ash says and it's only then, as he steps slightly out of my way that I see George cradled in the crook of one of Stephanie's arms. In her other hand, I see the thick slither of shiny steel.

'She's got a knife,' Rosie's voice, barely a whisper.

Stephanie is holding my carving knife. My best one, with

the longest and sharpest of blades, that I use to slice through tough chunks of meat for my casseroles.

'Don't you dare come anywhere near me.' The mirror-like shine from the blade reflects light up onto the ceiling above her, as she jabs ferociously with lethal procession, in Ash's direction.

'Stephanie!' I call out in warning.

Hoping that if she won't listen to Ash, she might listen to me. Only she doesn't waver. Her eyes flash with the same defiance I'd seen in her mother, all those years ago.

'Stephanie, darling. What are you doing?' I say, unable to hide the tremor in my voice as the feral scene plays out in front of me.

Ash standing just a few feet away from where Stephanie is waving the knife, as he begs for his son back. Stephanie is guarded, refusing. She shuffles backward, her eyes flashing with panic as she hits the sink behind her. There's no way out for her now, except through Ash. Only Ash, just as stubborn, inches closer.

'Give me my son, Stephanie,' he commands, extending his arms. Prepared to get hurt if he has to, ready to take George from her if she doesn't give him willingly.

'I said, keep the fuck away from me. I mean it.'

Her eyes are ablaze with fear as she slashes the knife wildly through the air in front of her, not allowing him into her space now that she has unwittingly backed herself into a corner. She's determined not to allow Ash anywhere even close to his son. I see it. How she is just like Amanda now. How the girl won't back down. Not when she believes she's right. Not when she thinks she is justified. Stephanie and Ash are both as unpredictable and volatile as each other and I know that this is not going to end well.

'Stephanie. Do as Ash says,' I say, praying that the girl will listen to me. That she'll see me as the voice of reason. She'll know I'm talking sense and that I have no other motive than making sure she and George are okay.

'Do as Ash says? He tried to kill me, Kay. He pushed me down the stairs. He was the one drugging me with those pills. And you just want me to hand George to him? Why won't you believe me?'

'I do believe you, Stephanie,' I say, glaring over at Ash, careful with my wording. Knowing that I can contain this whole situation if I can just get Stephanie to listen to me.

'I didn't at first, and I'm sorry for that too. But I see it now. You were right about them, Stephanie. They are not good people. I want them gone from my house. Give them back George, then they can leave.'

I feel Ash's eyes burn into the side of my face, and imagine the look of confusion on his face as he tries to work out if I really mean what I am saying.

'You're lying,' Stephanie says, a look of disbelief telling me that she is not falling for my act. There's something else there too. A quiet look of resigned disappointment.

'Just like you lied to me before when you said you'd help me. I heard you talking to Rosie, Kay. Telling her all of those horrible things about me being damaged and broken. Making out that I'm an addict too, *"just like my mum"*. Why would you say that, Kay? You know I'm nothing like her.'

'I only said those things to Rosie, to get her to open up to me. I thought if I gave her something, hinted at your secret, she'd think that she was on mutual ground. I only wanted to gain her trust, Stephanie. So that she would finally tell me the truth about why they were really here and about what Ash was doing to you.'

'So you believe that he pushed me. That when the fall didn't kill me, he drugged me. He put those pills in my porridge, to finish me off.'

I nod in agreement, only our conversation seems to rile Ash up.

'For fucksake, Stephanie. I didn't do any of those things. It's all in your head. None of that happened. I didn't go anywhere near your fucking porridge. Kay made it. You had the pills, they were in your pocket. They were yours. You're mental you are. Mental. Now give me George before someone gets hurt.'

Running out of patience, Ash's threat is loaded. He wants George back and he'll do whatever it takes to get him. I change tactics.

'Please, Stephanie, love. Listen to Ash. Give him the baby, darling. Come on, now. Maybe Ash is right, maybe this is all just a big misunderstanding. You've had a nasty bump to your head, Stephanie,' I say, hoping to calm whatever sporadic thoughts are spinning inside her head. 'The tablets you've taken have made you confused, love. It isn't you, sweetheart. Your mind is playing tricks on you. You're not well.'

'I'm not well?' Stephanie scoffs and I see how she falters. How she is no longer staring at Ash. She has turned her attention solely to me now. My advice is clearly not landing how I'd hoped it would, because there's something unnerving in her strange, twisted expression. Her brows furrow, causing a deep-set line to crease in the middle of her forehead.

'How could you?'

'How could I? How could I what?' I say confused, only the room blurs and warps into a mass of muted colours and I do a double-take as time slows and suddenly Stephanie is gone.

It's Amanda I see standing in front of me now. In that lovely violet dress that I'd buried her in.

'How could you, Mum? How could you do that to me?'

Her words are cold and laced with so much sadness that just hearing them now, breaks me in two. I miss her. My God, I miss her. I know in that moment that if I could turn back time, if I could have done things different. I would have tried.

'Amanda?' I mutter reaching out my hand, even though the rational part of my brain knows this can't be real. Amanda can't really be here. It's her ghost I'm seeing. She's haunting me. No, God no. It's just a trick of the light. My mind playing tricks on me. Only it feels as if she really is right here, standing in front of me.

'Amanda, my love... I'm sorry, my love... for all of it. All of it.'

As soon as I say the words out loud the vision of my daughter disappears like a puff of smoke and it's Stephanie who's there again, staring back at me as I sob now, with a baffled look on her face, as if I'm the one who's acting crazy. Not her, with a baby in one hand, a butcher's knife in the other.

'*You're not well,*' Stephanie continues, repeating my words. Undeterred as I try and compose myself. 'You said that to her too. I remember now. That one and only time I'd ever come here as a small child. We stood out on your doorstep, soaked through as the rain lashed down around us and still you wouldn't invite us in.' Stephanie shakes her head, as her mind whirls while she tries to piece it all together. The fragmented, scattered memories from so many years ago. Like an impossible jigsaw puzzle. She's forcing pieces in places where they just don't fit. Making her warped thoughts a reality in her head.

'She'd asked you for help, and you told her she wasn't well. That you wouldn't help her.'

'No. That's not what happened, Stephanie. Your mother didn't ask me for help. She asked me for money. And we all know where that would have been spent.'

'On drugs.' Stephanie nods in agreement, and I'm relieved she can see that too. Even if the memory is vague and blurred. That she believes what I am telling her.

'*What sort of a mother are you? Dragging the poor girl out in this so you can get your drug money.* That's what you said.' Stephanie's voice is calm and controlled now. A complete contradiction to the way I know she must be really feeling, which brings me a feeling of unease.

'She asked for your help to buy "drugs". Medicine for me. That's why I was there. She "dragged" me out in the rain that day, because she knew you wouldn't believe she was clean. So that you could see with your own two eyes I was really sick. Only still you refused.'

I shake my head.

'You've had a nasty shock, Stephanie. You've been through a lot the past few weeks. You're confused, love. You don't know what you're saying. That isn't what happened. You know the way your mother could be. With her constant episodes. How volatile she was.'

'I remember. The shouting, the name calling. The way you made my mother beg.'

Ash inches forward. Just a couple of feet away from Stephanie now. So close he can almost touch her. He can almost reach George. If I can just keep Stephanie focused, keep her eyes on me, Ash can take George. And this can all be over. All he wants is the baby, no one needs to get hurt tonight.

'There's no way you can remember all of that. You were too young. Barely five years old.'

'I was six. And I remember it all now. The shouting and crying and screaming. The calling each other names. I hadn't understood it at the time, too sick from whatever illness I'd had, too cold from the wind and the rain. Too innocent to have any inkling of what was going on all around me. You told her she wasn't well. You said that she was a bad mother! That she wasn't fit to look after me.'

'That's not what happened,' I say, firmly now. Because even though Stephanie claims to be nothing like her, she is every bit the same as her mother. Pig-headed and difficult. She's not going to let this drop.

'Isn't it?'

Fuelled with fury, she is about to say more. About to launch into a tirade of evidence against me.

Only Ash seeing her distracted takes his opportunity and lunges forward. Stephanie isn't ready for him. He is bigger than her, stronger than her. Even before her fall, before she'd ingested all those pills. Ash wrestles her for the knife. His fingers locked around her wrist as he twists it hard, overpowering her, though somehow Stephanie manages to turn her body away from him, her natural instincts to protect his child from getting hurt. To keep hold of George.

Before I have time to stop her, Rosie moves in, her motherly instinct only wanting to defend her child. To protect him from all danger.

I watch as the three bodies twist in an awkward violent dance, while George unable to comprehend what is happening around him continues to shriek out in distress.

Then I hear the awful sound of Rosie's blood-curdling scream.

36

ROSIE

'What have you done? What have you done?'

I am down on my knees. My fingers splayed out around the handle of the knife, as I press my palm down, applying pressure on the open wound. Blood pumps out from Ash's stomach. Disorientated, Ash tries to move, to sit up only the unbearable pain is too much for him and the low, continuous groan that escapes his mouth of reminds me of a dying animal.

No! He is not going to die. I will not let him die.

'Don't move, Ash. You're going to be all right; I promise. You just need to stay still.'

I glare over at Stephanie, stood over us now. Still holding my son. She's wide eyed and frozen to the spot as the pool of blood seeps out around Ash. She's in shock. The realisation of the horrific injury she inflicted on Ash only just hitting her.

'He didn't deserve this,' I spit. 'He only ever wanted to protect me. Everything he's done, he's done for me and George. To keep us safe.'

Stephanie doesn't answer. She can't. Her skin has paled and her mouth hangs slack. I see the blood splattered all over her clothes. Her foot twisted at an awkward angle. A huge bump protruding from her head. A crazed, demented look in her eye.

'I killed him.' Stephanie stares down at her blood-soaked hands and in that moment I see her for all the things she actually is. Unhinged. Deranged. And mentally unstable. She is falling apart in front of my very eyes. This is so much more than grief. This is guilt, eating her up from the inside out. She's losing her mind.

'She killed Amanda too, didn't she? That's her secret,' I say to Kay, not needing an answer.

I see it in both of their faces. That's the secret Kay has been keeping for the girl. Stephanie killed Amanda, and Kay, good, kind, caring Kay, had loyally protected her granddaughter for all this time. She'd stood by her, despite the fact that it was her only daughter that Stephanie had murdered.

Kay has done everything in her power to try and help the girl. Only Stephanie is beyond help. I see that now and I think Kay must too, the rapid mental decline Stephanie has suffered since we arrived here that day. She's tried so hard to hide it. So hard to stay guarded and cold and not let her feelings out, but the guilt of what she's done seeps out of every pore in her body regardless.

Kay was right. Stephanie has grown paranoid, terrified that she'll be found out, she hasn't wanted us here from the start, because she didn't want us bringing the police to Kay's door. In case they asked more questions. Questions Stephanie wouldn't be able to answer.

It was never personal. Stephanie was only trying to protect herself. Only the guilt she is riddled with is eating her alive. She hasn't got away with any of it, because even if there are no reprisals, Stephanie has to live with herself, knowing what she has done and she can't. I know this because I feel exactly the same. So when the pounding at the front door starts all I feel is relief.

'It's the police,' I say, looking up at Kay.

I know this too, because I am the one who called them. Worried for both Stephanie's and George's safety, as Ash had taken the stairs when we'd realised that George was gone. Scared at the lengths Ash was prepared to go to, to get our son back. I knew that I couldn't do this life any more.

'Don't answer it,' Ash slurs his speech, his breathing laboured now. His body growing weak. 'Get George and run, Rosie. Please, it's not too late.'

I look up at Stephanie once more. Still in her trance-like state and I wonder how much of it is shock and how much of it is all those pills she's taken still making their way around her system.

When the police come in here, they will get Ash help. They will get my baby away from this fucking mental woman.

I won't have my chance to say goodbye.

I stand.

'Time is running out for me. They're going to take him away from me, Stephanie. They're going to lock me up. For what I did to my mother. Please, Stephanie, just let me hold him one last time,' I beg, and to my surprise Stephanie steps forward and hands me my baby.

I hug George close and breathe in that beautiful familiar smell of his. Baby powder and creamy milk. George is sweet and soft and pure and as I stare around the room at the carnage that has unfolded around us, I know my decision is right.

I need to be a good mother.

'They're going to get you help, Ash. You're going to be okay. You and George...' I stutter, a ball of thick emotion in the back of my throat blocking the rest of the sentence from leaving my mouth. I can't bring myself to say it out loud. I can't talk about the fate that awaits me.

'Please, Rosie. No,' Ash begs me, but my mind is already made up.

'I can't keep running, Ash. It's not fair on him. I want this all to end. I want it all to be over. Life will never be the same after what I did, but I can't keep dragging my son through the debris of what's left of my old life.'

I look down at George and give him one last smile.

'Mummy loves you, darling. Always know that.'

I kiss my son gently on the forehead, unable to stop the single tear that runs down my cheek from dripping onto his pink, rounded face.

'Look after him for me,' I say, as I hand him over to Kay.

And Kay doesn't argue with me or try to persuade me otherwise. Instead she nods her head in understanding, before handing me the keys to the front door so that I can let the police in. She knows that I am doing the right thing. She only has to look at Stephanie to see the damaging consequences of keeping all these secrets. The resentment and turmoil our guilt can cause.

It's finally over.

For me, and for Ash and for Stephanie too.

It's time to pay for our crimes.

37

STEPHANIE

I stare down at Ash's blood-soaked body, in some kind of a trance, my gaze fixed on the knife that's still protruding out from his stomach. I did that. Me. I stabbed him. I am a bad person.

Liar, kidnapper. Murderer.

Only somehow my brain can't compute how it actually happened because one minute Kay was talking, the next, Ash was on me, trying to wrestle George from my arms. Only I couldn't let go of him. I *wouldn't* let go of him, unable to hand the boy over to a man that I know is capable of doing so much bad. I only struck out with the knife to warn him off, to get him away from me. Away from George.

I didn't mean to do it. Or did I? I'm not sure now, because I've killed before, haven't I? And I hadn't meant to do that then, either. What are the chances? What are the odds that anyone would believe me when at this point, I don't even trust myself?

There is noise and lots of commotion as police officers storm into the room, one of them going instantly to where Ash is. Crouching over his body, calling in urgent medical assistance on his radio. I hear the officer tell whoever the emergency dispatcher is at the other end of the call, that Ash has a pulse. That's it's weak and he's lost a lot of blood.

'Is he dying?' Rosie sobs loudly, before telling the officer who they are. About the tent in the park.

All of it.

I zone back out, not caring for the details as I stare at the dark pool of blood that seeps out around Ash and think of how I'd found my mother, the night she died. Unresponsive on the floor and foaming at the mouth after that last fatal dose of methadone.

The overdose that had killed her.

When she'd started having a seizure, I'd panicked. Part of me knew that I should call an ambulance. That I should get my mother some help. Another part of me had also known that it was me who had been at fault. That I had caused it. Scared and desperate, I'd called Kay instead. It was all such a blur after that.

'Go and pack a bag. You can come home with me.'

Kay's only thought had been protecting me.

'You're not yourself. You're sick.' The familiar, haunting words earlier that Kay had used, just before Ash had pounced, had thrown me. Causing the room to spin wildly.

An image of me and my mother, soaked through on Kay's doorstep.

'You're not yourself. You're sick, Amanda. Take this and give the girl to me.'

Kay had held out her hand and instead of giving my mother money, had offered her something else. Drugs. Kay had tried to bargain with her. She'd tried to sabotage my mother's attempts at staying clean. Offering her a bag of drugs as a swap for me.

'Who does that? I'm clean now, Mother. You nasty old witch.' My mum had spat with disgust, before dragging me away and telling me that we'd never see my grandmother again.

And we hadn't. Not until that last fateful day, when my mother passed.

I glare at Kay.

'That day on the doorstep, you wanted my mother to fail. You wanted her to cave into her addiction, to lose all her rights to me. So that you could gain custody instead,' I say, realising that I knew all of this, yet, somehow, I'd managed to block it out.

Good, kind Kay.

With my mother dead, Kay had finally got her wish, bringing me back here to her house. I think about my mother's bedroom upstairs, still full of all her things. Sweet Sixteen. My age now. As if it had been set up for all these years, just waiting for me. The good girl to replace my bad mother. Am I a good girl?

I zone back in, my ears pricking up when I hear Kay telling a police officer that my mother's pathology results came back this morning. That they found heroin in my mother's blood, as well as twice the dose of methadone.

'No. That's not right,' I mutter, shaking my head. Stunned that this is the first time Kay has mentioned my mother's autopsy results. That she is willingly offering this information to the police after everything we'd done. 'Apart from methadone my mother had been clean.'

Methadone had become her only addiction. A temporary fix that had in time become a lifelong intervention. I'd lived through it all with her. The withdrawals, the anxiety, her depression. I'd sat beside her in bed and held her hand when all the worst feelings in the world swirled around inside her.

That last day, she'd been struggling with her demons and the methadone hadn't been enough to stave off her cravings. Her need for something more had dominated her. I knew how her cravings for oblivion worked in these moments, how she'd be plagued with insomnia and muscle aches. Sickness and diarrhoea. How I'd be forced to watch her suffer. So when she'd begged me, I'd foolishly, stupidly given her that extra, fatal dose. She wouldn't have asked me for that if she'd gone back onto heroin. She wouldn't have needed it.

Besides, how had she got her hands on heroin? She hadn't left the house in days and we'd had no visitors either.

Except for Kay.

'Go to your room and pack your things. You're coming home with me.'

In shock and overcoming an almighty panic attack, I'd robotically done as I was told. In my mother's last final dying breath I had left her alone with Kay. When I'd come back she was no longer foaming at the mouth, vacant eyes rolling. She had stopped breathing. Eyes shut. Dead.

I was the one who killed her.

I've always believed that because that's what Kay had told me. I hadn't had time to think straight or process any of my thoughts. Kay had ushered me quickly from the house.

Two days we'd waited for the police to come and break the news to us that we already knew. Though my grief and tears and turmoil hadn't been an act. As soon as those words were said out loud it made it real. My mother was dead. She was never coming back.

I think back to earlier today when Kay had told Rosie that I'm damaged goods. That I'm closed off and guarded. That I get all of these negative traits from my mother. How the bond between me and Kay was never there. I needed her help and she needed me. Until she didn't. Until Rosie came along and offered her something that I never could.

George.

An opportunity for Kay to make amends and be the mother and nanny she was so desperate to be. Only Kay could never be any of those things.

'You did it,' I whisper and as Kay turns to look at me, I see it in her eyes. I am right. She was never protecting me. She was protecting herself.

Before I can think, I launch myself at her.

'You killed her. Oh my God, you fucking killed her.'

I am on her, clawing at Kay's shocked face, ripping out clumps of her straggly hair. Because suddenly everything makes so much sense. Kay had offered my mother drugs once before. She'd had them in her possession. She was capable of getting them again.

I feel the strong arms of two police officers as they drag me off Kay as Rosie tells the officers that I am deranged, that I've been acting crazy. That I'd kidnapped George and tried to murder Ash. She tells them I am suffering from delusions from all the drugs I've taken. That in one of my less than lucid moments I'd fallen down the stairs.

'I didn't fall, I was pushed. They drugged me. They're trying to kill me.' I am screaming now. Desperate for the police to listen to me. To believe me. 'They're the people from the tent in the woods. The ones you're looking for.'

Kay chimes in then too.

'She murdered her mother.'

There. I have hope. Despite the fact that I have just attacked her, Kay is staying true to her word and defending me until the very end. She is telling the police who Rosie really is. That her account can't be trusted.

I hear words like 'suspicious behaviour' and 'acting psychotic' and I feel vindicated that finally I have someone else to back up my story. That Kay finally sees how Ash and Rosie are not who they pretend to be.

Until I hear Kay telling the police officer that she fears I am a drug addict just like my mother. That I'm displaying all the same signs. That I am a danger to myself and to others.

'I can't do it, Stephanie. I can't keep your secret for you. You killed my daughter and then you begged me to help you cover it up.'

That's when the policeman tightens his grip on my arm and twists it up behind me, so hard that I think my arm might break as he slaps on a pair of heavy, metal handcuffs.

Kay isn't talking about Rosie at all.

She is talking about me.

'No. I didn't kill my mother. She's lying.' Straining against the hold, I fight, teeth gritted, fists clenched, like a wild, frenzied animal trying to escape its snare. I know I must look psychotic. Blood all down my clothes, a crazy look on my face as I direct my attention to Rosie, wondering why Kay is so set on protecting her and not me. 'Rosie killed her mother. She did! That's why they're running.'

'What are you talking about?' the officer barks. 'Rosie's mother isn't dead. She's the one who reported her missing.'

The officer turns to Rosie.

'She's worried about you, Rosie. She just wants you home.' Those are the last words I hear as I am led outside towards the awaiting police car.

Kay's words from the day previously chime inside my head. How I am jealous of Rosie. And in this moment, I am. Her mother isn't dead. Rosie didn't kill her. She can still salvage something from this mess. Unlike me.

Me, who is being thrown to the wolves by Kay, who in order to save herself is letting them feast on the little that is left of me. Good, kind, caring Kay. Though I know now, the woman was never any of those things. My mother was right about Kay. Telling me my entire childhood about how the woman was controlling. How Kay had been the one to drive her to drugs. Literally.

That there was a genuine reason she had kept me away from her. She wasn't lying. My mother hadn't got her all wrong.

She'd always told me the truth about the woman. Only I hadn't wanted to believe it.

There was something very wrong with Kay.

38

KAY

Rosie is feeding George the last dregs of his bottle, then we're going to put him in the pram and do a few laps around Highgate Park. It's our afternoon ritual now. Getting outside and getting some fresh air. It's good for the mind and the soul, as Rosie is forever telling me. The girl is all about doing as much as we can to help restore out mental health.

We'll take Max with us and let him have a run about to wear him out, before coming home and having a nice cup of tea. Well, tea for Rosie at least. Ovaltine will always be my drink of choice. The creamy, malty drink has always helped to keep the edge from my nerves, always managing to disguise the taste of the crushed up Xanax I've stirred into it. Extra sugar in Stephanie's tea has always worked to disguise the meds I slipped into hers too.

Stephanie has been admitted to a psychiatric unit for assessment, and I doubt very much that they'll be letting her out any time soon. It's a real shame for her that it didn't work out, but like my lovely Rosie keeps telling me, some people just can't be helped. Stephanie was too much like Amanda in the end. The life she'd lived had made her hard and bitter and untrusting.

When Rosie had come along with George, of course I knew that the girl had some kind of secret she was hiding. Because let's face it, we all have secrets. To me having secrets was never something negative. If you knew people's secrets you could use them against them as collateral if you ever needed to.

Only with Rosie, I'd never had to. The bond between us is natural. We're like mother and daughter, in fact, someone in the local cafe had only said that to us just the other day. How we looked so much like one another. Especially since I had my hair styled just like hers, and had a few blonde highlights added.

When Rosie had called the police, I'd used their presence to my advantage, confessing to them all about Stephanie killing her mother. How could I not when Stephanie had been so intent on putting on such a spectacular show? Showing the police and all of us how she was not of her right mind. That in her drug-fuelled haze she'd kidnapped baby George and stabbed Ash, almost killing him too, before she'd viciously turned her violent attack onto me.

It would have all come out in the wash eventually anyway. The truth always does.

I'd made a dreadful mistake in inviting Stephanie here. That's what I'd told Rosie afterwards. Believing that because we were blood related we would automatically have a bond. That the girl would make up for the loss of me losing my daughter. Only Stephanie was damaged and closed off. The trauma of killing her mother had seen to that. That and the scummy life Amanda had dragged her up in. The truth was, Stephanie hadn't warmed to me as I'd wanted her to, and the rejection I had felt in her company had been like living with Amanda all over again.

Rosie was different to Stephanie in so many ways. I preferred her, if I'm being brutally honest, and part of me felt so bad for even silently admitting that to myself at times. Stephanie could see it too, I think. How Rosie and I had effortlessly formed such a strong bond in such a short space of time, when Stephanie and I hadn't.

I feel like a motherly figure now to Rosie. Having her here makes me think of how different it would have been if things with Stephanie and Amanda hadn't been so distant and strained.

I expect that Stephanie's worked it all out now. How I was the one who had pushed her down the stairs and drugged her. I never set out to kill her though. I'd only intended on scaring her into a submissive silence. Only the more she'd proved herself to be such a problem, the more I'd come around to the idea that getting rid of her for good wouldn't be such a bad idea. I'd thought my game was up, once she'd found an empty packet of pills next to the pot of porridge I'd made her.

She'd been blinded by her hatred of Ash by then. So shrouded by her fear of him and what he was capable of doing to her next, that she hadn't suspected me at all. That I was the one who had taken her phone, taken the evidence she had of Rosie and Ash breaking into that car. I'd cut the internet wires, to cut Stephanie off and make it impossible for her to reach out for anyone. I was the one who'd double locked the front door to keep her from getting help.

She wouldn't have realised any of that until it was too late.

When she'd turned on Ash, I'd used her hatred of him in my favour. That was all too easy too. Setting Ash up to look like the bad guy hadn't exactly been a difficult feat. Not when the man was so naturally overprotective and controlling. Not with his temper.

He meant well. Rosie only ever insists on this, and I'll let her have that if it makes her feel better for not believing Ash all the time he'd protested his innocence about the shady goings-on in this house. It's a shame I couldn't blame everything on him. Killing two birds with one stone and all that. Only making out that it was all Stephanie's doing works so much better for me.

The problem with Stephanie was that she had a conscience. I could see it, how she was gradually falling apart as the guilt of what she'd done to her mother ate away at her. One day she'd talk. I was sure about that. She'd give away her secret. She'd worked it out in the end, that I hadn't just covered up Amanda's murder for her sake. That it had never been about protecting her. I only ever wanted to protect myself.

Stephanie didn't kill Amanda.

I did.

I think about all the disgusting people and places I'd had to go to in order to get my daughter that awful drug. Heroin. In preparation that one day Amanda might cave and relapse.

I'd done it out of love, though Stephanie would never understand that. How I'd put my daughter out of her never-ending misery once and for all. Ending her suffering. Because Amanda would never be free of her need for that poison, not really. No matter how many years she'd claim to be clean. Amanda always went back to it eventually. Once an addict, always an addict. She is at peace now. Safe. Visiting me in my dreams so often in fact, that it almost feels in a way as if I've got her back.

'Can you grab that for me?' Rosie says as her phone beeps.

And I do so, gladly. Only too happy to help Rosie, so that she can continue winding George before dressing him in his warm coat and strapping him up in his pram.

'Who is it?'

'Oh, it's just that annoying weather App. Again. Apparently it's eight degrees today. What would we do without our phones, huh? Such clever devices. Though I have no idea what half the things on mine can do,' I lie, pretending that even the simplest actions are too complicated for me to navigate, as I stare at the text message from Rosie's mother, Susan, inviting her and George over for Sunday lunch. No mention of me, I note as I press delete. I'm not surprised.

I hadn't liked the woman on sight when I'd met her, and after an emotional, tear-filled mother-daughter reunion I'd taken great delight in making no pretence of that fact, the minute Rosie had left the room. Leaving us both sitting in a stoney silence, as I glared at the woman. Making her feel intentionally uncomfortable so she was under no illusion that she wasn't welcome here.

I click on the 'recently deleted folder' and erase the message in there too, so there's no trace of it should Rosie look, before switching Rosie's phone to silent.

It's the third time I've deleted text messages from Susan this week and I wonder when the woman will finally get the message and stop bothering the girl. She's relentless. Trying to build bridges. To have some sort of relationship with Rosie and George after the way she'd behaved when she'd found out about Rosie and Ash's relationship.

Trying to redeem herself by telling Rosie how she'd never told the police about Rosie pushing her, or the twenty stitches she'd needed in the back of her head. She'd never mentioned Ash's name at all, either, which was why there was no mention of him in any of the missing person appeals. It was as if he never existed. Because Rosie's mum knew if she made a fuss about his age, drew any attention to him at all, she'd lose her daughter for good.

I place the phone back down on the side and vow that if she texts Rosie again, I'll send her a nasty text from her daughter cutting all ties with her, before I permanently block her number.

Rosie doesn't need the woman. Not now. Rosie is sixteen and a mother herself, so she's more than capable of choosing where she wants to live.

Besides, she has me now.

And I know how she's grown to love this house, now that we've completely decluttered every room and I've agreed to give free rein to Rosie on decorating for me. She wants to be an interior designer she's decided. She wants to go back to college and sit her final exams and then enrol in an interior design course. She'll do it too, I have no doubt about that. And of course I'll be only too happy to help her. Minding George for her while she studies and works. Waiting with a nice home-cooked meal for her at the end of each day.

We often joke about how I act like I'm the one looking after Rosie, but really it feels as if sometimes it's Rosie looking after me. Because as far as she knows, I'm still in shock, now that the secret my granddaughter had been harbouring is finally out in the open. That Stephanie is responsible for Amanda's murder. That she'd tried to kill Ash too, though thankfully (Rosie's words, not mine) Ash is alive, in hospital. He is expected to make a full recovery. For now. Only I have big plans for him once he gets out... Accidents happen all of the time. Don't they? Should anything happen to Ash in the near future, I'll be ready. Patiently consoling Rosie for her awful, tragic loss.

'Right, George is ready and waiting when you are, Kay,' Rosie calls out to me and I beam with happiness as I make my way towards the front door, grabbing Max's lead on the way.

It's so lovely having a baby in the house. Being such a big part of it all.

Just the three of us. And Max of course.

Finally, a family all of my own.

A LETTER FROM CASEY KELLEHER

Dear reader,

I want to say a huge thank you for choosing to read *The Perfect Guest*. This is my sixth psychological thriller, and I really enjoyed how dark and claustrophobic this one felt at times.

As always, I started my writing process with such a small seed of an idea, a vision actually – of a young couple and a tiny baby, sleeping in a tent in the local park.

When Kay Wyldes lets complete strangers into her home, we worry about the secrets the young couple are keeping from her and the dangers she's exposed herself to. Only we quickly learn that it's Kay's secrets that are the worst of all... I really hope you enjoyed this one.

If you would like to keep up to date with all my latest releases, just sign up at the following link. Your email address will never be shared and you can unsubscribe at any time.

www.bookouture.com/casey-kelleher

I'd love to hear what you thought of *The Perfect Guest* so if you have the time and you'd like to leave me a review on Amazon it's always appreciated. (I do make a point of reading every single one.)

I also love hearing from you, my readers – your messages and photos of the books that you tag me in on social media always make my day.

So, please feel free to get in touch through social media or my website.

Thank you

Casey Kelleher

www.caseykelleher.co.uk

 facebook.com/officialcaseykelleher
instagram.com/caseykelleher

ACKNOWLEDGEMENTS

Many thanks to my new brilliant editor Ruth Jones. This is our first time working together and I have thoroughly enjoyed every minute of it. Thank you for all your hard work in helping me pull this story together so perfectly.

Thanks as always to my brilliant publishers, Bookouture, and all of the fabulous team.

Special thanks to Kay Bull – for the amazing £250 bid you placed for a signed copy of my last book, *The Missing Mother* – raising money for the incredible Healing Paws Animal Rescue in Greece.

Kay Wyldes is named after you and in honour of your lovely mum and aunt.

Special thanks also to the amazing bestselling author and all-round GEM, Angela Marsons – who on seeing Kay's generous online bid, matched it. Wow!

£500 is just out of this world – THANK YOU BOTH!

And to Tracy Howard for nominating Max's name for the little dog in this story. In tribute to your late sister Pam x

As always I'd like to thank my extremely supportive friends and family for all the encouragement that they give me along the way. The Coopers, the Kellehers, The Ellises. And to all my lovely friends.

Finally, a big thank you to my husband Danny. My hero!

Much love to Ben, Danny and Kyle.

Ben, the Ovaltine was a nod to you, as yourself and Kay are the only people I know that drink the stuff ;)

Not forgetting little Miska. My most favourite child.

And to you, my lovely reader. I say this every single time, because it's true. You are the very reason I write, without you, none of this would have been possible.

Casey x

PUBLISHING TEAM

Turning a manuscript into a book requires the efforts of many people. The publishing team at Bookouture would like to acknowledge everyone who contributed to this publication.

Commercial
Lauren Morrissette
Hannah Richmond
Imogen Allport

Cover design
Aaron Munday

Data and analysis
Mark Alder
Mohamed Bussuri

Editorial
Ruth Jones
Nadia Michael

Copyeditor
Deborah Blake

Proofreader
Claire Rushbrook